STRICTLY BUSINESS

"Please don't scold me, Mr. Ryerson. I know what you're thinking—"

"You can't possibly know what I'm thinking," Jack corrected her. Then he took a deep breath and managed a firmer tone. "This is completely unnecessary, Miss Standish. I don't regard your—your physical appearance as an asset of this project."

"You see it as a liability?"

"Good God, no," he began, then caught the twinkle in her eyes and relaxed for the first time since she'd entered the room. "It's clear we need to talk, but you'll need to put your robe back on first, or all you'll hear from me is incoherent babbling."

He leaned down to retrieve her garment, but again Trinity restrained him. "You asked me to consider your plan and I've done so carefully. You also told me that if I found your solution unacceptable, we'd explore other alternatives. That's what we're doing now. Exploring the alternative of marrying for six months. I have a strong need to respect my grandfather's dying request. And if you have needs that I can meet—" her cheeks turned crimson—"then I will do so gladly, with every asset I possess."

Dear Romance Reader,

In July 2000, we launched the Ballad line with four new series, and each month we present both new and continuing stories set everywhere from medieval England to the American West—the kind of passionate, romantic stories you love best, written by the most gifted authors. At the back of each book, we tell you when you can find subsequent books in the series that have captured your heart.

This month, Kelly McClymer continues her sparkling *Once Upon a Wedding* series with **The Impetuous Bride.** When a spirited young woman flees England to avoid matrimony, she never imagines that she'll be forced to wed in America's Wild West—or that her new husband will be quite so appealing! Then the ever talented Linda Lea Castle concludes her dramatic saga, *The Vaudrys,* with **Embrace the Sun.** A Scottish lass harboring a dangerous secret risks everything when a wounded Englishmen falls into her dooryard . . . and into her heart.

Next up, Sandra Madden introduces the second book in her wonderfully atmospheric *Of Royal Birth* series, **A Prince's Heart.** A British lieutenant fighting the Irish rebellion loses his heart to the enemy—a lovely Irish lass leads him on a journey of discovery that he'll never forget. Finally, Kate Donovan concludes her sweetly romantic *Happily Ever After Co.* with the charming tale of a woman looking for a husband to save her ranch—and a man who can't resist playing the hero in **Fool Me Twice.**

These are stories we know you'll love! Why not try them all this month?

Kate Duffy
Editorial Director

The Happily Ever After Co.

FOOL ME
TWICE

Kate Donovan

ZEBRA BOOKS
Kensington Publishing Corp.
http://www.kensingtonbooks.com

ZEBRA BOOKS are published by

Kensington Publishing Corp.
850 Third Avenue
New York, NY 10022

All Kensington titles, imprints, and distributed lines are available at special quantity discounts for bulk purchases for sales
promotion, premiums, fund-raising, educational or institu-
tional use.

Special book excerpts or customized printings can also be created to fit specific needs. For details, write or phone the office
of the Kensington Special Sales Manager: Kensington Publishing Corp., 850 Third Avenue, New York, NY 10022. Attn.
Special Sales Department. Phone: 1-800-221-2647.

Zebra and the Z logo Reg. U.S. Pat. & TM Off.

First Printing: November 2002
10 9 8 7 6 5 4 3 2 1

Printed in the United States of America

*This story is dedicated to Amy Garvey,
who made every step of the writing and editing
process feel rewarding and effortless.
Thanks!*

One

"Once again, you've transformed a modest investment into a fortune." Owen Talbot was beaming as he lowered himself into a guest chair in Jack Ryerson's spacious wood-paneled office. "Our arrangement suits me perfectly, but aren't *you* beginning to tire of it? Using your talent to make other men wealthy rather than yourself?"

Jack gave his friend and sometime-associate a cheerful grin. "These ventures have proven lucrative for us both over the years. Don't forget that I take a percentage of every profit I earn for you. And in the meantime, *you* assume all the risk. All in all, a fine arrangement from my point of view."

Owen seemed unconvinced. "The only reason you hesitate to put your personal funds at risk is because your orphaned sisters are still so young. And now you've taken responsibility for young Louisa as well. It's admirable, Jack—keeping the inheritance intact until they're old enough to take their share and find good husbands. But surely, your father never intended—"

"I doubt Father intended any of this, but Fate didn't consult him before taking him and Mother so prematurely. And you're correct—it falls to me to safeguard his legacy for Jane and Mary, and to look out for Louisa as well. And you're correct about one other thing," he added ruefully. "The day I marry off the last of those girls will be a relief, as much as I love them."

"You could set an example for them, by having a wedding of your own." Owen raised a hand to ward off Jack's protest. "Again, you don't want to take risks— this time, to risk your heart again, after that disastrous engagement to Erica. But she was an unusual woman, my friend. It almost certainly won't happen again."

"I won't allow it to happen again," Jack agreed, hoping his interruption would warn his friend away from this annoyingly familiar topic. Yes, Erica had turned his life upside down by breaking their engagement and running off with a sailor, but Jack had made his peace with that. If only the rest of Boston society would do likewise!

But his visitor persisted. "Suppose I told you I've heard of a young lady who is particularly well-suited to your tastes and needs?" Removing a packet from inside his jacket, Owen proffered it across the desk.

Dismayed that people were now apparently bringing him photographs of prospective brides—had he become as pitiable as all that?—Jack winced and shook his head. "She is no doubt lovely, Owen. And I appreciate the sentiment, but—"

"But who am I to choose a bride for you?" Owen's smile had developed a mischievous bent. "I agree. I wouldn't presume to try."

It wasn't in Owen's nature to be evasive or manipulative, or, at least, not with close friends, so Jack gave him a steady stare. "What's this about?"

"You're a professional. You match failing businesses with willing investors, and the results are invariably successful. No one but another professional could presume to make matches—especially of a romantic nature—for someone like yourself."

"Stop!" Jack knew he was scowling but didn't care. This particular line of reasoning sounded familiar in the most obnoxious and unappreciated of ways. "You're referring to Russell Braddock? Don't tell me you've gone so far as to hire a *matchmaker* on my behalf! And not just any matchmaker, of course, but the selfsame meddler who introduced Erica to her sailor? Are you profoundly deranged?"

Throwing the packet onto his desk, Jack jumped to his feet and began to pace. "Whenever Erica and her insufferable husband come to visit, she implores me to contact Braddock, claiming, as you've just done, that his business parallels my own—that he matches a man to a woman in much the same way as I match an investor to a business. It's rubbish of the most obnoxious sort."

Owen chuckled. "Apparently, Erica has been subjecting Russell Braddock to the same rubbish."

"Pardon?"

He motioned for Jack to retake his seat behind the desk. "According to Braddock, Erica has been singing *your* praises, too. And begging the poor fellow to find you a bride. But he had no intention of doing so, until a candidate presented herself who—well, I'm sure it's all in there. I haven't opened it, but it was accompanied by a letter addressed to me, in which the matchmaker asked me to act as go-between. Anticipating your reaction, it seems."

Jack pursed his lips, annoyed that the matchmaker had predicted his reaction, and perplexed that he had chosen Owen Talbot as a romantic intermediary.

His friend seemed to read his mind. "Erica apparently told him that she first heard about his mail-order bride company from me. Do you remember the dinner party where—"

"Don't remind me." Jack gave the thick bundle a wary glance. "I can just imagine the misinformation Erica has invented about me. Even assuming this Braddock is truly talented, which I doubt, he must rely, as I always do, on accurate information. But Erica—"

"She knows you better than anyone," Owen said, his tone gently chiding. "And apparently she still loves you in her own particular way. Why else would she devote herself to ensuring your happiness? Guilt? I don't believe Erica is familiar with that emotion."

Jack had to smile at that. "She cares about me—the brother she never had, as she so insultingly labels me these days." Turning his full attention to the packet, he hefted it and murmured, "The perfect candidate? Is that all he said in his letter to you? No glowing description of her alleged beauty and grace?"

"She has qualities of another sort."

Jack looked up in time to see that his friend's eyes had begun to twinkle again. "What sort of qualities?"

"Braddock says the prospective bride has inherited a failing enterprise which she hopes to restore to its former glory."

Jack had to laugh at the matchmaker's provocative approach. "What sort of business?"

"He didn't say. I'm sure he doesn't reveal personal

details about the brides to just anyone. Whatever else you may think of him, he's a professional with a sterling reputation and a rate of success that rivals your own."

Jack arched an eyebrow in warning. "Enough."

"You won't even consider it? Frankly, I'm surprised. You've always been a practical fellow. And I've never known you to be stubborn or to ignore an opportunity. What harm can come from simply considering Braddock's proposition?"

"If I were looking for a bride, I might. But at the moment, the last thing this household needs is another female. Oh!" He grimaced, noting for the first time that his housekeeper had appeared in the doorway. "My apologies, Margaret. I wasn't referring to you with that complaint."

The servant gave a quick curtsey. "Forgive the interruption, sir, but I thought you'd want to know—Miss Louisa isn't in her bed."

"At this hour?" Jack fought a wave of annoyance. "It's hardly your responsibility to control that girl, but if you don't mind, give her a message for me, won't you? Tell her if she isn't in that bed immediately, there will be no outing this Sunday. And since she is undoubtedly visiting one or both of my sisters, give the message to them as well. I want each of them to get into their respective beds and stay there." To Owen he explained, "Louisa isn't content with disrupting the household. She insists on *cor*rupting it as well, by constantly drawing Jane and Mary into her pranks and misbehavior. They were perfectly well-behaved before she arrived, and now—well, never mind."

"Sir?" Margaret's voice was apologetic yet firm. "She

isn't in Miss Jane's room, nor Miss Mary's. As far as I can tell, she isn't anywhere in the house. And her bedroom window is wide open. And so . . ."

Owen was on his feet, clearly alarmed. "Shall I alert the authorities?"

"Margaret?" Jack drawled. "Do you suspect foul play?"

The housekeeper winced before admitting, "I imagine she's off on mischief of her own making, sir. You know how she is."

"I do indeed," Jack said.

"We can only pray she has sense enough not to leave the grounds."

"Sense? Louisa?" Jack shook his head, wondering what he had done to deserve the constant diet of aggravation his sixteen-year-old cousin had been serving up since her arrival four months earlier.

Then he shrugged to his feet and asked the housekeeper, "Would you do me the favor of waking my sisters? Bring them to Louisa's room. I'll interrogate them there."

Margaret seemed about to object, but something in Jack's expression must have warned her it would be futile, so with another quick curtsey, she hurried from the study.

The kindhearted servant was correct to protest, Jack knew. There were gentler ways to deal with this situation, but he had tried such tactics without success. It was time to take a stricter approach, for everyone's sake. Louisa's behavior was growing bolder by the minute, and could result in true peril, for herself or even for Jack's sisters, if left unchecked.

Exhaling sharply, he offered a handshake to his

friend. "I'd best see to this. And you'd best get home to Elizabeth."

"I'm more than willing to help you search for the girl, Jack. You're amazingly calm about her disappearance."

"I've learned to keep a level head where Louisa is concerned. How her grandmother in Albany tolerated her for as long as she did is beyond me. The girl's incorrigible."

"Still, it's dark and dangerous out there—"

"And safe and sound in here? Not anymore," Jack said, only half in jest. "I've tried not to punish her for these antics, knowing that she lost her mother in the same tragedy that made orphans of Janie and Mary—"

"And of you."

Jack shrugged. "It's different for a child. That's why I've indulged my sisters, just a bit. And I'm sure Louisa's grandmother tried to do the same for her, until the poor woman's patience reached its breaking point. Now she's my responsibility, and I'm not sure I'm equal to it." He flashed a rueful smile, just to show his friend that it wasn't nearly as grim as he'd painted it, then inclined his head toward the door. "I'll see you out. My apologies for the abruptness of all this."

"Nonsense. You gave me marvelous news this evening—Elizabeth will be pleased to hear we'll be taking another, grander trip to the continent next year, thanks to your business acumen. I'm grateful as always, Jack."

"We both profited," Jack reminded him.

"Speaking of mutually beneficial arrangements . . ." Owen reached for the packet from Russell Braddock and handed it to Jack again. "You could save this

woman's family business, while she helps you raise the
girls."

"As I said, the last thing this household needs is another female."

Owen chuckled. "I'll see myself out. Best of luck
with your rambunctious cousin. If I see her on the way
to my carriage I'll send her inside."

Jack followed his friend into the entry hall and
watched until the carved oak doors had closed behind
him before turning to the main staircase. Taking the
steps two at a time, he burst into Louisa's bedroom, hoping to present an intimidating figure, then grinned in defeat at the sight of his two sisters snuggled under the
lacy covers of Louisa's bed.

They were too adorable to scold, and he realized that,
for all his annoyance, he had had a strong need to see
that they were safe and sound. Sitting on the edge of the
mattress, he jostled Mary's arm gently. "Wake up,
sweetheart. I have something to ask you."

She opened her huge, trusting blue eyes and struggled to a seated position. "I forgot where I was," she
murmured. "Mrs. O'Shea says Louisa went out the window again. Are you cross with us, too? We'd never do
any such thing, Jack."

"We're good girls," Janie added, although she hadn't
yet opened her green eyes.

Jack grinned. "Are you asleep, Jane?"

The little girl nodded.

"Well, wake up for just a minute, won't you?"

One eye opened. "Mrs. O'Shea said you're cross. But
we didn't do anything at all. I can't even open the window without help."

He tried not to laugh. "I'm not angry. Just worried. And frustrated. But not with either of you."

Janie smiled and wriggled out from under the covers, then wrapped her arms around Jack's neck. "I don't ever want you to be cross with me."

He embraced her with reassuring firmness. "Tell me something, sweetheart. Did Louisa mention anything to either of you about this? About where she was going?"

"No," the girls chorused, then Janie added with a pout, "She wouldn't even tell us his name. She said we might tell *you*, but we never, ever would."

"Shh!" Mary gave her sister a disgusted glare, then told Jack simply, "We don't know anything."

"So? She went to meet a boy? Is that what you're saying?"

"We didn't say any such thing," Mary protested, but when Jack arched an eyebrow, she changed tactics and insisted sweetly, "She isn't meeting him, Jack. *He's* meeting *her*. And please don't tell her we told you, or she'll never trust us again."

"She isn't meeting him, but he *is* meeting her? That doesn't make any—oh." He grinned in reluctant amusement. "You're saying he's come out here to meet her? To the house?"

Mary nodded. "He told her it wasn't safe for her to come to the wharf."

"The *wharf*?" His heart sank. "How in God's name did Louisa manage to meet a sailor? What do you know about him?"

The older girl shrugged. "We only know he's handsome. And he's in love with Louisa. And if he proves his love to her, she'll marry him."

"And we'll miss her," Janie added, her tone woeful. "And she won't even be able to visit, because you'll be so cross with her."

"Even though you shouldn't be cross at all, because you *want* her to go away," Mary said. "So wouldn't it be best if she married him?"

The childlike logic almost made sense, Jack had to admit. If Louisa were just a little older, and her prospective suitor were a respectable boy from a respectable family—anyone but a sailor, in fact!—he'd be celebrating the idea of marrying her off.

"You're absolutely certain she didn't go to the wharves?"

The girls nodded solemnly.

"And how exactly did Louisa want him to prove his love to her?"

"By bringing her candy and kissing her," Janie explained. "Louisa says you can tell whether to marry a boy or not by the way it feels when he kisses you."

"Fascinating." Jack's voice was closer to a growl than he'd intended, and when his sisters' expressions clouded, he gave them a quick, reassuring smile. "Time for your big brother to carry you back to your safe little beds."

"Yay!" Janie scooted behind him and wrapped her arms around his neck, but Mary didn't budge.

Instead, she told him, "I'm not a baby, Jack. You shouldn't act as though I am."

He stared, taken aback by the proclamation. She was only nine years old, after all. Not a baby, perhaps, but certainly a little girl, at least for a few more years, assuming Louisa didn't corrupt her prematurely.

He wasn't about to allow that to happen, and so he instructed her, "Stay here while I take Janie back to her bedroom." Without waiting for a reply, he jumped to his feet and bounced the little one down the hallway, enjoying her gleeful shrieks.

Depositing her into her bed, he grabbed one of her rag dolls off the bedstand and tucked it, along with its owner, under the covers. "Sweet dreams, Janie. I love you more than you'll ever know."

"I love you, too," Janie assured him. Then she eyed him sternly and added, "So does everyone."

"Is that so?"

The little girl nodded.

"Well, everyone loves you, too," he said, his throat tightening unexpectedly. "Pleasant dreams, sweetheart. I'll come back and check on you in a while."

Janie beamed, then closed her eyes and cuddled her doll to her chest.

Leaning down, Jack brushed his lips across her cheek, then turned back toward Louisa's room, all too aware that two tougher challenges awaited him. He had almost bypassed Mary's room when her voice called out his name; he realized sadly that she had disobeyed him, but only slightly, in order to make a point that apparently meant quite a bit to her.

Stepping into her room, he was humbled to see her propped up against her pillows, trying to look older than her tender years. And trying to appear less vulnerable than her gentle spirit could manage.

Jack gave her a respectful smile. "Are you sleepy, sweetheart?"

She sighed, clearly relieved he wasn't angry. "A little."

"I didn't mean to imply you were a baby. You'll always be my little sister," he explained, moving carefully toward her bed, then sitting on the edge. "But it's obvious you're becoming a young lady, and I couldn't be more proud."

"Oh, Jack!"

To his dismay, she threw her arms around his neck and burst into tears. "I was so horrid!"

"You were no such thing," he said, gathering her against his chest. "Can I tell you something, Mary?"

She choked back a sob, then nodded without pulling her face from his shirtfront.

"When Mother and Father were lost at sea, I was determined to provide you and Janie with idyllic childhoods. But no childhood, idyllic or otherwise, can last forever. Yours will continue for a good long while—no arguments on that score, young lady—but perhaps it's time I began to prepare myself for something more."

"Louisa says you want us to be children forever, so you don't ever have to have children of your own."

"I beg your pardon?"

"Because of Erica," she explained diplomatically. "Louisa says Erica broke your heart, and you'll never trust another female. So you'll never have children of your own. But we want to have our *own* babies, Jack. So you have to let us get married."

"When exactly would you like this to happen?" he drawled. "Next week?"

Mary gasped. "No. Just someday."

"Fine." He kissed her cheek, then urged her back under the coverlet. "Someday, you may marry. I give you my word. But not soon."

"Not soon," she agreed. "Not for me. But for Louisa—"

"Not soon for her, either," Jack corrected her. "But eventually, you will all marry, as will I. Although it's difficult to imagine Janie as anything other than a sweet little baby."

Mary giggled. "All she cares about is dolls and chocolate."

"Good." He grinned. "I shall see that she has both for as long as that satisfies her." Sobering slightly, he asked, "Is Louisa unhappy in this house?"

"She's unhappy everywhere, I think. Because she misses her mamma and papa."

"She says that?"

"No. But I know she does, because—" The little girl flushed. "Well, I just know."

"Because you miss *our* parents so much?" Jack patted her hand. "So do I, sweetheart." Clearing his throat, he dared to ask, "Do you suppose it would be better for you and your sister—and for Louisa, for that matter—if I had a wife?"

The child seemed confused by the question. "Wouldn't it be better for *you*?"

Jack chuckled, then he stroked a stray hair from her cheek and rose to his feet. "Pleasant dreams, Mary."

"Good night, Jack. I love you. So does Janie. So does Louisa."

He watched her snuggle into her pillow, then whispered softly that he loved her, too, before edging out of the room and back into the hall.

"Now for the toughest female of all," he reminded himself.

His first instinct was to stride down the staircase, pull open the front entry doors, and bellow Louisa's name, along with some choice threats. But she was such a stubborn girl, she might just run off for the wharf with her candy-toting admirer. Perhaps it would be better to simply sneak about the grounds until he discovered the two together.

And then what would you do? he asked himself, wandering back into her room and staring at the open window. *Punch the lad in the jaw? Carry her back here, kicking and screaming? It would only be a matter of time before she ran off again, and this time, she wouldn't content herself with an innocent meeting here at the house.*

What would Louisa's parents have done? Or his own parents? The grandmother in Albany had reportedly been strict without success. Jack, on the other hand, had employed patience and evenhanded rules, but Louisa had thwarted him and those rules at every turn.

Moving to sit on the edge of her empty bed, he spied the package from Russell Braddock. "What would *you* do?" he asked the matchmaker grimly. "According to Erica, you are an expert in human nature, with an infallible sense of what a person wants.

"What do you suppose a pretty little orphan like Louisa wants? More importantly, what do you think *I* want? A bride with a failing business? No. But one who could ensure happiness for Louisa and for my sisters? If you could find such a woman, I would gladly pay your full fee!"

Tearing away the brown paper wrapping, he found a bundle of documents accompanied by a lengthy letter crafted in exquisite penmanship. But not one photograph, which he found inexplicably intriguing. Settling back against a lacy pillow, he began to read:

My dear Mr. Ryerson,

Allow this letter to serve several purposes, ranging from introduction to apology to solicitation. You have heard of me—of that I have no doubt. I can only suppose that you have been subjected to a barrage of compliments on my behalf second only to the praises our lovely Erica sings at every mention of your name.

Jack grinned at that, pleased that Erica's antics had annoyed the matchmaker as much as they had Jack. Then he turned his attention back to Braddock's words.

Which, of course, leads to the apology. I believe I played havoc with your plans to marry Erica. You could not have chosen a more beautiful or charming bride, and I know it is small comfort to realize, as you undoubtedly have, that her thirst for constant upheaval and danger would have made the match less than blissful from time to time. Still, I believe you and she would have made the best of it, and because of me, that aspect of your life remains unresolved. For that I apologize.

On the other hand, it does present you with an opportunity to seek a bride more particularly suited to your needs. You are not yet prepared to take that step, however. I know this from Erica's account of your mood on her last visit to Boston. When you are ready to find the perfect bride, I can only hope you will do me the honor of allowing me to assist you.

In the meantime, I have a business proposition for you. A young woman of my acquaintance recently inherited a cattle ranch from her grandfather. This enterprise was once profitable, but a series of mishaps in the last two years has thrown it into a precarious state. Still, the house and stock are relatively solid, and the land alone quite valuable. This woman, whose name is Trinity Standish, would like to restore the place to its former glory in honor of her grandfather.

I thought of you immediately. As you can see, I have included some initial information concerning the ranch in hopes of piquing your interest.

There is one complication. The grandfather conditioned Miss Standish's inheritance on the following: she and her lawfully wedded husband must live on the ranch for at least a full six months during the year following the old man's death. Odd, is it not? But apparently, he knew only too well that his granddaughter was not attracted to ranch life.

His assessment was accurate. While Miss Standish will do everything necessary to restore the ranch, she has no intention of being the wife of a rancher—or of any man, for that matter. She therefore finds herself in the odd position of needing a temporary husband as well as a business manager.

There is one further complication. The grandfather's will provides that the ranch must never fall into the hands of a neighboring family named Crowne. It seems that a feud exists between the two clans. Miss Standish is of the opinion that a man named Walter Crowne was responsible for her grandfather's death, which of course makes her doubly determined that they never touch one acre of the land despite the fact that they would pay her a tidy sum for it.

There are further nuances to this situation, but given your broad experience in these matters, I'm sure they will present only minor obstacles.

Miss Standish was delighted when I told her about you and your successes. She asked me to tell you that if you can assist her, she will gladly give you 50 percent ownership of the ranch. The marriage must be a valid one, but one that can be neatly dissolved after six months. After that, the two of you can hire a manager, and simply return to your old lives, reaping your profits year after year, or find an eventual buyer—on the condition, of course, that it not be a Crowne.

Given the fact that the marriage will be temporary, I will not dwell on Miss Standish's suitability as a prospective bride, other than to mention that she is a healthy young woman and an entertaining conversationalist.

My dear Mr. Ryerson, I cannot begin to guess at your reaction to this communication. I can only hope you will accept it in the spirit in which it is offered—as an opportunity, and, to a lesser but equally sincere extent, as an olive branch.

I look forward to your reply.

> *Warmest regards,*
> *Russell Braddock, Proprietor*
> *The Happily Ever After Company,*
> *San Francisco, California*

Jack shook his head as he reread the more provocative passages from the letter. "A healthy young woman and an entertaining conversationalist?" he quoted, grinning reluctantly. "Not exactly a beauty then, eh, Braddock? I can only imagine the myriad flaws you've finessed with this rather diplomatic phrasing."

Not that it mattered in any event. Even if Jack were interested in the proposition—which he wasn't—he knew that neither he, or any other experienced businessman, could sail a schooner through a loophole as broad as the one reflected in these documents. There was no need for Miss Trinity Standish to endure a six-month sham of a marriage, and out of prudence, Jack would send a brief note to Braddock, suggesting that the poor girl consult an attorney immediately.

As for the viability of the cattle ranch itself . . .

Jack sifted through the documents, intrigued by the history—financial and otherwise—outlined therein. Established in 1852, the ranch had grown from a modest enterprise into a phenomenal success, and would have continued as such had a series of calamities not subverted it. But the raw materials were all still there—hundreds of acres of prime grazing land, along with ample supplies of fresh water.

And Jack suspected there was also an endless supply of willing workers, now that the winners and losers in the gold rush had been chosen. Some of those losers had turned their attentions to the silver strikes, where once again, they were failing miserably. But in the meantime, hungry miners and hungrier railroad workers needed to eat. Why not eat steak?

His reverie was interrupted by the rustle of branches outside the window, and he set the papers on the bed, then moved into the shadows just as a small foot in a delicate calfskin boot poked through the curtains. One long leg in lacy pantaloons, and then another, and then with a thump, Louisa Jane Ryerson arrived. Brushing dirt and bark from her dark green skirt, she straightened, then tossed her loose brown locks in a gesture of defiance that might have annoyed Jack had he not also noticed the tracks that had been made by tears through the dusty residue on her cheeks.

His first thought was to thrash the bastard who had made her cry. On the other hand, she seemed physically unharmed, so he adopted a neutral demeanor as he stepped out of the shadows and drawled, "Welcome home, Louisa."

"Oh!" She stepped back from him, then seemed to regret the submissive movement, jutting her chin forward in a belated show of bravado. "How dare you lurk in my room."

"That's all you have to say for yourself?"

"I don't owe you an explanation. And even if I did, I'm too tired to bother now. Can't we discuss it in the morning?"

"We'll discuss it now." He gestured toward her bed. "Sit down."

She grimaced but complied. "If it's any consolation, I see now I made a wretched mistake."

"Because you shouldn't have gone out the window at all, or because your young man disappointed you?"

"Janie and Mary told you about him?" She grabbed a coverlet and pulled it over her dusty clothes, then cuddled into her pillow. "He was supposed to meet me at the foot of the tree, but he was injured today in a fall from the mast and wasn't able to come."

"If he didn't come to meet you, how did you hear about his fall?"

Louisa's lip began to quiver. "He sent his friend to tell me."

"I see." Jack sat on the edge of the bed and took her hand into his own. "Are his injuries serious? Is that why you're so upset?"

"I can only hope his injuries are very, very painful, and extremely fatal."

He could see the hurt in her huge blue eyes, and again wanted to strangle the boy. "Why is that?"

"I promised him I'd kiss him—I know it was naughty, but he seemed so sweet. So harmless. But he wasn't sweet at all. He actually believed I'd entertain his friend in his place!"

Jack's temper flared. "Unbelievable. I'm so sorry, Louisa. If he laid one finger on you—"

"He didn't. He brought me candy, and apparently thought I was such a harlot, I'd fall into his arms. But instead, I slapped him. With all my might," she added, her lip quivering again.

"There, there." Jack pulled her into a comforting embrace. "I'm sure he'll think twice before he'll insult a lady in the future. These sailors are the lowest form of mankind, sweetheart. They don't know any better. Promise me you won't entertain their advances ever again, no matter how harmless they seem."

Louisa wriggled free and patted his cheek. "We've both been wronged by sailors, haven't we? And we'll hate them until our dying days. It's a wonderful bond between us, Jack. So much more meaningful than simply being cousins."

"I agree. Although I'm quite fond of being your cousin. Being your guardian, however, is proving to be a challenge."

"Pardon me for being such a burden," she said, sniffing disdainfully. "Send me back to Grandmother if you'd like. I'll be glad to go. I miss her terribly."

"And I'm sure she misses you." He tried not to let her read his thoughts as he remembered the grandmother's frantic entreaty that Jack never again ask her to take responsibility for their wild little Louisa.

Louisa touched his cheek. "You aren't really considering sending me back to Grandmother, are you? I know I've been difficult. I'll try harder to be good. I promise."

"Nonsense. I was just wondering what I could do to make these next few months easier for you. To entertain you, and help you grow safely into womanhood, without boring you to tears, or driving you into the arms of sailors."

"You *are* boring," she admitted with a sigh. "But that doesn't give me the right to be ungrateful."

Jack chuckled. "Boring, am I?"

She gave him an apologetic smile. "It's not your fault. There's simply nothing to do here. Haven't you noticed? You're content with your dull books and dreary accounts, but I want to have exciting experiences, and so do Janie and Mary. They're just too polite to say so, for fear it might hurt your feelings."

Jack had never before noticed how much like Erica she was. Sweet and lovely, but so very easily bored. And dangerous, to herself and to *his* sanity, when sufficiently ignored. She might as well have sung Erica's perpetual refrain: *I want an adventure!*

He had ignored Erica, and had paid a high price, although in a sense, he was sure Russell Braddock was correct: they hadn't been well-suited to one another.

But Louisa was his blood relative, which meant he didn't have the luxury of driving her away. He had to find a way to keep her safe while still satisfying, to a rational extent, her thirst for excitement.

And so, with a rueful smile, he sandwiched her pretty face between his hands and asked her simply, "How would you like to visit a cattle ranch in California?"

Two

Trinity Standish tugged at the collar of her stiff black dress, feeling suffocated despite the fact that the fit was not at all tight. "You can't really intend to meet your future husband in this dreadful outfit," she told her reflection in the bedroom mirror. "One look at you and he'll head back to Boston on the very next stage."

Or would he? According to Russell Braddock, this Boston accountant understood the arrangement perfectly, and wasn't expecting romance. Instead, he was making this long trip, by steamship and stage, in hopes of making a tidy profit. The marriage would be a temporary one, more akin to a business partnership, despite the fact that it would be sealed by marital consummation rather than a handshake.

Still, the last thing Trinity wanted to do was confuse the poor man by appearing in the doorway dressed in something soft and alluring, and so she was taking advantage of the fact that she was in mourning, and had dressed accordingly.

"Grandpa would roll over in his grave at the thought of you dressed this way. Even when Papa died, you never wore anything so severe. Of course," she added philosophically, "Grandpa would be shocked by more than just this. To be murdered before his time, by his sworn enemy, and to remain unavenged while his beloved ranch fails more with each passing day."

She could only pray that Russell Braddock had chosen the correct business manager for the Lost Spur. If her new "husband" could restore the ranch to its former glory, Trinity would take care of the rest by somehow proving to the world that her grandfather's "accident" had actually been cold-blooded murder, and by bringing Walter Crowne to justice for that crime.

Jack Ryerson . . .

She frowned as she pulled her pale gold locks into a severe knot behind her head. Again, it was an unfamiliar image for her, but one she was determined to project, at least initially, if only to demonstrate to Ryerson that she intended a no-nonsense relationship. Of course, to be fair, Ryerson might be worried that just the opposite was true—that Trinity might prove to be a clinging female who might insist on following him back to Boston when his work at the ranch was completed.

Don't worry, sir, she thought with a disdainful sniff. *I have no desire to live out my days with a pasty-faced accountant who spends his life indoors, poring over facts and figures. Six months to the day after we wed, you will be rid of me as a wife. As a business partner, perhaps it will take a while longer, but rest assured, I will be no burden to you. Or to any man.*

For a moment, the absurdity of the situation threatened to overwhelm her, as it had more than once during the sleepless nights since Braddock had told her about Ryerson. Could she really rely on a stranger, even one who came highly recommended by a professional matchmaker? Could she trust the stranger to be gentle? To be reasonable? And most importantly, to be true to their bargain, bizarre though it might be?

He's as worried as you are, she reminded herself again. *Do you suppose a successful Boston businessman wants to jeopardize everything he's built for himself by marrying a strange, impoverished girl? You act as though you're the prize! Imagine instead the women he must admire—society ladies with impeccable breeding, content to sit and do needlepoint while he studies his accounts. Not the daughter of a vagabond, and certainly not one who intends to follow in her father's footsteps by traversing the world before she even considers settling down with a family.*

If there was one thing she knew for certain about Jack Ryerson, it was that family was of paramount importance to him, so much so that he was actually bringing two little sisters and a cousin along with him from Boston! It had impressed Trinity when she'd first heard about it, but it had also warned her that she and her fiancé had precious little in common.

In contrast to Ryerson, she had absolutely no interest in raising children. Still, on a practical note, it pleased her that he took his responsibilities so seriously. And she assumed the children's presence would be a convenient impediment to any attempt by the bridegroom to take more than token advantage of his intimate relationship with Trinity.

Her brooding was blessedly invaded by the sound of shouts from the yard as Elena, the ranch's cook, announced, "*M'ija*! They're coming! I can see the carriage!"

"Oh, dear." Hurrying to the open window, Trinity poked her head through billowing curtains and peered into the distance, where a cloud of red dust was moving briskly toward the ranch from the east. At that rate, the newcomers would be on her doorstep in ten minutes or less, which meant Trinity needed to put her useless worrying aside and hurry downstairs to greet them.

As she was about to turn away, her attention was grabbed by something else in the distance: a horse and rider coming out of the west on a path intersecting that of the carriage. The horseman cut a dashing figure—tall in the saddle, wearing a long, dusty coat and wide-brimmed hat. As Trinity watched, he drew up alongside the vehicle and appeared to be conversing—shouting, no doubt—with the occupants. Apparently satisfied with what he'd heard, he then urged his steed forward, galloping toward the ranch house with the carriage falling quickly behind.

Trinity's imagination danced as she studied the stranger's confident bearing. Although she couldn't quite see his face, she imagined him to be tanned and ruggedly handsome. A cowboy or lawman, born to ride the length and breadth of the untamed West and to sleep out under the stars.

Who could he be? A tingle of excitement shot through her, and without thinking, she turned back to the mirror for an instinctive check of her appearance, then groaned in self-reproach.

Had she completely lost her mind? Fantasizing over some stranger, when another, more important man was about to ride into her life? In a carriage, not on a huge black horse, but that certainly wasn't *his* fault.

Stop this nonsense immediately! she scolded herself.

*The rider is undoubtedly a friend of Clancy's, and will
probably turn out to be old and ugly and completely un-
heroic. Jack Ryerson, for all his pasty-faced ways, is the
man you should be thrilled to see—and if he manages
to save the Spur, he'll be a true hero, whether he travels
here by steed, carriage, or turtle.*

Smoothing her hair one last time, she flew down the
stairs and out onto the broad wooden porch, where various members of the ranch house staff had already as-
sembled.

Elena arched a disapproving eyebrow. "This is how a
lady greets her betrothed?"

"Never mind all that. Do you know who that rider is?"

"I've never seen him before."

Trinity turned to the ranch foreman. "Clancy? Do
you recognize him?"

"No, miss." The elderly man's eyes twinkled. "Can't
say I recognize you, either."

She laughed in appreciation of his gentle teasing.
"I'm in mourning, am I not?"

"You think that dress'll discourage your new husband's attentions? Not likely, honey. Them prim dresses
have a way of perking a fella's imagination in some real
unexpected directions."

She wanted to scold him, but her attention was fixed
again on the approaching rider, who was now so close,
she could see that he was neither old nor ugly. Instead,
he was alarmingly handsome, with skin that was tanned
but not at all weather-beaten. As he grew closer, he
raised his gloved hand in greeting, flashing the group a
lopsided, seductive smile.

Trinity felt another sharp stab of excitement, and this

time, she didn't even bother to shake herself free of it. So what if she was technically engaged to someone else? She could still avail herself of one last opportunity for an innocent flirtation, at least until the carriage arrived.

And so, as the rider pulled up alongside the porch, she smiled and stepped forward, conscious of the approving gleam in his vibrant green eyes as he rapidly assessed her.

"Welcome to the Lost Spur Ranch, sir." She almost giggled at the sultry tone in which her words had emerged, and cleared her throat before adding more practically, "I'm Trinity Standish, the owner of this spread."

The man's grin widened as he swung off the horse and looped its reins over the porch rail. Standing at ground level, he surveyed her for a long, flattering moment, then swept his hat off and bowed slightly. "It's an honor, Miss Standish. My condolences over the loss of your grandfather. And my thanks for making us feel so welcome."

"Us?"

His grin faded. "I thought Braddock told you—damn!" He glanced back over his shoulder at the carriage, then shook his head. "Your driver didn't seemed surprised to see the girls, so I just assumed—"

"Wait!" Trinity hurried down the steps and stood before him. "You're Mr. Jack Ryerson?"

The newcomer nodded, clearly confused. "I assumed you knew."

She could hear Clancy chuckling in the background, and knew her cheeks were crimson. "Forgive me, won't you? I thought you were in the carriage with your sisters and cousin, who, of course, are welcome. I would have been disappointed if they hadn't accompanied you. I'm so sorry, Mr. Ryerson. I just didn't expect you to be so—well, so tall."

"Or so dusty?" His boyish smile returned. "You're not quite what I expected, either." Taking her hand, he kissed her fingertips lightly. "Jack Ryerson, at your service. And your confusion is completely understandable. The only reason I hired a horse was to get a closer look at the ranch. I was able to cover quite a bit of ground without losing sight of the carriage. Unfortunately, that same ground is now coating my clothes, so it's no wonder my appearance startled you."

Trinity moistened her lips, desperate to say something intelligent or reassuring, but she was too confused to manage either. It had been odd enough when she had thought him a handsome interloper. But he was her fiancé! The man she had hoped to keep at a distance except as absolutely necessary to honor her grandfather's will.

The touch of his lips against her hand had sent her insides reeling, and her plans for discouraging him were now disintegrating into an irrational need to bolt back into the house and up the stairs, to pull off her unattractive garb, loosen her long, golden hair, and dress herself in her finest and most feminine gown.

Clancy came to her rescue, although not without another knowing chuckle as he insinuated himself between Trinity and her fiancé, pumping the latter's hand and announcing, "I'm Bob Clancy, the closest thing to a foreman the Spur has for now. We're mighty glad you're here, sir. I just hope half of what Miss Trinity heard about you is true."

"It's a pleasure, Mr. Clancy. I've read enough about you in the information from Russell Braddock to know how valuable you are to this ranch."

"And this here's Elena. She and her kinfolk do all the cooking and cleaning, and generally keep us outta trouble."

Jack inclined his head toward the servant, who had stayed at the top of the steps. "I'm very pleased to meet you, Elena. My apologies for all this grime I collected along the trail." Taking off his calf-length coat, he gave it a brisk shake, then studied the still-dusty results with a grimace.

"Nothing I don't see every day," Elena assured him, beaming. "Like Clancy said, we're all so glad you're here. Miss Trinity more than any of us, as you can plainly see."

Trinity shot the woman a glare, then turned her attention to the carriage, which was just pulling to a halt a dozen or so yards away. Anxious to make a better impression on the sisters than she had on the brother, she summoned a gracious smile that widened with true delight as the door sprung open and two darling girls halffell to the ground without waiting for assistance.

"We're here!" the smaller of the children announced, her round face glowing. "Where are the cows?"

"They're roaming the pastures, so you'll just have to settle for us at the moment," Trinity told her, dropping to one knee to look her in the eyes. "I'm Trinity Standish. Welcome to the Lost Spur."

"Allow me to present Miss Jane Ryerson," Jack said

from behind her. "She's been talking of nothing but cows for the last six weeks. If we're not careful, she'll name each and every one of them."

"I'm pleased to meet you, Jane." Trinity hesitated, then gave the girl's hand a tentative squeeze. "We have a nice room fixed up for you. And once you've had a good night's sleep, you and I will ride out and see the herd." Straightening, she turned to the second girl and smiled. "Hello, there."

"This is Mary," Jack supplied quickly. "She's pleased to be here, too, although she shares her big brother's wariness for livestock."

Trinity laughed and patted the taller girl's shoulder. "You should have seen me the first time I visited the Spur. I had never even owned my own cat or dog, and suddenly, I was surrounded by animals!"

Mary smiled shyly. "Thank you for inviting us to your ranch, Miss Standish. I'm not at all afraid of cows. And neither is Jack. I don't know why he said such a thing."

"I never had a brother, but I'm told they feel compelled to tease their sisters whenever possible," Trinity said with a sympathetic wink. Then she looked up at the carriage in time to see a third girl emerge, stepping onto the foot rail cautiously. Jack was there in an instant to offer his hand, helping her to the ground.

"That's Louisa," Janie told Trinity. "She's our cousin."

"How fortunate you are to have a sister, a brother, *and* a cousin."

"Louisa complains about everything," Jane confided in a whisper. "But she hardly ever means anything by it."

"I'll remember that," Trinity promised. Then she

straightened and walked over to where Louisa was standing. "Welcome to the Lost Spur, Louisa. We'll do our best to make you comfortable here."

"I'm pleased to meet you, Miss Standish," the girl insisted, as though trying to convince herself in the process. "I hope you don't mind Jack bringing me along. He could have left me at school—"

"I would have been disappointed if he had," Trinity interrupted, adding silently that she herself had been "left at school" far too frequently in her childhood, when she had wanted nothing more than to travel around the world with her wandering father.

On impulse, she gave Louisa's shoulder a warm squeeze, and was pleased when she didn't pull away. Then she turned back toward the house, only to find herself face-to-face with Jack Ryerson, his smile more charming than ever as he offered his arm to escort her back toward the steps.

Warmth flooded her cheeks as she tucked her hand into the crook of his elbow. Had she honestly believed they could engage in this quasi-romantic relationship without becoming hopelessly confused? It had seemed possible when she had imagined him as a serious, squinty-eyed weakling with a talent for facts and figures. But this dashing man had another talent, namely sending shivers of anticipation through unsuspecting women with one glance from his emerald eyes.

The thought of spending a wedding night in his arms and emerging the next day with a cool head was ludicrous, and yet her grandfather's will, combined with her own plans for her future, left her no choice.

Jack apparently was having no trouble adjusting to

the notion, so she decided to follow his lead for the moment. But at the first opportunity, she would find an excuse to escape to her room, so that she could gather her wits and decide how to handle this unexpected development.

And to change into something prettier.

Jack and the girls had spent seven long weeks travelling to San Francisco, where Russell Braddock had housed and entertained them for another ten days before sending them off on the last leg of their journey.

And in all that time, Jack grumbled to himself as he escorted his hostess onto the porch, *that wily matchmaker never once mentioned the fact that Trinity Standish is a stunningly beautiful girl. Thank God she's in mourning. Or rather,* he corrected himself hastily, *thank God she's still dressing in black, to remind you of her loss. And to remind you further that even though a matchmaker brought you together, you're here for business reasons only.*

If he had had any lingering doubt about whether Braddock was a genius, this had effectively settled it. Not only had the matchmaker neglected to mention Trinity's beauty, he had studiously avoided any description other than "healthy" and "good conversationalist," thereby leading Jack to believe that she was probably plain, or perhaps even unattractive.

But what was the matchmaker's motive? To manipulate Jack into relaxing his guard, so that he would be even more impressed at the first meeting with his new business partner? It made a certain amount of sense.

After all, Jack had made it clear that he was coming to the ranch to evaluate the potential investment, without any commitment on his part to actually take on the ranch as a project. He wanted a chance to objectively judge the ranch's strengths and weaknesses.

Had he known one of those strengths was the pleasure of spending time with a beautiful girl, he could have prepared himself accordingly. Instead, his business instincts were being subverted, at least for the moment, by more primal urges.

The black dress was thus a godsend, reminding him why he was there. Still, he couldn't help wondering how he would have felt, seeing her there on the porch for the first time, if he had been planning on marrying her, as Braddock's first letter had suggested. That complication had been put to rest, thanks to Jack's expertise in finding loopholes. But seeing her now, a part of him couldn't help but fantasize about a wedding night— even a wedding night that was part of a business arrangement that included divorce within six months.

He could only imagine how Trinity Standish would have felt had the wedding still been part of the plan! As it was, she seemed nervous and apologetic. How much more nervous—or worse, despondent or even frightened!—would she be if she thought she was going to find herself in bed with a strange man.

And a tall one at that, he added to himself with a grin, remembering how she had reacted when she'd first seen him. She had been alarmed when the much-heralded business expert had arrived in so dusty and unceremonious a manner.

Better a dusty business partner than a dusty lover, he

told her in silent amusement as he escorted her into the long, red-tiled entry hall of the modest two-story ranch house.

Trinity returned his smile, but to Jack her expression seemed somewhat forced. "Elena has prepared some refreshments for you and the girls, but I'm sure you'd like to freshen up first. And if you'd like to rest until dinner, we'd understand perfectly. I'll show your sisters and Louisa to their rooms. You'll be taking Grandpa's old room. It's the nicest by far." She grimaced slightly. "He didn't die there, but if you have any reservations about . . . well, about such things—"

"If it's the nicest room, shouldn't it be yours?" he asked carefully.

Trinity's smile warmed. "I lived in Maryland when Grandpa built this house, but he was already planning my visits, so he designed perfectly lovely accommodations for me. Grandpa's room is the room of a rancher, and since you're going to step into his shoes and manage the ranch—"

"Since there's a *likelihood* I'll be managing the ranch," Jack corrected her quickly, "I'd be honored to use his room. Thank you."

A small, petulant crease appeared across Trinity's forehead, and Jack forced himself not to laugh. "Mr. Braddock made that clear to you, did he not?" he asked.

"He was quite clear," she agreed. "You need two full weeks to conduct an inventory, examine the books, and ask questions, and then you'll make your decision. But the fact is, until two years ago, this ranch was more of a gold mine than most of the *actual* goldmines in these parts. If you're half the manager Mr. Braddock claims you to be, it won't take two weeks to discover that this is a wonderful opportunity for you." She flushed and added quickly, "It has its complications, of course. But if we're respectful of one another, we should emerge with a substantial profit. And hopefully with our dignity intact."

"Our dignity?"

Her blush deepened. "I didn't mean to imply that I was ashamed, sir. Nor that you should be. Grandpa forced us into this peculiar arrangement, but if we follow Mr. Braddock's advice—"

As Jack watched, amazed, she dropped her lovely violet gaze to the floor and added unhappily, "Perhaps we shouldn't discuss this in front of the children."

"Discuss what?" he asked, but as the words were leaving his mouth, he somehow knew, and the realization made him groan. "You're not talking about the marriage, are you? Surely Braddock told you my position—" Jack stopped himself, acutely aware that Louisa was hanging on his every word. With a nervous smile, he suggested, "You offered to show the girls to their rooms, and that sounds like an excellent plan. I'll find your grandfather's room on my own, and perhaps once we're all settled in, you and I could speak in private? Perhaps in the parlor?"

Trinity was staring at him as though he'd suddenly switched to an obscure Latin dialect. "Your position?" Her eyes began to blaze. "I'm no fonder of this arrangement than you appear to be, sir, but the marriage is integral to our success. You need only read Grandpa's will to know that. If I've disappointed you in some way—"

"Certainly not!"

"Let me finish!" She backed away as though she didn't trust herself to be within slapping distance of his face. "If you expected me to greet you with some sort of flirtatious or seductive attitude, I apologize. But I see this as a business relationship, and I urge you to do the same."

The fire in her eyes lapped at Jack's senses, and for a moment he was speechless. Never before had he stood so close to wild, untamed beauty, made all the more amazing by the contrast with her matronly dress and severely coifed hair.

And then he understood everything—her manner of dress; her nervousness; her embarrassment.

A proud young woman, believing she needed to submit to indignity in order to honor her grandfather's memory. If it hadn't been so immediate and so completely bizarre, it would have touched his heart. As it was, he needed to keep his heart out of it, and his wits about him, if he wanted to salvage this deal.

Turning to Louisa, he instructed, "Take your cousins and go upstairs. This instant. Elena?" He locked eyes with the housekeeper, who was literally gawking in his direction. "Might I impose on you to show the girls to their rooms while Miss Standish and I discuss a business matter in private?"

"N-no, Señor Ryerson. I mean, *si*! Yes, sir." Whirling toward the girls, she insisted, "Come along now, little ones. I've made up your rooms with fresh flowers and linens. Hurry now and I'll show you."

Trinity was nodding in emphatic agreement. "Go with Elena, girls. Once you've settled in, we'll all have tea and cake in the sunroom. Thank you, Elena," she added sincerely. "Whatever would I do without you?"

The housekeeper shrugged her shoulders, in helplessness rather than response, then shooed the three girls up the stairs, leaving Jack alone with his new partner.

"Believe me, Miss Standish—"

"Hush!" She took him by the arm and pulled him toward a nearby room dominated by a shiny mahogany desk. Once they were inside, she pulled a pair of sliding doors closed then turned to face him, her face pale, her expression stricken. "I can't imagine what you intend to say after all this time. I trusted you and Mr. Braddock—"

"And if you'll listen, for just five minutes, your trust in me will be renewed. And your opinion of Mr. Braddock—well, we'll discuss that, too, eventually. For now—" Jack gave her his most reassuring smile. "Have a seat, won't you, Miss Standish?"

She didn't seem at all reassured, and Jack grew uneasy. Despite years of persuading male investors to trust him, he had had little experience placating females. And on the few occasions where a client's wife or daughter had quizzed him on his investment strategies, they had responded to his reassurances with contented smiles, and even, once or twice, with flirtatious offers of thanks.

There was no danger of that happening here. Trinity Standish's eyes had gone from blazing to cold. And her hands were on her hips—a clear sign that she was about to snap his head off, if he remembered his days with Erica accurately.

She wasn't going to sit, and so he would stand as well, but he allowed himself to lean against the desk, hoping the casual attitude would convey a comforting confidence. Then he began, as gently as possible, hoping to find words that would quell this angry bride's fears. "There's a loophole in your grandfather's will. If we take advantage of it, we can own the ranch, free and clear of the charity's interest, without the need to marry."

"A loophole?"

Her soft-spoken response encouraged Jack to continue. "In Mr. Braddock's original letter to me, he insisted you would lose your interest in this ranch unless you lived on the premises with your wedded husband for six consecutive months during the first year after your grandfather's death. Is that your understanding as well?"

Trinity nodded. "If I don't marry, and marry soon, title passes to the Delta Valley Home for Boys. I've read the will myself, Mr. Ryerson. It's there on Grandpa's desk. Perhaps you should familiarize yourself with it."

He gestured again toward one of the leather chairs facing the desk. "Shall we discuss this calmly?"

Trinity hesitated, then nodded and took a seat. Relieved, Jack moved around the desk and settled into the well-worn seat that had clearly served Abe Standish well for a decade. Forcing himself to ignore how vulnerable and lovely his hostess appeared at that moment, he leaned forward and locked his gaze with hers. "Since you've read the will, let me ask you this: if you and I marry this month and then live here together as man and wife for the next consecutive six months, what will the Delta Valley Home for Boys receive?"

"I beg your pardon?" She cocked her head to the side, clearly confused. "They won't receive anything—at least, not anything under the will."

"Precisely." He paused to smile. "I imagine they'd rather have something than nothing, wouldn't you say?"

Trinity moistened her lips, then nodded.

"And so, if we were to go to them, and to tell them we intend to marry, but we're willing to consider other means of resolving this dilemma, they'd be interested, wouldn't you say?"

"Other means?"

Jack nodded. "My intention, if I decide to become involved with this business, is to offer them a percentage of the ranch's current value—out of my share, I might add—in exchange for their agreement not to enforce their interest under the will's condition subsequent. Do you understand what I'm saying?"

She bit her bottom lip as she again nodded.

"What do you suppose their answer will be?" Jack continued.

"I'd like to think they'd reject that proposition, Mr. Ryerson."

"Reject?" He collected himself and explained more gently, "I'm not sure I made myself clear—"

"You made yourself perfectly clear," Trinity assured him. "My grandfather invested everything he owned into a piece of bare ground and spent ten long years developing it into a successful cattle ranch. I'd like to think the owners of the orphanage respect his right to determine its disposition. He earned that with sweat, and blood, and more than a few tears along the way. Who are they—and who are *we*?—to conjure up a loophole to thwart his wishes?"

It was happening again—she was livid, and in her anger, her untamed beauty was assaulting his senses, making him want nothing more than to spring across the desk, take her into his arms, and swear never again to mention such a godless concept as circumventing her grandfather's dying wishes.

And he might have done so, had *she* not sprung to *her* feet first, her vibrant stare locked on him, imprisoning him. "May I say something, Mr. Ryerson?"

"Of course," he answered, his tone strained and unfamiliar.

Her chin jutted forward proudly. "I don't blame you for reacting to me the way you have. The truth is, I dressed this way for the sole purpose of appearing unattractive. It never occurred to me—" Her voice had begun to shake slightly, and so she visibly steeled herself before continuing. "I see now it was a mistake." Reaching behind her head, she pulled several tortoiseshell hairpins free, then shook her pale gold tresses, allowing them to swirl around her shoulders and down her back.

Jack stared, mesmerized by the display, not daring to imagine how it would feel to bury his face in those soft, silky tresses, whispering words—any words—that might win her affections.

Then he realized her fingers were busy again, this time working the row of buttons that ran down the back of the dreary black dress. Still proud, but also trembling, she insisted, "I'll do my best to please you, Mr. Ryerson.

Within reason, of course. I'm n-not a prude, but I'm also not a whore—"

"Of course you aren't!" Rushing to her side, he grasped her hands in his own. "My God, Miss Standish, do you honestly think I don't find you attractive? You're the most beautiful woman I've ever had the pleasure to offend! If it were simply a matter of taste—or temptation—I would have been on my knees the moment I first laid eyes on you. But I have a fiduciary duty, as your potential business advisor, not to take advantage of such opportunities at your expense. You see that, don't you?"

She studied his expression for a moment, then smiled a tremulous smile that tugged at his heart. "Am I really the most beautiful woman you've ever had the pleasure to offend?"

"Absolutely."

A spate of light laughter bubbled from her throat. "What a lovely thing to say. Silly, but lovely. Thank you."

He grinned and released her hands. "At the risk of offending you further, may I suggest that it's actually Russell Braddock who should be ashamed of himself?"

Trinity pursed her lips. "He knew you were going to propose this solution, and yet he said nothing to me. Why would he do such a thing?"

"He's a matchmaker," Jack reminded her.

"True, but . . ." She frowned. "All this effort to arrange a marriage that would end in six short months? Or are you saying . . . ?"

"I can't think of another explanation, can you?"

Her eyes flashed again, and for once, he could relax

and enjoy the colorful display, knowing this time it was Russell Braddock who had drawn her ire. "I've never seen eyes like yours before, Miss Standish. Violet, are they not?"

"Like my mother's."

"She must have been exquisite."

"I'm told she was." Trinity sighed. "I'm so disappointed in Mr. Braddock. He has our best interests at heart, of course. But I explained to him, in no uncertain terms, that I had no intention of settling down with a husband until I'd traveled to my heart's content. And that will take years. Why would he try to manipulate me otherwise?"

When Jack just shrugged again, she smiled and echoed his earlier observation: "He's a matchmaker. He simply can't help himself, can he?"

"I suppose not."

Clearly mollified, she returned to her chair. "I wish he had prepared me for this."

"So do I. But it's good news, is it not?"

"I don't know," she mused. "I mean, it's wonderful that we don't need to—well, to enter into a marriage for purely business reasons. But it was Grandpa's dying wish, Mr. Ryerson. Even if your plan succeeds, I'm not sure I can ever feel right about it."

Jack sat on the edge of the desk closest to his hostess. "Listen to what you're saying. Do you really believe it was your grandfather's dying wish for you to marry a stranger? To subject yourself to a wedding night with a man who married you purely for economic gain? Not that it would be purely for economic reasons," he added hastily. "I only meant—"

Trinity burst into laughter. "You poor man, you must think me a lunatic. I know what you're saying, and I agree, at least to an extent. I'm sure, deep in his heart, Grandpa hoped my husband and I would fall in love with this ranch, and choose to live out our lives and raise our family here."

"That's right." Jack nodded in encouragement. "But you want something else from your life. To travel, apparently. And whether or not I manage to reverse this ranch's fortunes, I have no doubt that I'll return to Boston once it's functioning smoothly. I'm not a rancher, believe me."

Her eyes began to sparkle with mischief. "You needn't worry, sir. I'm not asking you to be a rancher, nor to be my lifelong husband. But I can see why Mr. Braddock couldn't resist finding you a bride. You're so charming and tenderhearted. I'm tempted to find one for you myself."

"And I'll find a husband for you who wants to travel the world to your heart's content," Jack countered lightly. "Have you thought of asking Braddock to find that fellow? He knows just where to look. I know that from personal experience."

"Oh?"

He coughed, annoyed with himself for the unnecessary reference to Erica and her sailor. "Didn't Braddock tell you how he happened to hear of me?"

"He told me the two of you have a mutual friend who holds you in the highest regard."

"She adores me," Jack said with a wry smile. "In fact, she would have *married* me had Braddock not interfered. It's a long story. If I decide to stay, I'll tell it to you one day, if only to convince you that Braddock knows how to find adventurous men for women who crave such nonsense."

"Oh, dear."

He grinned. "Do I sound bitter?"

"Ever so slightly," she told him, standing to look more evenly into his eyes. "It sounds as though he did you a favor."

"So he says."

"And it's true, is it not? You deserve a woman who wants a man like you."

Jack laughed at the succinct observation. "Don't look so distressed, Miss Standish. Braddock fully intends to see that I live happily ever after. He's awaiting my permission to begin the search for another, more suitable bride."

"You're still in love with the mutual friend?" Trinity frowned. "Shouldn't you be furious with her for allowing Mr. Braddock to come between you?"

"Furious with Erica?" Jack exhaled slowly. "Yes, I suppose that would be a more useful reaction. But I never really could stay angry with her for more than a moment, although God knows she drove me mad with some of her—" He stopped himself, conscious suddenly that he was confiding in a stranger—a beautiful stranger, with eyes that seemed to make him babble without restraint, but a stranger nonetheless—who was also a potential business partner. It was time he began to respect that relationship for both their sakes.

Trinity was eyeing him intently. "It's obviously difficult for you to talk about her, especially to a stranger. So why don't we change the subject. And perhaps one day, when we've become friends as well as partners, you can cry on my shoulder, or rage at the unfairness of it all, or perhaps simply talk it through until your bitterness begins to fade."

Touched, Jack motioned for her to sit back down while he leaned against the desk. "For now, we should focus on this matter of the loophole in your grandfather's will. You need time to think it through on your own. After that, if you're honestly not comfortable with my advice, we can discuss alternatives. In the meantime, I should look in on the girls. They've had a long, hard journey."

"Of course! Here I am, monopolizing your attentions, when those sweet children are all alone in a strange house. Where are my manners?" Trinity was halfway to the door before Jack could protest. "I'll take you to them immediately. And you must promise to tell me if other accommodations would be more suitable for them. We gave each her own private quarters, but perhaps they'd feel more comfortable sleeping together. You need only tell Elena, and she'll have Clancy or Little Bob move the beds—"

"Miss Standish?"

"Yes?"

"I'm sure the girls are fine. And believe me, if they decide they want other arrangements, they won't be shy about letting us know—or at least, Janie and Louisa won't."

"Louisa, who complains about everything?" Trinity laughed lightly. "She reminds me of myself at that age. Nothing my father did pleased me. And then, when he passed away, poor Grandpa was saddled with the impossible task of making me happy." Her smile faded. "I'm sure they each looked forward to a time when I would be more agreeable—more interested in *their* needs than my own. But neither of them had that pleasure."

"They had the satisfaction of knowing they raised an intelligent female who wasn't afraid to look out for her own interests," Jack reminded her. "Whenever life with Louisa begins to tax me, I ask myself if I'd rather she suffer in silence, pretending to be happy, while crying into her pillow at night. I've known women like that—who were grateful just to have a roof over their head and a man to protect them, and didn't realize they were entitled to demand more from life than that."

"What a noble thing to say." Trinity's eyes were shining as she added, "They're so fortunate to have you in their lives."

"Actually, it was Erica who taught me that," Jack confided with a wistful smile. "For all her faults, she knows how to be happy, and insists on everyone around her being happy, too. She instructed me in no uncertain terms on how to raise the girls, and a surprising amount of her advice was solid. The rest was insane, but that's another story."

"I can't wait to hear it," Trinity said, her voice dripping with sarcasm. "I'm beginning to see that the next six months will be quite rich with tales of Erica. I only hope I can prove worthy of hearing them."

Before Jack could react, or better still, apologize, his hostess had sailed to the double doors, throwing them open and disappearing into the entry hall as though she couldn't suffer his presence for even one more instant.

He was tempted to pursue her, but decided against it. He'd probably just say something else to offend her, he reasoned warily. A wiser course would be to spend a minute or two reviewing this bizarre conversation, so that he could avoid making certain mistakes in the future.

Assuming he stayed at the Lost Spur, of course. He could only hope his tempestuous partner-to-be understood that the only promise he had made thus far was to evaluate the ranch as an investment. Only if he found it potentially profitable would he proceed with the partnership, which would entail a substantial investment of his time, and an even more substantial investment of money, either from one of Jack's associates, or more daringly, from Jack himself.

Until now, the information presented to Jack had made this particular investment ideally suited to his needs. But had he known of Trinity's volatile temper and irrational desire to obey the terms of her grandfather's will to the letter, that balance might have shifted.

You're here now, he reminded himself with half-hearted resolve. *It's simply another factor to consider. Another detail to cover in the partnership agreement if you decide to accept this project. It's not as though you don't have experience with irrational females. Success with them? Certainly not. But it's safe to say, you've had more than your share of experience.*

He chuckled at his predicament, reminding himself that it would have been infinitely worse had the loophole to the marriage condition not existed. That would have been a frightening prospect, Trinity's pretty face and graceful body notwithstanding. Fortunately, this was just a business arrangement. And like all of the challenges he had faced in his career, it presented unique obstacles, including finding a way to communicate productively with his partner.

She undoubtedly wanted that as much as he did. After all, she was willing to give him fifty percent of the ranch in exchange for his expertise and advice as well as for investment capital. She appeared to be an intelligent woman, despite her occasional outbursts of illogic, and so she would be as anxious as Jack to find a way for them to coexist.

And if she's half as mercurial as the other females in your life, he told himself as he ambled into the entry hall and over to the staircase, *she's completely over her tantrum by now. In fact, she's probably feeling grateful to you, for having found a way to avoid an ill-fated wedding night.*

Three

Slamming her bedroom door behind herself, Trinity stripped off her black dress and kicked it across the room. So much for her plan to discourage her new partner's lustful attentions! If only she had known he was a lovesick fool who was blind to every woman on earth except some heartbreaker named Erica.

Mr. Braddock should have warned you! she told herself in disgust. *You could have approached the whole matter so differently. Better still, you could have found someone else—someone willing to marry you despite your innumerable flaws.*

It was too late for that now. And even if it weren't, she wanted Jack Ryerson. Or rather, she wanted his expertise. Fifteen minutes alone with him had confirmed the rumors of his logical mind and ability to focus on business to the exclusion of everything but his family and his precious lost love. And she still couldn't forget the confident way he had handled his horse—as though he'd spent a lifetime in the saddle, when nothing could be further from the truth. He was perfect for the task of saving the Lost Spur Ranch. Which meant he was perfect for the dual role of business partner and temporary spouse.

Which means, you must apologize to him immediately. And try to win the support of the little girls. If they want to stay, it will be difficult for him to decide otherwise. And most importantly, you need to talk to him about Grandpa. Help him see how grand the ranch was before everything began to go wrong. Mr. Ryerson wants to make a profit—it's as simple as that. Prove to him that he can make a fortune here.

And in the process, he'll begin to appreciate Grandpa, and he'll be offended by the way those awful Crownes are trying to steal all this from us, after Grandpa poured every ounce of strength and love into it. If Mr. Ryerson can see that, then he'll also see that we shouldn't try to circumvent Grandpa's wishes. We can reap huge profits from this ranch, but only if we do so honorably.

Her thoughts were interrupted by the sound of someone knocking on her door, and she smiled in relief. Hoping this was an opportunity to appear more rational—not to mention, more attractive—to her prospective partner, she quickly slipped into a modest but flattering pink dressing gown, then threw open the door, only to find a darling little girl on the other side.

"The lady says you must come right away and have cake with us," Janie announced solemnly.

"The lady? Do you mean Elena?" Trinity smiled. "Cake sounds lovely, doesn't it? But first I must find something pretty to wear. Would you like to stay and help me?"

Janie nodded and wandered into the room, taking in everything with huge green eyes. When she reached the open doors to the balcony, she murmured, "Are children allowed to go out there?"

"Of course." Following her out into the brisk afternoon air, Trinity said teasingly, "If you're looking for the cows, they're just beyond that rise."

The little girl peeked through the slats in the rail. "That's where we're going tomorrow?"

"Yes."

She nodded her approval, then turned to study her hostess. "Are you cross with Jack?"

"Oh, dear. You heard us arguing? I hope we didn't upset you."

The child shrugged her narrow shoulders. "No one ever raises their voice to Jack. Except—" She caught herself and grimaced. "Never mind."

"I suppose you were going to say Erica?" Trinity asked, fighting an illogical wave of jealousy at the repeated intrusions of Jack's former fiancée.

Janie's eyes widened. "No. Erica *never* raises her voice. She says it isn't ladylike. That's the first reason we mustn't do it."

"The first reason?"

"The second reason is, we must never let a man see that he has upset us."

Intrigued despite herself, Trinity asked, "Why not?"

"I don't remember. But Mary will. She remembers everything better than me."

Trinity laughed sympathetically. "So? Who is it that *does* raise their voice to your brother?"

"Louisa. She's awfully nice, but awfully rude."

"And now that I've raised my voice to him," Trinity asked, "do you think me rude also?"

Janie considered the question carefully. "You didn't sound rude at all. Just upset, and I know why."

"Oh?"

"You feel all alone because your grandpapa went to heaven. But Jack's here now, so you needn't be upset any more."

Charmed, Trinity led the child over to the bed. "Sit up here and we'll chat while I dress."

"Oh!" Janie had spied one of the maps Trinity had drawn in preparation for her travels. "How pretty. Did you make it?"

"Yes. It's a map of the world."

"The *whole* world?"

"Yes. Why?"

"It doesn't say Boston."

"Well, we can fix that, can't we?" Fetching a pen from her desk, Trinity carefully made a new mark. "There's Boston. And see this?" She drew a small dot just east of San Francisco. "This little circle shows where we are right this instant—the Lost Spur Ranch."

"A circle." Janie nodded. "But not a star."

"The stars are for special places. Places to which I intend to travel one day."

"Boston is special, too."

"So I'm told, and I believe it. But these places—the ones marked by stars—are special because my father visited them, and when he was there, he wrote me letters. I've kept the letters all these years, and I've promised myself I'd retrace his footsteps one day."

"Is he in heaven, too?"

"Yes. With my mother."

"My mamma and papa are there, too. But Jack takes care of us."

Trinity sat next to the child and gave her a little hug. "And in your own way, you take care of him, too, don't you?"

Janie nodded. "Tell me about the star places, please?"

"We really should join the others, but . . ." Trinity bit her lip, pleased for an opportunity to indulge in her favorite subject—the wondrous places to which she one day intended to travel. Aside from the feud, and her obligations under her grandfather's will, these plans were her whole life.

And so with a wistful smile she began, "Have you ever heard of a place called Morocco?"

"Howdy."

"Good afternoon." Jack shielded his eyes from the sun, wishing he had remembered to wear the hat Russell Braddock had given him on the last day of their visit to San Francisco. Braddock had predicted Jack would need its wide brim to ward off the blazing San Joaquin valley glare, and he'd been right. "This is an incredible enterprise, Mr. Clancy. I didn't expect such diversity of livestock."

"Yeah, we've got us some of everything here. Sorta like Noah's ark without the nice, steady rain to keep 'em all cool."

The homespun observation amused Jack. "How many horses does the ranch have at any given time?"

"Too many," Clancy replied. "I reckon we've got forty in the corrals, and it's my job to train 'em all. That was my *only* job when Abe was alive, and now that you're here, I'm hoping it'll be that way again. Never did want more responsibility than that." His smile became a wide grin. "So when I tell you you're welcome here, I mean it."

Jack met the older man's gaze directly. "For the moment, you're still in charge. I'll be spending the first week or so assessing the ranch's potential. Did Miss Standish explain all that?"

"A smart fella like you wouldn't come all this way if he wasn't pretty danged sure it was worth his time. And seeing as how a pretty girl like our Trinity is willing to marry you if you stay around, I figure you'd be a fool not to."

Jack cleared his throat. "I'm not at liberty to discuss the details, but I may have found a way to secure title for Miss Standish without the necessity for a wedding."

"No wedding?" The foreman scowled. "If you're thinking you can have her without making it legal first—"

"Good God, no! The relationship would be a formal business partnership with no need for Miss Standish to become involved on a personal level."

"You reckon?" Clancy cocked his head to the side and told him, "If you can do that, you'll have our gratitude, Mr. Ryerson, pure and simple. And my personal loyalty. I've been worried sick over this mess Abe made with that will of his. Stubborn ole mule. He wanted his way, but didn't have the guts to try and tame that granddaughter of his when he was alive, so he thought he'd do it when he was safe in his grave."

Jack grinned. "You make her sound fairly formidable."

"She's pure sunshine most of the time. But she's got her grandpa's stubborn streak. Her father had it, too, rest his soul. Traipsing all over the world, leaving his little girl all alone. Never visiting his own pappy—not once—to see what he'd created here from sweat and dreams."

"It's hard to believe Mr. Standish built all this in less than ten years," Jack agreed.

"And for what? A son who turned his back on it all, and now a granddaughter set to do the same. Not that I blame her. This place has nothing but bad memories for her. Did you know she first came here when her papa died unexpectedly? Grieving then, and grieving now. Mighty poor legacy, wouldn't you say?"

"Yes."

"Old Abe thought he found a way to trick her into loving the place the way he loved it. But it ain't right to force that sorta thing. So if you've figured how to set her free of that, I'll be the first one to thank you kindly."

"Once I decide to invest, I believe I can arrange it so that Miss Standish can leave right away, if that's how she wants it. I'm not sure what her financial situation is, so she may want to stay until we start generating a profit, but otherwise, yes—she'll be free of any obligation to the Lost Spur."

Clancy pursed his lips. "We'd all miss her, but it'd be for the best. She's got herself a burning need to go wandering the world. Looking for something special, I reckon. Something she thinks she can't find at home."

"Believe me, I'm familiar with that particular affliction in females," Jack said with a chuckle. "If Miss Standish wants excitement and adventure, I'll be the last man to stand in her way. It's not only futile, it's down-right hazardous."

Clancy burst into laughter. "That's a fact. I'd rather be caught between a fence and a buckin' bronc than within spittin' distance of that girl when she's all riled up. Wait till you see that, mister. You'll wish you'd never heard of the Spur."

Jack had a fleeting urge to reveal that he'd already witnessed Trinity's worst—or what he could only hope was her worst! But instead he gave the foreman a reassuring shrug. "As I said, I've known my share of temperamental females. And if Miss Standish would rather be travelling around the world, I'm impressed that she's here instead, dealing with all this responsibility."

"That girl may not give a hoot about this ranch, but she's as loyal to Abe as a girl can be. I sure hope you decide to stay on, son. For her sake."

"I'll be relying on you to provide information I'll need to make that very decision. Starting with a tour of the ranch tomorrow, if that's convenient."

"I 'tour' the danged place every day," Clancy said with a grin. "You're more than welcome to come along. Are you fixing on riding that stallion of yours?"

Jack noted a twinkle in the old man's eyes. "I hired that horse in Stockton. He performed well."

"That's what he was bred for," Clancy agreed. "Performing. Not much use on a cattle ranch, though. I'll fix you up on Ranger over there."

Jack looked in the direction the foreman had indicated, and saw an ordinary quarterhorse with a dark brown coat and a jet-black mane and tail. When Clancy whistled, the animal's ears perked up and he trotted over to the fence line, tossing his head as though greeting an old friend.

"Hey, buddy." Clancy scratched the horse behind the ear. "Mr. Ryerson, meet Ranger. The best danged cow pony I ever trained."

"Seems only fair that *you* should ride him tomorrow then," Jack said. "I'll take Pluto out again. You might just be surprised at what an excellent horse he is."

"Blue Toe? What sort of name is that?"

"Apparently he was named for the Roman god of the underworld. Pluto."

Clancy burst into laughter. "Ain't much need for a Roman god out here, son, but have it your way. Ride old Blue Toe on the 'tour' tomorrow, and we'll see how he does."

Jack could see that the old man was having fun at his expense, but didn't mind. He imagined there weren't many Arabian stallions of Pluto's caliber in the valley, so it was logical that Clancy would view them as useless luxuries of spoiled Easterners. It had been a visiting Easterner, in fact, who had reportedly died of heart failure in Stockton several months earlier, resulting in the sale of Pluto to pay for his room and for shipping his remains to San Francisco.

"You might just be surprised, Mr. Clancy."

The foreman grinned. "I might. Then again, it's hard to surprise me, horse-wise that is. What time do you want to take your tour?"

"When do you usually start out?"

"Sunup."

"That's fine."

"Bring that big, black hat of yours. And them fancy new gloves, too."

Jack exhaled sharply before nodding. "Anything else?"

Clancy's grin became a warm smile. "You take a ribbing pretty danged well, son. That's a good sign where I come from."

"It's a good sign where I come from, too."

"Boston? I was worried about that," the old man admitted. "Figured you'd be some pale-faced little runt of a fella talking numbers and drooling all over Miss Trinity. But I knew different the minute I saw you ride up. She knew it, too. You sat that big ole stallion like you were born in a saddle, and tipped your hat to her just right. Like you're the boss, but you ain't gonna lord it over her. It was a real relief for me, and I could see it made her feel better, too. And now hearing you don't plan on making her marry up with you . . ." He thrust his hand toward Jack. "I mean it when I say, welcome to the Spur. You just let me know what you need and I'll git it for you. I'm bound and determined to convince you to stay on."

Jack shook the old man's hand briskly. "As you said, I wouldn't have come all this way if I didn't think there was a very good chance I'd stay. I appreciate the cooperation, and I look forward to reviewing the ranch at sunup."

"Do you see this, Jane? My father drew it in Egypt. Do you know what it is?"

"A kitty?"

Trinity smiled. "It's called the Sphinx. Part lion, part

man. The legend is, he asked travelers to solve a riddle. Do you like riddles?"

Janie yawned, shaking her head, then nestled herself into a pile of pillows at the head of Trinity's bed. "I never know the answers."

"No? Let's try something simple. My grandfather used to love this one: what do you call a cow who doesn't give milk?" When the little girl just grimaced, Trinity explained quickly, "An udder failure. Do you see? *Udder* rather than *utter.*"

"I *never* know them," the child repeated, her tone revealing complete dejection.

Oh dear, see what you've done? Trinity scolded herself silently. *It's you who's an utter failure—with children, that is. Now the poor child—a guest in Grandpa's house—is miserable.*

Determined to repair the gaffe, she patted the child's hand. "Would you try one more, just for me?"

Janie winced again, but nodded.

"Who has long brown braids, huge green eyes, and the sweetest face of any houseguest this side of the Mississippi?"

Cocking her head to the side, the child asked cautiously, "Is it me?"

Trinity grinned. "Very nicely done."

"Oh!" She squealed with delight, then threw her arms around her shocked hostess's neck, hugging her with fierce insistence. "You're such a wonderful lady!"

"My goodness." Stroking her little guest's back, and unsure of what to do next, she reminded herself once again that she and children were not a good mix. And this one was at least five or six years old! What would she do were she ever confronted with a crying baby?

You'll just make certain that never happens, or at least, not unless you one day marry a man willing to hire an army of servants for all his children's needs, she decided, as she'd done so many times in the past.

"I never, never guessed a riddle before," Janie was murmuring, her voice filled with reverence.

"And I have never, ever been hugged by a little girl before."

The child drew away and stared in disbelief. "Only little boys? They're so horrid! Don't you like this much, much better?"

Trinity laughed lightly. "I've never been hugged by a little boy, either. I've known very few children, and none of them well."

Janie seemed baffled, so Trinity explained, "My mother died when I was just about your age, and after that, I spent most of my life in boarding schools, with students close in age to myself. The younger children attended another school nearby. Sometimes my friends' little brothers and sisters came for visits, but I had no brothers or sisters. So for me, it was—well, I never had the experience."

"Did your mamma and papa visit you?"

She felt her cheeks warm under the child's sympathetic gaze. "Father traveled endlessly. He visited every two years or so, and that was wonderful, but . . ." She stopped herself and grinned weakly. "You're a very sweet child, do you know that? And we'll have time in the next six months to share stories from our pasts. For now, I need to get dressed, and you need to close your eyes and rest for just a few minutes. Then we'll join the others for tea. How does that sound?"

"I'm not sleepy."

"You needn't sleep. Just rest. Here, let's clear all this away." She gathered up her maps and sketches, stuffing them back into their velvet-lined case. "Settle back now. You can advise me on which of my dresses would please your brother most."

"Why do you want to please Jack?" Jane asked as she dutifully snuggled into the bed.

"Because I want him to decide to stay. And I want to make him forget how I raised my voice to him."

The child nodded. "Jack doesn't approve of shouting."

"Well, I was hardly—never mind. I don't approve of shouting, either." Jumping to her feet, she shrugged out of her dressing gown, then rustled through the contents of a whitewashed armoire: eight dresses, any of which was more alluring than the dreadful black outfit she had kicked across the room. Remembering how her grandfather had always complimented her when she wore pink, she pulled out a soft, flowing gown of white lace over pink silk and spun back around toward the bed. "What do you think of—oh . . ." She sighed, enchanted at the sight of the little girl who had curled into a ball and succumbed to sleep in what seemed like seconds.

A light tapping at the bedroom door further amused Trinity. Another little visitor? Thank goodness her bed was so large and fluffy. She wouldn't want the elder sister—pretty little Mary—to feel at all slighted. Pulling the lacy gown over her head, she crossed quickly to the door and opened it, fearing that the knocking might grow louder and awaken Janie.

"Oh!" She stared into Jack Ryerson's big green eyes and murmured lamely, "What a surprise."

"I've managed to misplace a sister," he explained with an apologetic smile.

Trinity smiled in return. "She's here. See for yourself. Honestly, Mr. Ryerson, she is so perfectly adorable." Taking him by the elbow, she pulled him toward the bed. "Have you ever seen anything more darling?"

Jack cleared his throat. "I should carry her to her own bed."

"Nonsense. The poor child is exhausted. Let her sleep here for a while."

"If you're sure you don't mind." He took a folded quilt from the foot of the bed and covered his sister, then brushed his lips across her flushed little cheek.

Trinity watched with sincere admiration, wishing she could be half as comfortable and loving with children as this man was. "Are the others waiting for us in the sunroom, Mr. Ryerson?"

"Yes. If you're sure you don't mind, I'll leave Jane here and join them while you finish dressing."

"Wait just one moment, won't you? Here . . ." She turned her back to Jack. "Could I impose on you to button me up?"

He cleared his throat again, and she was glad she couldn't see his face. Was he blushing? Or, more likely, annoyed or shocked that she would allow him to touch her when she was barely half-dressed? She was rather shocked herself, but if they were to be married in two short weeks, wasn't this an opportunity to accustom themselves to such interaction? Hadn't Russell Brad-dock—an experienced marriage broker—suggested this very sort of thing to her?

Use those first two weeks to gradually increase your interaction with him. Not just intellectually, but also your physical familiarity, he had counseled her. *Some of my brides marry their new husbands on the same day they meet them. Treat this as an opportunity. If you make good use of the time he spends evaluating the investment, the wedding night will be less intimidating.*

Trinity had been mortified at the thought, but had been forced to agree that Braddock's advice made sense. And it wasn't as though she was naked under the dress. Her silky white chemise formed a definite, albeit provocative, barrier, did it not?

His fingers began to work the tiny round buttons that stretched from the neck of the dress to well below her waist, and his quick, expert movements convinced Trinity he had fastened the dresses of countless women. A wave of jealousy, reminiscent of her reaction to his repeated mentions of his former fiancée, flooded her.

You're a goose, she chided herself silently. *Be grateful he's an experienced man with such a gentle touch.*

Relaxing slightly, she began to enjoy the sensation of his fingertips working their way up her back, brushing momentarily against her silk-covered skin whenever a button resisted him. By the time he had reached the neckline, she was positively tingling.

"All done," he announced finally.

She whirled, anxious to catch some hint that he, too, had found the experience provocative, but his face was expressionless as he asked, "Shall we join the others?"

"In a moment. I'd like a word with you alone first. Outside, so we don't disturb your sister," she added, taking him by the elbow once again and pulling him toward the balcony doorway.

He seemed to resist her effort, if only for a second, and she realized her behavior must be confusing him. But wasn't that for the best? He had come here so committed to one particular plan, and while she didn't blame him—his decisiveness was undoubtedly the key to his successful career—she hoped to find a way to convince him to explore every option before forcing her to disregard her grandfather's wishes.

"This is nice," he admitted, staring off into the distance, where the snowcapped Sierra Nevada Mountains formed an inspiring silhouette against the late afternoon sky.

She backed away until she was flush against the railing, then fixed her gaze on her guest. "I owe you an apology, Mr. Ryerson. Can you ever forgive me for the way I acted in the study earlier?"

"It's forgotten," he assured her.

"I had no right to react the way I did. I sounded like a jealous female, and I believe that's exactly what I was."

"Pardon?"

She gave him her warmest smile. "Isn't it silly? But true nevertheless. For six long weeks I've considered you my fiancé. Apparently, I'm much more possessive about such things than I have any right to be under the circumstances."

A hesitant grin spread over his features. "I see what you mean. I suppose the same would have been true for me, had I not realized from the start that the arranged marriage wasn't necessary." With a playful bow, he insisted, "Forgive me for discussing my ex-fiancée so cavalierly when our own nuptials had not yet been officially cancelled."

Trinity laughed. "You're forgiven, sir. And feel free to mention Erica to your heart's content. As you said, you caught me unawares at first. But now I'm actually fascinated by the subject."

"Oh?"

"I want to spend the next two weeks learning all about you. What better way to learn about a man than to learn about the woman he fell in love with? For example, your sister tells me Erica never argued with you."

He coughed into his fist before smiling warily. "You discussed Erica with my sister?"

"I wouldn't call it a discussion. More a passing reference. You and she never quarreled?"

Jack shifted his weight from one foot to the other. "We quarreled incessantly, but it's true that she wouldn't argue with me in the traditional sense. Whenever I displeased her—which was often—she would begin a campaign to change my mind. Flirting, pouting, twisting a man's words, teasing—those are Erica's weapons, and she actually wields them quite well, so she rarely resorts to actually arguing, which is not her strong suit."

"She sounds so very beguiling. I'm afraid you'll find my approach unattractively direct," Trinity drawled.

"Are you jealous again?" Before she could respond, he dropped the teasing tone and assured her, "I much prefer a direct approach, especially from a business partner."

Trinity bit her lip, embarrassed at her behavior, then took a step closer and dared to look up into his eyes. "Do you regret coming here?"

"No," he murmured. "Not at all."

"I was concerned I might have alarmed you with my temperamental outburst, when that's the last thing I wanted to do. I so desperately need for you to stay, Mr. Ryerson. Just tell me what you want me to do, and how you want me to act, and I'll do it. You have my word."

He seemed to consider her words carefully before resting his hands on her shoulders, offering reassurance with his steady stare. "I caught you by surprise with that loophole. And in any case, it was unpardonably rude to ramble on at length about my former fiancée. Shall we begin again?"

"I'd like that."

"Feel free to be as direct as you wish. Potential business partners should be nothing less than candid with one another at all times."

"That's true," she agreed, relaxing under his warm, green gaze. "I'm grateful to you, sir, for your patience."

"Shall we join the others now?"

"The others? Oh!" She backed away, her cheeks burning. For that one brief moment, she had literally forgotten that "the others" even existed, and was mortified to think he might have noticed. "Of course we should join them. Right away."

"After you." He stepped aside, granting her access to the doorway.

Still flustered, she managed a dignified, impersonal expression as she swept past him; then she gathered up her skirts and dashed for the safety of the hall.

Four

While little Janie slumbered, Trinity was joined by her other three guests in the sunroom, which was in fact bathed in warmth on this sunny afternoon. Elena plied them with delights, from tiny, frosted cakes to flaky, scone-like *pan dulce*, tinted to a vibrant rose hue in accordance with her family's cherished recipe. Mary and Louisa sipped hot chocolate, while Trinity and Jack enjoyed fresh, tart lemonade as they warily traded information.

"According to Braddock, your father was some sort of antiquities dealer. Is that correct?"

"Yes. He was employed by a man named Darien Porter." Trinity noted with satisfaction that Jack's eyes had widened. "You've heard of him?"

"Sugar imports, I believe."

"That's his business," she said, nodding. "But his passion is collecting rare and unique artifacts. Mr. Porter is quite a traveler in his own right, but prefers to spend his time in London and Paris, so he paid Father to roam the rest of the world in search of precious objects for his collection."

"Fascinating."

"When Father died, I wrote to Mr. Porter, asking if

he'd hire me to do Father's work. It amused him. More particularly, it amused his wife, who began corresponding with me. They scoffed at my suggestion, of course, but Emelia Porter took note of my interest in travelling and eventually offered me a position as her personal appointments secretary. They arranged for me to return to the East Coast. From there I accompanied them to London and Paris."

"An impressive opportunity. You gave that up to come back and save the ranch?"

"Actually . . ." She paused for a sheepish smile. "I had already 'given it up' a month before Grandpa was killed. I was on my way back to California when I received news of his death."

"Why did you quit your position?" Louisa asked, clearly amazed that anyone could abandon so exciting a life.

Trinity smiled. "London and Paris—and all the other cities the Porters visit—are lovely. But my tastes run to more exotic locales. Baghdad, Cairo, Cuzco, Athens, St. Petersburg. I intended to ask Grandpa to finance my travels, on the understanding that I would repay him from sales of the antiquities I acquired."

"Fascinating," Jack repeated, and something in his tone caught Trinity's attention. Disapproval? Or downright annoyance?

Louisa had also noticed it. "Jack doesn't approve of adventures for women. He believes we should be docile and unimaginative, while men take all the risks and enjoy all the excitement."

Trinity watched Jack's expression closely, remembering what he had said: that he didn't want his sisters and cousin to feel they must pretend to be docile.

It was no surprise when he muttered, "Is that not precisely why I brought you to this ranch, Louisa? For excitement and adventure?"

"That's true," Mary interjected. "We've had adventures for weeks. On the ship, and especially in the jungle in Panama! And there are horses here, and miles of open land to ride on. If Jack wanted us to be docile, he would never have brought us with him."

"I agree." Trinity gave her prospective partner an encouraging smile. "I spent my entire childhood begging my father to take me with him—just once!—to someplace exciting or dangerous. But he always told me to be patient. And then it was too late. Mr. Ryerson is to be commended."

"He only brought us because he was afraid we'd run off while he was away," Louisa declared. "His fiancée ran off last year. And last month, I myself went out the window to meet a boy. *That's* why he brought us. To keep his eyes on us so we *wouldn't* have adventures."

"Every day with you is an adventure," Jack assured his cousin dryly.

Struggling not to laugh, Trinity turned to Mary and asked, "What about you, honey? Do you want to travel and have adventures?"

The girl pursed her lips. "I'd rather read books. And I want to get married and have dozens of babies one day. Don't *you* want to get married and have children?"

Glancing at Jack to confirm that he wasn't amused or annoyed, Trinity explained, "I'm not opposed to marriage or children, but I've had my heart set on travelling since I was your age, or perhaps even younger, so I'd like to accomplish that before I settle down."

"If you want to travel by ship, we could introduce you to a very good friend of ours named Erica," Mary offered. "She and her husband have their own boat."

"I see."

"So much for Erica," Jack interrupted. "Girls? Why don't you go upstairs and rest until supper. Miss Standish undoubtedly has things to do, and I'd like to start looking over the ranch's books."

Surprised, Trinity suggested, "Shouldn't you rest, too, sir? You've had a long journey."

"Jack never rests," Louisa interrupted with a petulant toss of her head. "He just works and works, and reads and reads, and works and works."

Jack reached over to rumple his cousin's hair. "I believe we've established how dull I am."

"Saving this ranch is far from dull," Trinity protested. To the girls, she added sincerely, "Mr. Ryerson will be a true hero if he can find a way to save the Lost Spur. Do you know why? Not just because it's my family legacy, but because it will prevent a monumental injustice from being perpetrated."

Mary's blue eyes widened. "What sort of injustice?"

"There's a foul and hideous man who lives on a ranch south of here. His name is Walter Crowne and he was always jealous of my grandfather's success. So he did everything he could to hurt Grandpa. He even brought in diseased cattle and mingled them with our herd, just so our stock would get sick and die. Then he tried to force Grandpa to sell the Spur to him, and when he refused, Crowne murdered him."

"Oh, dear," the girls chorused.

"If we lose the Spur, it means Crowne has won. But if Mr. Ryerson finds a way to save it, Crowne will be defeated. That's why, in my opinion, Mr. Ryerson's work is not at all dull. It's a hero's task, and I'm grateful to him for attempting it." Turning to Jack, she added softly, "If I haven't said so before, I say it now. Thank you for coming."

A flush spread over Jack's face. "I appreciate the sentiment, but—"

"I know exactly what you're about to say. You haven't yet decided to stay. That's perfectly fine, Mr. Ryerson. I simply wanted to be sure you knew what was at stake."

He cleared his throat. "As far as these allegations of murder are concerned—"

"That's right," Louisa interrupted. "If Mr. Crowne murdered your grandfather, why didn't he go to prison?"

"He will," Trinity assured her. "I intend to see to that personally."

Jack cleared his throat again. "I may have some bad news for you in that regard, Miss Standish. I spoke with the sheriff in Stockton while your driver was transferring our bags from the stage. He told me he had concluded his investigation and is convinced your grandfather died of natural causes."

"He's mistaken."

"How, exactly, did it happen?" Louisa demanded.

"He fell to his death," Jack replied. "Miss Standish believes he was pushed. But the sheriff found no proof of that. And Mr. Standish's own doctor says his patient had been complaining of dizzy spells—"

"How very convenient," Trinity interrupted. "The truth is, Doctor Clark and the sheriff and everyone else in Stockton are hopelessly intimidated by Walt Crowne. In their heart of hearts they know it was murder, but they didn't aggressively pursue the truth. So I'm going to find proof that simply can't be ignored."

"I beg your pardon?"

Trinity eyed Jack sternly. "I've begun my own investigation. Unlike the sheriff, I won't abandon it prematurely."

"I see." He glanced toward the children, then lowered his voice. "I understand how you feel, Miss Standish, but these matters are best left to the authorities. If Crowne is guilty, you'll be endangering yourself. And if he's innocent—"

"He's not. Don't concern yourself with this, sir. I have no intention of involving you in it. Concentrate on saving the ranch, while I solve the crime."

"Assuming there *was* a crime."

"Assuming you *can* save the ranch," she quipped, annoyed by his arrogant attitude.

"Won't you please let *me* help you?" Louisa interrupted. "It sounds so exciting! And I hate mean old Mr. Crowne. He killed your cows, and then your grandpa! He's a horrible man."

"I'll help, too," Mary declared.

"That's enough!" Jack shook his head. "Louisa? Mary? Go upstairs and check on Jane. She's in Miss Standish's room. Now!"

Clearly startled, the two girls jumped to their feet and scurried out of the room.

"Really, Mr. Ryerson. If you don't want the girls involved—"

"I don't want *anyone* involved," Jack retorted. "The sheriff has concluded his investigation. Whatever your private feelings—"

"Feelings? It's more than that. I'm convinced—"

"Based on what? Some feud?" he drawled.

"It's more than that," she repeated.

"It's exactly that." He inhaled and exhaled slowly, as though fortifying himself. "If you'd like, I'll speak with the sheriff again. If he admits his findings were inconclusive, I'll urge him to reopen the investigation. But if he was thorough and his results logical, you'll need to accept it."

"Never! I won't rest until I see Walter Crowne brought to justice. It's none of your business—"

"It is precisely my business. What point is there in investing my time and energy in this ranch if you're intent on putting it all in jeopardy?"

She was furious, but also wary. "I don't understand."

"You just told the girls in no uncertain terms that Crowne murdered your grandfather."

"He did."

"I assume you've said as much to the sheriff?"

"Of course."

"And to others?"

"I didn't tell them anything they didn't already suspect. Everyone in town knows how much Crowne hated Grandpa."

"Everyone in town? There! Do you see?" Jack shook his head, clearly agitated. "You cannot make these wild accusations. Crowne has been cleared of wrongdoing, for the moment at least. Calling him a murderer all over town is actionable defamation. He would be within his rights to sue us, and he could end up owning this ranch in satisfaction of a judgment. The very result you fear, yet it could happen."

"Defamation?" Trinity winced. "How can he sue me for telling the truth?"

"Truth is a defense," Jack agreed. "But only if you can prove it. And the sheriff and doctor would testify otherwise."

"You're suggesting we allow that monster to go free?"

"I'm suggesting we be prudent. Wait until the ranch is turning a profit. We could hire professional investigators—"

"All the clues will have disappeared by then!"

Jack fixed her with a steady stare. "I'm going to say something, and I want you to listen carefully. Try not to lose your temper."

She grimaced but nodded. "I'll try."

"When Braddock described you to me, he said you were a healthy girl and a good conversationalist. He failed to mention how pretty you are. He also failed to mention how headstrong and impulsive you are. Had he told me about that—had he said one word about this blood vengeance you crave—I would not have come."

"I see." She jutted her chin forward in a halfhearted show of defiance. "I apologize, sir. Mr. Braddock should have been more forthcoming with you."

She wanted to exit the room in a sweeping show of disdain, but her burst of bravado had faded, and so she sank back into her chair instead. "What was he thinking? He must have realized we couldn't possibly get along, much less be partners."

"I agree. He should have told us everything, right from the start."

She nodded, then gave him a weary smile. "I won't apologize for being passionate and loyal."

"And I won't apologize for being practical." He switched seats so he could face her, their knees inches apart. "So?"

"I can't bear the thought of Crowne walking free while Grandpa lies cold in his grave."

Jack took her hands in his own. "The way I hear it, the feud began when Walter Crowne's father, Randolph, left half of his land to your grandfather. The son never forgave his father, and did everything in his power to convince your grandfather to sell the land back to him. Isn't that so?"

"Randolph Crowne had good reason to reward Grandpa in his will," Trinity informed him coolly, pulling her hands free as she spoke. "Have you heard *that* part of the story?"

"I look forward to it," Jack assured her dryly. "But for the moment, I have a point to make."

"Go on."

"Everything Walter Crowne has done has been to try and regain ownership of this land. If we prevent that from happening—if the Lost Spur becomes a profitable enterprise again—Crowne will have lost. Isn't that so?" Taking her hands in his own once again, he added firmly, "Once we've accomplished all that, we'll hire those detectives, and we'll see what we can do about getting him behind bars."

His quiet, steady confidence flooded into her, and she nodded gratefully.

"So? We have an understanding?"

"Yes, Mr. Ryerson." Grasping his hands more tightly, she murmured, "I truly hope you'll decide to stay."

"Well then . . ." He cleared his throat. "The sooner I start examining those books, the better."

He started to tug his hands away, but she held onto one firmly. "I meant what I said earlier, sir. If you can save the Lost Spur, you'll be a hero in my eyes."

"And if I can't, I'll incur your wrath?" His boyish smile resurfaced. "You certainly know how to motivate a fellow, Miss Standish. Now excuse me, won't you? I'll see you at dinner."

She watched in dismay as he hurried out of the sunroom after bowing slightly in her direction.

If I can't, I'll incur your wrath?

"That's how he sees you," she scolded herself aloud. "Some wrathful, vengeful, wild-eyed female. And jealous, too! It's so unfair. So untrue. Or at least," she amended carefully, "it's a recent development, brought on by your responsibilities to Grandpa. You simply *must* find a way to keep the ranch out of Walter Crowne's murdering hands.

"Which means," she added philosophically as she gazed in the direction of the study, "you simply *must* convince Jack Ryerson to stay."

She prepared for their next encounter by brushing her long, golden hair to a lustrous sheen, and by reminding herself again and again *not* to lose her temper with him.

Not ever again. She had to be agreeable, if not down-right flirtatious, no matter what he said or did.

Unfortunately, he stayed behind closed doors in the study right up until dinnertime, and even then, seemed preoccupied, leaving it to his sisters and cousin to respond to Trinity's attempts at conversation. He didn't seem to notice her appearance or her good behavior, saving all of his compliments for Elena's spicy pork stew and fluffy white tortillas.

And then, true to his reputation, he was excusing himself from the table, bowing graciously, and thanking Trinity for her hospitality. Then he reminded his family that while he might be buried in facts and figures well past midnight, he expected each of them to come and kiss him good night, and wouldn't go to bed himself without looking in on them one last time no matter how late the hour.

When she was sure he was out of earshot, Trinity scanned the faces of her remaining guests. "You know his moods, so tell me what you think. Is he interested in this project? Discouraged? Have I frightened him away with my shrewish temper and thirst for revenge?"

To her surprise, the three girls squirmed in their chairs, then Louisa murmured, "Mary, you go first. You always seem to know what he's thinking."

The nine-year-old moistened her lips. "He wouldn't have traveled all this way if he weren't interested. I believe this is his favorite pastime, Miss Standish. Poring over books and records. It aggravated Eri—I mean, his former fiancée—no end."

"Oh?"

Mary nodded. "Erica always tried to convince Jack

not to spend so much time in his study. It was only because she cared for him, and was certain he would enjoy
himself more elsewhere. She didn't understand that he
was happy just as he was."

"And you're advising me not to make the same mistake? Thank you, Mary. I truly appreciate it."

"My turn," Louisa interrupted. "I believe you worried
him when you talked about pursuing the murderer on
your own."

"That's true." Trinity sighed. "He's concerned that
Mr. Crowne will bring a lawsuit against us—against our
partnership and the Lost Spur Ranch—if I keep insulting him."

"No, that's not it." The pretty girl pursed her lips. "He
wants to keep you safe. That's how he is. He protects *us*
because we're his family, and now he's protecting *you*
because you're his hostess. He believes you'll put yourself in danger if you try to bring Mr. Crowne to justice."

"I see."

"Jack doesn't understand that he can't protect us from
our destinies. You must avenge your grandfather, just as
I must find my true love and have a tempestuous affair."

"And I must have a husband and children," Mary
added, obviously enjoying the game.

"What about me?" Janie demanded. "Mustn't I have
a turn, too?"

Trinity smiled. "A turn?"

"It's my turn to say something about Jack."

"Oh, of course. What do you think? Does he want to
stay? Or go?"

"He wants to stay."

"That's wonderful. How can you be so certain?"

"Because you're so pretty."

When Mary and Louisa giggled, Trinity gave them a warning glance, then told the little girl, "That's a lovely thing to say. But I don't think your brother came here looking for a pretty girl. If anything, he came here to escape the memory of one. Erica, to be blunt."

"Then why were you talking about marrying him?"

Trinity winced. "That's a complicated question."

"Because Mr. Braddock usually makes marriages, not partnerships. Isn't that it?" Mary asked.

"Something like that."

"Mr. Braddock is so-o-o nice," Janie said with a sigh.

"Oh? Did you enjoy your visit at his house?"

"It was fun. He told us silly stories. And he asked us lots of questions."

Trinity smiled, imagining the matchmaker gathering information from these adorable future brides. "When I learned that my grandfather had been killed, I was heartbroken. I was also wild with vengeful emotions. Mr. Braddock soothed me by telling me stories about a wonderful man named Jack Ryerson. He said he was the man to ensure the survival of Grandpa's legacy."

"He said something else, too," Janie told her.

"Oh? What was that?"

"He said you'd let me play with the cows."

Trinity laughed. "One doesn't play with them, exactly. That's what the piglets are for."

"Piglets?" The child's eyes began to dance.

Trinity grinned. "I believe a litter was born just last week. If you ask Clancy nicely, he'll let you feed the runt with a bottle. And in another week's time, when they're stronger, you can play with them."

"Will they grunt?"

"Absolutely. You've come to the Lost Spur at the perfect time of year, Janie. We'll go out to the pastures and see all the new calves, and Elena tells me the goat is about to give birth as well. Have you seen a baby goat? They're darling."

The little girl squirmed with delight. "Are the piggies beddie-bye already?"

"Hmm?"

"She means, are they still awake," Mary translated. "If they are, Louisa and I could walk her out to the yard to peek at them. Would that frighten them?"

"We'll all go. You really mustn't wander outside after dark unless an adult is with you."

"*I'm* an adult," Louisa reminded her.

Trinity gave her a reassuring smile. "An adult for some purposes, but for wandering around a ranch, it's a different matter. Most of the men are respectful, but occasionally Clancy hires a buckaroo who simply doesn't know how to behave around girls. They're careful with me, because they know I'm the owner. But with you—well, it might be otherwise."

"Buckaroo?" Janie cocked her head to one side. "That sounds like an animal, not a man."

"Exactly." Trinity grinned. "In times past, the men who worked the ranchos were called *vaqueros*. When the Easterners descended on the place, they twisted the word into buckaroo. It all means the same thing—cowboy. When I first saw your brother, I thought *he* was a cowboy. Can you imagine that?"

"Miss Standish?"

"Yes, Janie?"

"Have you forgotten about the piggies?"

"What was I thinking? Run and fetch your wraps, girls." She watched with amusement as Jack's sisters bolted from the table and into the hall, their braids flying in the air. Predictably, Louisa was more reserved, and Trinity took advantage of that fact to ask her to stay at the table for just a moment longer.

The girl settled back into her chair, her expression wary.

"I just wanted to assure you that I don't see you as a child. I was your age when I made my first visit to the Lost Spur, and I made it very clear to Grandpa that I expected to be treated as a lady, not a baby. You can expect nothing less from me."

"Thank you, Miss Standish."

"That being said . . ." Trinity licked her lips, wondering just how to phrase what was on her mind. "I was seventeen when I came here. I had lived a sheltered life, despite my fervent wishes otherwise. A cattle ranch wasn't exactly the answer to my prayers—my ambitions turned more toward Cairo or Baghdad. Still, I saw this as an opportunity to prove that I was a grown woman who could take care of herself."

Louisa nodded, but the wariness had returned.

"Grandpa told me not to wander around alone at night, nor to venture far from the house even in daylight. I disobeyed him constantly. During one of those transgressions, I learned a sobering lesson at the hands of a young brute from a nearby ranch. I'm going to tell you about it, but first I'd like your word that you won't repeat it. I've never told another living soul this story."

"Really?" Louisa's eyes sparkled with curiosity. "But

you're telling me, even though we just met? Just to keep me safe?"

"And because, in some ways, we're kindred spirits. I strained at the bonds of childhood much as you did. And because of my recklessness, I put myself in peril."

"Tell me."

Trinity glanced about to ensure that Elena wasn't hovering nearby, then began. "It's a familiar story, I'm afraid. I rode out to the foothills, looking not so much for adventure as for beauty. Even in the heat of summer, it's beautifully green here if you go high enough above the ranch. I found a lovely spot by a stream and settled down to read a book of poetry."

"That's when the brute came?"

"Yes. I was closer to the boundary of the Crowne ranch than I'd realized. Walter Crowne's son, Frank, was chasing down strays. He found me instead, and began to romance me. It was flattering, and I probably wasn't as discouraging to him as I should have been. But I didn't encourage him, either. At least, not to take the sort of liberties he began to demand."

Louisa's mouth had tightened into a worried line. "How frightening."

"It honestly was. I struggled to escape him, but he threw me down, and—" She stopped herself, realizing that she was trembling at the memory of Frank Crowne's roving hands and smirking mouth. "I couldn't have stopped him on my own, Louisa. But by some miracle, his father's voice called out from the distance, scolding him for disappearing from sight and reminding him that they had work to do. Had Walter Crowne ventured further and discovered us together, I have no doubt that he would have joined in his son's disgusting game, but as it was, Frank's fear of his father's temper was greater than his lust for me, and so he left. I was bruised, and terrified, and violated in spirit, although blessedly, his intrusions had not been as successful as might otherwise have been."

"You didn't tell your grandfather?"

"No. I knew he'd lecture me. And he'd never allow me to go riding again. So I kept the secret, but it spoiled the Spur for me. It's one of the reasons I went off with the Parkers. I swore I'd never again step foot on this ranch. My humiliation . . ." She shook herself free of the emotion and tried to smile. "You mustn't tell Mr. Ryerson this, nor anyone else."

"I'd never tell that story to Jack. He would say it proves he's been right all along."

"Would he be so wrong? You mentioned that you sneaked out of your house once or twice? Do you see now why he's concerned?"

"There aren't any buckaroos in Boston," Louisa said with a smile. "But there are sailors, and in Jack's eyes, they're the worst of the lot."

"Because a sailor stole his fiancée's heart?"

Louisa nodded, and seemed about to say more, when the pounding of tiny feet in the hall announced the return of the little girls.

"Piggies," Trinity reminded Louisa with a grin.

As they herded the girls through the kitchen and out into the yard, the hostess forced herself to forget about Frank Crowne's aborted attack on her innocence three years earlier. As unpardonable as that sin had been, it was dwarfed by the sins of Frank's father in destroying the Lost Spur and murdering Abe Standish.

Wasn't that the reason she didn't want Jack Ryerson to hear the story of Frank's attack? Her prospective partner might misunderstand. He might assume that Trinity's desire for revenge was born of Frank's conduct that dreadful afternoon, rather than that of his father, when nothing could be further from the truth.

He already believes you're prejudiced when it comes to the Crownes. If he knew about this, he'd be certain you can't be rational, or accept the rational verdict of the sheriff, because of it.

No, she wouldn't tell Jack about the incident, but she was glad she'd shared it with Louisa. The girl was moody, just as Trinity had been at that age. Fortunately for her, Abe Standish had been patient. And Louisa was also fortunate to have an understanding guardian in Jack.

An odd parallel, she decided. Jack and her grandfather had patience and business acumen in common. Was there more? Probably not. Her grandfather had had a profound love of the land and of ranching. And he'd been a bona fide "adventurer"—a word Jack associated with bride-stealing sailors and heartbreaking women.

She smiled, knowing it was absurd to think of herself in such a light, but knowing also that in Jack's eyes, her desire to travel, along with her thirst for blood-vengeance, put her in the same category as Erica. She was the last woman on earth he'd ever consider marrying. Which paradoxically made him the perfect bridegroom for a six-month marriage of convenience!

After all your worries that the husband might decide to make the arrangement permanent, or worse, roman-

*tic! Mr. Braddock was a genius to choose Mr. Ryerson.
Now if only you can find a way to convince your handsome guest that his "loophole" is an ignoble tactic, disrespectful of Grandpa. Mr. Ryerson would never
knowingly be either ignoble or disrespectful.*

She remembered what he'd said that afternoon: once
she'd given his loophole suggestion serious consideration,
if she still insisted on obeying her grandfather's wishes,
they would discuss "alternatives." Wasn't the most logical alternative for them to marry, with the clear understanding that the union would be dissolved in six months
to the day, with no lingering entanglements of any sort?

Now if she could only find a way to assure *him* that
it was logical.

Jack rubbed his burning eyes, conscious of the fact that
he'd devoured an ungodly amount of information in just
three short hours. It was his way, of course, but in this
case, he felt particularly driven to arrive at his assessment
quickly. For a variety of reasons, it would be difficult to
tell Trinity Standish that the Lost Spur Ranch had proven
to be an unsuitable investment. On the other hand, it
would be folly to invest in an enterprise that had less than
excellent chances to make a profit.

So far, he was encouraged by what he'd discovered,
not only here, but also in the time he and the girls had
spent in San Francisco before traveling to Stockton.
While his sisters and Louisa had been entertained by
Braddock, Jack had consulted an attorney who special-
ized in California land grants. That conversation alone
had been worth the long voyage, as Jack learned about

the California missions that had controlled the land until a group of men known as the *Californios* gently wrested it away to form their sprawling ranchos. That had been a time of hospitality, gentility, and abundance, with California existing blissfully apart from its nominal owner, Mexico, and its future destiny with the United States. Had it not been for the gold rush of 1849, the culture and influence of the *Californios* might have continued indefinitely.

Instead, the influx of "Yankees" had been disastrous for them, as well as for their land titles. Despite the efforts of a seemingly reputable Land Commission, the large ranchos had been torn apart. While the *rancheros* retained title to some of the land, most of it had fallen into the hands of settlers.

The Lost Spur had once been a part of a grand rancho, but the owner had needed money for a series of court battles brought by unscrupulous challengers to his title. Desperate, the family had sold a rugged expanse outside Stockton to an old man named Randolph Crowne, who also acquired a partial interest in thousands of acres of pastureland.

Three years later, the elderly Crowne passed away, leaving one-half of his holdings to his foreman, Abe Standish, "for loyalty and services rendered." Crowne's son Walter fought the devise bitterly, but without success. Not only did Standish acquire the better half of Crowne's ranch, he also became a tenant in common in regard to grazing land used by Crowne and the few remaining relatives of the original ranchero.

Thus had begun the "feud"—with a father's slap in his son's face. Bad blood had further developed when

Crowne purchased 100 head of Texas Longhorns infested with ticks that carried a virulent disease. Crowne's longhorns were immune to that disease. Standish's shorthorns were not. Weakened by a two-year drought, the Standish herd had been decimated. Various other calamities had befallen the Spur in that same eighteen-month period, converting the thriving business into a precarious and highly mortgaged liability.

And then Abe Standish had fallen off a cliff. Had he not, would the Lost Spur have recovered? To Jack, this was the pivotal question. Standish had been a sophisticated entrepreneur who almost literally created something out of nothing. With a handful of gold dust, he had turned bare land into a gold mine of a different sort. Every decision he'd made in the early years of ranch ownership had been nothing short of brilliant.

Then, without warning, he had suffered a dramatic reversal of fortune. Even worse, his decision-making had become suspect, compounding the disasters. Why?

Based on preliminary research, Jack had three theories for the downward spiral: bad luck; bad luck plus mindless feuding; and bad luck, feuding, and the "dizzy spells."

Were you sick, Abe? he asked the absent patriarch. *It would explain so much. Why, for example, did you mortgage the ranch, when you could easily have raised enough cash by selling off the northwest quarter, while still retaining excellent water and grazing position?*

Jack suspected the answer was in one of seven journals Abe Standish had meticulously kept over his ten years as a rancher. Jack couldn't wait to devour them, but first had to wade through accounts, bills, and legal documents. *In their own way, just as dramatic,* he reminded himself with a wry chuckle.

"Mr. Ryerson?"

He whirled toward his hostess's voice, amazed that he hadn't heard the doors to the study being opened. He found himself startled anew at the sight of her dressed in a provocative, curve-hugging satin robe. The pale peach color contrasted richly with her wavy golden tresses. And while the floor-length, long-sleeved garment covered almost every inch of her body, the belt was so tightly cinched, and the fabric so clingy, it left little question as to the grace or proportions of the body beneath.

Realizing that he had been staring most particularly at her hips, Jack cleared his throat and started to stand, but she moved quickly to confront him, then rested a hand lightly on his shoulder, insisting, "Please don't get up."

Acutely aware of her nearness, he slowly moistened his lips. "I didn't hear you come in. Is there something you need from me?"

Trinity exhaled softly. "I started thinking about what you said—that you need to evaluate every asset and liability before you can decide whether to invest in this partnership. That's why I'm here."

"Pardon?"

"I know you like to be thorough, so . . ." She loosened her sash with one hand, then slipped the robe off her bare shoulders, allowing it to spill to the floor.

Five

For one mind-numbing instant, Jack thought she was actually naked, and a jolt of anticipation shot through him that he was certain she could read on his face. And she might as well have disrobed completely, given the revealing nature of the elegant nightgown she now wore. Two slender satin ribbons were all that held its ivory lace bodice, complete with plunging neckline, in place, while the waltz-length skirt of peach satin conformed seductively to her hips.

He opened his mouth to speak, but it was too dry, and so he settled for shaking his head as he rose to his feet, trying earnestly not to notice how high and full her breasts were as their rosy nipples strained against the sheer lace.

"Please don't scold me, Mr. Ryerson. I know what you're thinking—"

"You can't possibly know what I'm thinking," he corrected her. Then he took a deep breath and managed a firmer tone. "This is completely unnecessary. I don't regard your—your physical appearance as an asset of this project."

"You see it as a liability?"

"Good God, no," he began, then caught the twinkle in

her eyes and relaxed for the first time since she'd entered the room. "It's clear we should talk, but you'll need to put your robe back on or all you'll hear from me is incoherent babbling."

He started to lean down to retrieve her garment, but again she restrained him. "You asked me to consider your plan for using a loophole to circumvent Grandpa's will, and I did so carefully. All evening, in fact. You also told me that if I found your solution unacceptable, we'd explore other alternatives. That's what we're doing now. Exploring the alternative of marrying one another for six months. I have a strong need to respect Grandpa's dying request. And if you have needs that I can meet—" her cheeks turned crimson—"then I will do so gladly, with every asset I possess. I—I just wanted to make certain you understood that. For six months, I would dedicate myself to pleasing you."

"That's enough," he told her, his voice hoarse but gentle. "You're speaking from desperation, when there is no reason for you—for either of us—to feel desperate. How can I convince you of that?"

He rested his hands on her hips, and to his guarded relief, his touch made her jump. If he had had any question as to how experienced this girl was, she had just answered it. And thankfully, it was just the reaction he needed to keep his baser passions firmly in check.

"What would your grandfather say if he saw you like this? Offering yourself to a strange man—"

"In marriage," she reminded him nervously. "Don't misunderstand, sir. I'm willing to submit to your inspection tonight. Nothing more. But the moment you marry me, I will submit to anything you ask."

"I see." Keeping her gaze locked with his own, he slid his hands behind her and down, until they were lightly caressing her buttocks.

Steady, Jack, he warned himself, confused by just how good she felt through the cool satin. Then he repeated, "What would Abraham Standish say if he could see this? His innocent granddaughter, offering herself to a stranger—a man motivated solely by greed and lust."

"I welcome your lust," she insisted, her voice dangerously akin to a moan. Sliding her arms around his neck, she stepped into him, moistening her lips in clear anticipation of his kiss.

"Good God," he groaned. "Now you truly do remind me of—" He caught himself, aghast that he had almost mentioned Erica.

And Trinity knew it. He could see that from the flash of hurt in her luminous gaze. Yet she still didn't pull away. Instead, she whispered, "Close your eyes and pretend you're kissing Erica, if that's how it has to be."

"Kissing Erica is the last thing I want or need at this moment," he assured her, gripping her buttocks firmly with one hand while the other slid up behind her neck. Then he lowered his mouth to hers and allowed himself to kiss her with deep, hungry insistence.

Trinity raked her fingers through Jack's thick hair, grazing his scalp with her nails in imitation of the shocks of delight shooting through her. She had prayed their first kiss would be a tame and respectful one, and knew she should protest or resist this passionate onslaught at least a bit, but his tongue was seducing her while his hand on her backside forced her to accommodate the raging need she had somehow managed to awaken in his loins.

Breathless, she pulled her mouth free for a few quick gasps of air, and was further seduced when his lips moved immediately to her neck, nibbling their way up to her ear, which he nuzzled as he told her with fervent appreciation how soft she was and how very, very sweet she smelled.

"Jack," she answered, her voice low and throaty. "We can marry tomorrow if you wish. I'll do my best—"

"Don't say that." His hand slid up from her buttocks to the small of her back, patting her gently as his other hand eased her face against his shirtfront. She could hear his heart beating fiercely, and could also feel the deep breaths he was forcing himself to take in order to overcome his lust. "I'll need just a moment, if you don't mind," he told her simply.

Stifling a sympathetic laugh, she untangled her arms from around his neck but continued to rest against his chest, amazed at the effort it was taking them each to regain their composure. For all that she had dreaded giving her innocence to a stranger, she actually found herself imagining their wedding night, when Jack would take it from her with no need to restrain himself.

"There now." He exhaled as he stepped back from her; then he bent down to grab her robe, which he held open for her to don. "It's imperative that you listen to me now."

She complied gratefully, and once she had cinched her belt, she settled into a chair and nodded for him to continue.

"I'd like to establish two points. The first is awkward, but has to be said."

"Speak freely," Trinity urged. "I'll do my best not to take offense."

"I appreciate that." He flashed an apologetic smile. "When I said you reminded me of Erica, it wasn't because you resemble her. You don't. Not in the slightest. I was referring to something else—her habit of trying to seduce me."

"She had to *try*? I thought you were engaged."

Jack chuckled. "It seemed to me that a respectful gentleman would wait for the wedding night, regardless of his fiancée's willingness to indulge him earlier. But more often than not, especially when I was engrossed in my work, Erica would invade my office to make provocative suggestions that we should steal off into the woods, or behind a hedge, or somewhere equally inappropriate, and surrender to our passion."

"But you resisted?"

"I wanted nothing more than to make love to her," he admitted. "But I believed it was a compliment to her that we wait. I had a good friend once who was killed in a riding accident on the eve of his wedding. His fiancée found herself in something of a predicament during the early months of mourning."

"Oh, dear."

"And even aside from that, Erica's father had entrusted her to me on his deathbed. I took that responsibility seriously. Too seriously for Erica's liking."

"If only you had made love to her during the engagement, she never would have looked at that awful sailor."

Jack arched an eyebrow. "Don't be so certain."

"You're forgetting that we just kissed. Although," she

added with a frown, "I suppose you kissed Erica with much more passion."

"I doubt I could survive a more passionate kiss than the one you and I just shared," he said, his green eyes teasing her. "In any case, when you came in and proceeded to seduce me, it reminded me of some of Erica's antics. That's my point. You're an amazingly attractive woman, and I didn't want you to misunderstand my remark."

"You did seem somewhat attracted to me during the kiss."

Jack laughed. "Yes, I imagine that was abundantly clear. Which leads us to the second point I'd like to discuss."

She curled her legs up under herself, then gestured for him to proceed, intrigued by his serious expression. Was he reconsidering their marriage of convenience? Or was he simply going to regale her with more annoying tales of Erica?

Jack began to pace. "From the moment I read Braddock's first letter, I was convinced I'd be able to find a way around the marriage clause in the will. These things happen all the time. Men want to control their property, even after death, but when their restraints are unreasonable or overly emotional, civilized men—and at times, even the courts—find a way to ensure that the heirs are not placed in untenable positions."

"I don't agree that he was unreasonable or overly emotional."

Jack studied her for a moment, then continued. "If I had believed, when I read that first letter, that the marriage clause couldn't be handled in a civilized manner,

I would have advised Mr. Braddock to seek investment advice elsewhere."

"Oh."

His tone softened. "But instead, I was confident that it wouldn't be an obstacle, so I proceeded to study the remainder of the information he sent me. And I was intrigued by the project, but also somewhat wary, given the nature of the business."

"I don't imagine there are many cattle ranches in Boston."

Jack nodded. "And that leads to another drawback. While I often visit the site of a project, even if it's hundreds of miles from home, I rarely take so extended a voyage when I'm not even certain yet that it is potentially profitable. But in this particular case, the distant location actually appealed to me, because it offered me a chance to spend some time with Louisa and the girls away from Boston. Louisa in particular seemed bored and moody, and I believed a change of scenery would improve her spirits."

"How sweet of you."

"It was self-defense," he countered quickly. "I've learned from experience how dangerous a bored female can be."

"Erica again?" she asked, trying for a light tone but failing completely.

He shrugged. "Didn't you tell me yourself this very afternoon that you have a burning need to travel the world before you settle down into a boring domestic routine? At the moment, you're consumed with honoring your grandfather, but in a few months, this ranch will bore you, will it not?"

She grimaced but nodded. "According to your theory, I'll be dangerous then. Is that it?"

Jack cocked his head to the side, as though confused, then a grin spread slowly over his handsome features. "I hadn't thought of that, but I appreciate the warning. My point in all this is that I seized the opportunity to take the girls on an adventure. A tame one, and one that would hopefully prove a financial success, but an adventure nonetheless. I want their childhood to be filled with good memories. I want to raise them with good judgment, self-respect, and strong morals. And—" he arched an eyebrow—"I can't think of anything worse than teaching them that a marriage between two strangers based on nothing but mutual financial interests is acceptable. I'd never knowingly set so poor an example for them."

Trinity bit her lip, then said quietly, "My motive is not financial gain, sir."

"But mine would be. You see that, don't you?"

She had to admit it was true. She couldn't really ask him to marry a stranger in front of three impressionable little girls for something as crass as monetary gain. "Couldn't we pretend—?"

"Lie to them? I make it a point to avoid such behavior, for various reasons."

She squirmed, certain now that she had been judged. "I'm sorry you see me as so morally depraved. I don't make a habit of lying, either, Mr. Ryerson, although obviously I have my faults. I just thought it would be best for the girls. But you're correct, of course."

Jack exhaled slowly. "A woman who is willing to dedicate every resource at her disposal to honoring her grandfather is nothing short of noble in my estimation. If I seemed to be criticizing you, I apologize. There is no right or wrong in this. Just an awkward situation, created—if I may be blunt—by your grandfather and Russell Braddock. Had Braddock simply passed my advice on to you, you would have asked him to find another candidate, and I would have taken the girls on another, less controversial adventure. You'd be married by now, and with any luck, your new husband would be hard at work turning the Lost Spur into a thriving enterprise once again."

"But instead, we have an awkward situation." Trinity nodded. "I agree completely. And I'm willing to discuss alternatives, if you have any to suggest."

"I'm relieved to hear that, because—" he exhaled again—"it's vitally important—for my own peace of mind if nothing else—to make certain you understand all conceivable options, even the repugnant ones."

"Repugnant? Is that how you view the prospect of marriage?"

"I was referring to the option of selling the ranch to Walter Crowne—wait!" His expression grew stern. "I'm not advising it. Just describing it."

"You needn't bother," Trinity replied, but another arch of his eyebrow warned her to cooperate, so she added with a huff, "Fine. Describe it."

His expression softened. "With the money Crowne has offered on numerous occasions, you could pay off the mortgage, make a generous donation to the orphanage, and still be financially comfortable for life. You could travel—not extravagantly, but comfortably. That's the life you want, is it not?"

"Please proceed to the next option."

"You could sell a portion of your acreage to Crowne—"

"Oh, for heaven's sake!"

Jack chuckled. "With the proceeds, we could repay the mortgage and clear your title. You'd still retain the choicest pastures and ample water. Within weeks, the Lost Spur Ranch would be a profitable enterprise. You could reinvest some of that profit, and use the rest to travel."

"No."

"Fine. We could try to find another buyer—"

"A buyer who would turn around and sell it to Walter Crowne? No."

"We could structure the sale in a way that prevented that result."

"Unless, of course, they found a loophole?" she drawled.

"Touché." Jack flashed a charming grin. "Assuming my review of these books persuades me to take this project on, I'm sure we'll find a way around our dilemma. The first being the simplest: we'll offer the orphanage an attractive sum of money out of my share, just as I planned. Over time, the ranch will begin to turn a profit, and you'll use your share to travel. You'll meet some lusty adventurer with an appreciation for beauty and intelligence, and you'll marry him. Then you'll bring him back to the Lost Spur and live here with him for six months. Doesn't that meet the spirit of your grandfather's request, if not exactly the letter?"

"That's a lovely suggestion, Mr. Ryerson," she admitted.

Jack smiled again, this time with evident relief. "It's infinitely more acceptable than the only other viable alternative, which would involve your marrying some other man for an immediate six-month marriage."

"That would bother you?" she asked, intrigued that he might be experiencing some jealous twinges of his own.

But Jack dashed such hopes by explaining, "He'd undoubtedly want a share of the profits."

"If it came to that, I'd pay him out of my share, just as you were willing to pay the orphanage out of your share."

"I appreciate that, but my objection runs somewhat deeper." Jack sat down on the edge of the desk. "I don't relish the thought of another man as part owner. If I take on this project, I want to have final say in every decision. Not that I won't solicit your input on every important decision," he hastened to assure her.

For a moment she thought he was teasing, then realized he was perfectly serious. "That's unexpected, Mr. Ryerson," she murmured. "Thank you."

His green eyes finally began to twinkle. "I wouldn't have it any other way, for fear you'd become bored, and grow dangerous."

"You have me confused with Erica again," Trinity said, scolding. "I'm beginning to wonder if you'll ever recover from this broken heart of yours. It's as though she occupies your every waking thought, and, I'm sure, your every dream."

"If you think I'll be dreaming of Erica tonight, you have too small an opinion of your own charms, Miss Standish," he said with a mischievous bow.

She felt her cheeks redden, and tried for a casual smile as she scurried to her feet. "I'm only glad little

Mary or Jane didn't wander down here while I was making such fools of us both. Shall we pretend it never happened? I'd be ever so grateful."

"Of course. As long as you accept my apology for taking advantage of the opportunity."

"It was just a kiss," she assured him, trying not to blush again.

"An elaborate one, and wrong of me."

"It's forgotten," she began, but then had to smile and admit, "or, at least, that's what we'll pretend. Either way, you mustn't blame yourself. After all, I did my very best to seduce you. It would have been terribly insulting if you'd been able to resist too easily." She hesitated, then touched his arm. "I dearly hope you decide to stay."

He cleared his throat before replying, "So do I."

"Good night, sir."

"Good night, Miss Standish."

From the moment she'd heard about the will, Trinity had gone to bed each night with the specter of a temporary, loveless marriage looming over her future. At first, her fears had been dwarfed by her grief due to the loss of her grandfather, but as the weeks had passed, the idea of sharing a bed with a strange man had monopolized her every sleepless thought and haunted her every restless dream.

Thanks to Jack Ryerson's loophole, she could now snuggle into her pillow and relax, knowing she had been freed, albeit reluctantly, from that fate. Although she knew her grandfather would disapprove of the deal with the orphanage, she also knew he would have wanted her to do whatever was necessary to convince Jack to stay and save the Spur. And since Jack would almost surely leave if Trinity insisted on a wedding, she really had no choice but to give in to her handsome advisor.

"Mmm . . ." She sighed again, remembering their kiss. Giving in to him was proving to be a paradox, she decided with a nervous laugh. He would undoubtedly be a wonderful lover. Not that she was ready to take a lover, even a wonderful one, and certainly not one who was in love with another woman!

A kiss is one thing, she reminded herself. *But to allow him—or any man, for that matter—to take your virginity in a loveless marriage? That would be a bleak moment, his green eyes and beguiling smile notwithstanding. Be grateful he has provided you with a means of saving the ranch without sacrificing your pride. Assuming he decides to stay, of course.*

She bit her lip, disturbed at the prospect of losing his valuable assistance. Even if Russell Braddock could find her another bridegroom in time, it seemed doubtful he could find an advisor of Jack's caliber. She just *had* to find a way to convince him to stay.

He has already told you what to do, she scolded herself. *First and foremost, try not to remind him of Erica. Which means you mustn't talk about travelling. Or complain. And don't make slanderous remarks about Walter Crowne, even though you know in your soul he's guilty. And most of all*, she told herself playfully, *you mustn't ever again try to seduce the poor man. Even though . . .*

Sighing wistfully, she turned down the lamp, then allowed herself to remember, for just a moment, how he

had kissed her. Then she shook herself free of temptation, snuggled into her pillow, and willed herself to
sleep.

Jack's pre-dawn breakfast in Elena's kitchen was an
adventure in itself, as she plied him with pungent
mashed beans and soft, scrumptious tortillas alongside
his eggs. Even his coffee was different, with a hint of
chocolate that Clancy assured him happened only in the
morning, "and don't bother trying to talk her out of it.
More likely, she'll convince you to have the chocolate
without the coffee."

Jack learned that Elena's aunt had been the cook for
a sprawling rancho during the reign of the *Californios,*
and she seemed determined to perpetuate as many of
the customs as possible. Most especially, she continued
the rich tradition of abundance and hospitality, treating
Jack like royalty despite the ranch's austere financial situation.

Just as Elena dictated the atmosphere in her kitchen,
Clancy's habits and philosophies dominated the ranch
itself. If Jack had had any doubts as to that, they were
banished when he stepped into the yard and saw that
both Pluto *and* Ranger—"the world's finest cutting
horse"—were standing ready for him.

"We've got a long day ahead of us," Clancy explained. "No *vaquero* worth his salt would ask one
horse to work that hard. When old Blue Toe there gets
tuckered out, Ranger'll be ready."

"Assuming Pluto tires as easily as you think he will,"
Jack countered, returning the old man's easygoing grin.

As they rode together, Clancy entertained Jack with tales of the Lost Spur's early days, when an enterprising miner named Abraham Standish had set out to build himself an empire. Both Clancy and Abe had worked for Walter Crowne's father until the patriarch died, leaving one half of Crowne Ranch to his foreman Abe, infuriating his own son. Everyone had chosen sides, and Clancy swore he hadn't spent even a minute regretting his choice to follow Abe to the Lost Spur.

"Abe was something special, right from the start. We were friends—the kind of friends who'd take a bullet for the other if it came to that. But it was pure selfishness on my part that made me up and go with him. I could see he had a vision, and the gumption to see it through. He was going to build a ranch that put the Crowne place to shame, and I wanted to be a part of it all."

"I started reading his journals late last night," Jack admitted, "and I saw just what you're talking about. He *did* have a vision. And he was a genius when it came to organization."

"I only wish you coulda met him," Clancy murmured. "He'd be relieved, knowing it's you who's gonna git the Spur through these bad times. And to look out for his little girl, too."

"I haven't decided—"

"I know, I know. But Abe always said: when there's only one acceptable alternative, then there ain't any alternatives at all. Just one true course, and you oughta just ignore the rest. That's how it seems with you staying here."

Jack grinned, wondering if Trinity had ever heard that particular folk wisdom. Probably not, or she would have used it the night before, when he was trying to delineate her options.

"Why don't you tell me what it is we're going to see," Jack suggested finally. "You call it a roundup, so I'm assuming it's just that. You're gathering the herd into one spot, rather than having them wandering and grazing?"

Clancy nodded. "It feels good to have a real one again at all. Last year, there weren't nearly enough young'uns to brand. And we were buying, not selling. It all felt wrong."

"So the purpose of the roundup is to brand the new calves? And fill orders for beef?"

"Brand and dehorn the calves. And send the strays on their way. Some of the fellas—our hands and some from the neighboring ranches—set up camp this week so they can git right to it at daybreak. In case the sun starts gitting too hot."

"They work together? How do they know what brand to use for each calf?"

Clancy grinned. "We try to catch 'em while they're still trailing after their mama, so we can brand them same as her."

"That makes sense."

"The fellas are also trying to cut out any strays. In perticular, we keep a close watch for Crowne cattle—they were never welcome, but after that Longhorn mess, we send them running these days with a vengeance."

"I can imagine."

"Abe built a fence a few years back—cost time and money we didn't have, but he was determined to make it as tough as could be for Crowne cattle—or any other critter, human or otherwise, to wander onto Standish land."

"In other words, the Crownes aren't part of the joint branding effort?"

"Not hardly. They've got their own operation with a few of their neighbors to the south. The Spur is the dividing line for a lot of things around these parts."

"Does the bad feeling filter down to the ranch hands?"

"If you mean, do our hands hate the Crownes, I guess I'd say they can't afford to. They gotta go where the work is, and the Spur still isn't steady on its feet. And Walt Crowne is a smart man. He pays the best hands double just to keep 'em loyal. Abe used to do that sometimes, too." Clancy winced as he added, "I've just paid 'em straight wages myself. Seeing as how money's so tight, I didn't figure it was my place to pay extra. I didn't know if Miss Trinity could afford it."

"Can she afford not to?" Jack shrugged. "It's my experience that well-paid labor, especially skilled labor, is a bargain for most enterprises."

"I'm glad to hear you say that."

"And I'm glad to hear these sorts of details. This is precisely the information I need from you, Mr. Clancy."

Clancy's smile turned to a grin when Pluto suddenly pulled up short and whinnied as though in distress. "His nose tells him we're gitting too close to the cattle for his liking," the foreman told Jack.

Scowling, Jack touched the Arabian with his heels, and was relieved when the horse dutifully sprang forward, approaching the top of the long, low rise that they'd been ascending.

Then they reached the apex and Clancy gestured broadly. "There it is—your empire, if you want it."

Jack nodded his approval as he surveyed the herd of cattle, meandering and grazing under the watchful eyes of a sprinkling of hard-working cowboys. The soft, soothing sound of lowing, punctuated by an occasional anxious bray, filled the crisp morning air.

"Watch and learn for a spell," Clancy advised. "See over yonder? That buckaroo's gonna cut that steer out of the herd. Or rather—" he paused for emphasis—"his *horse* is gonna cut the steer out. Watch."

The cowboy and his steed moved as one with quick, decisive movements that isolated and directed the huge steer away from the others. A second man rode up on cue to block the animal's path, preventing it from gaining too much momentum. Thus subdued, the target was herded toward a makeshift corral.

"Look there, Jack. Little Bob Parkins is gonna rope himself a bullcalf. See how him and his pony're matching their pace to the calf? Like they've got all the time in the world. See that?"

Jack nodded, studying the nonchalant technique. It did indeed seem as though the cowboy had no immediate plans other than to guide his prey toward the branding camp. Then he began to twirl a rope over his head with the same lazy air, until finally with a flick of his wrist, he landed the loop neatly around the calf. In an instant, the horse stopped short, the slack in the rope tightened, and "Little" Bob Parkins—a veritable giant of a man—jumped to the ground, sprinting forward with a shorter length of rope in his hand. In seconds, the yearling had been expertly landed and immobilized.

"Ranger could've dropped that calf for him, so's all he'd have to do is truss him up," Clancy told Jack.

"Damn."

"Think you could do that?"

Jack laughed. "If the Lost Spur's future depended on my ability to catch one of those cows, we'd be finished before we even started." To himself he added, *Before I leave here, I'm going to master at least one of these techniques, if only for the sheer sport of it.*

Clancy seemed to guess his thoughts. "I can teach you a trick or two, just for fun. It takes a fair amount of practice to rope a calf. But cutting, like I said, is mostly the horse's job. If you want to give that a try on Ranger—"

"I'm sure Pluto can handle it." Jack chuckled at his own defensive tone, then clicked his tongue at his mount. "What do you say, old chum? Shall we give it a try?"

The horse burst into action, racing toward the herd as though he had no thought other than to perform like the champion he was. Unfortunately, as they neared the huge, odorific animals, Pluto seemed to reconsider, and while he didn't completely balk at Jack's directions, he began to prance and dally, while tossing his head as if sensing danger.

"Steady, Pluto," Jack said, hoping to soothe the Arabian. "We'll work together on this. There, do you see that steer's brand? A crown, which tells us all we need know. Shall we send the interloper back home?"

He urged the thoroughbred into the herd, but succeeded only in terrifying the hapless animal, until finally Jack pulled up on the reins, murmuring, "It is rather daunting, isn't it? Who would have suspected these brutes would be so massive? We'd best retreat while we can."

By the time they'd regained the edge of the herd, Jack saw that several hands had gathered with Clancy, huge grins on their sunburned faces. It was no time for false pride, so Jack rode right up, a grin on his own face, and shook hands with each and every man while cheerfully interrogating them as to their skills, backgrounds, and loyalties.

Trinity knew she should be patient while her prospective partner completed his inspection of the ranch, but she didn't want the matter of the loophole to linger in the air, giving him unnecessary doubts as to the wisdom of this investment. She needed to put his mind at ease as soon as possible.

And she had promised little Janie a visit to the cows, hadn't she? What better time to do so than when Clancy and Jack and the rest of the men were out on the range, offering protection.

She grinned, acknowledging that the real reason for this excursion out to the herd was the chance to see Jack again—or, more precisely, to see him on horseback, his clothing coated with dust, his green eyes sparkling from under the wide brim of his black hat. That image had pleased her long into the night as she had imagined his mouth on hers and remembered the eagerness of his touch, all the while protected by the knowledge that he would never take advantage of his effect on her. He was too honorable to act on lustful urges. Not only that, he was determined to set a proper example for his sisters and cousin, so that they would come to respect the institution of marriage as fully as he did.

Trinity respected it, too, of course, but she also respected her dead grandfather's wishes. And the more she thought about it, the more certain she was that Abraham Standish would have wanted Jack Ryerson to take the reins of the Lost Spur, if not as grandson-in-law, then at least as business manager.

"There they are, Elena! Do you see them?"

"*Si*. There they are. Working," Elena said, emphasizing this last as though rebuking her employer for daring to disturb the men at such a time.

"The harder they work, the more they need food for strength. Which is why we've brought this picnic, so stop scowling and let's set out the chicken and biscuits, shall we?"

"I see the cows! And I see Jack!" Janie waved her arms over her head with delight.

When the child began to dash down the hill, Trinity grabbed her, laughing. "It's farther than it looks, and cattle are unpredictable. What would you do if they suddenly started running at you with all their might?"

"I'd give them a biscuit," Janie replied.

"Wait for your brother or Clancy. They'll take you down for a closer look. Oh . . ." She felt her cheeks turn crimson. "I believe he has noticed us already. Do you see, Jane? He's riding this way. Have you ever seen a more magnificent stallion?"

"And the horse is fine also," Elena drawled.

"Elena!" Trinity glared. "What will the girls think? Please behave."

Trinity had worn her long hair loose around her shoulders, and she tossed it while dragging her fingers through the locks, hoping it would present the perfect combination of grace and effortlessness. She had chosen a peach-toned frock with a lacy white shawl for the same reason, wondering if Jack would notice that it was similar in color to the seductive nightgown she'd worn the night before, although the neckline of her present garment was infinitely more respectable.

When he tipped his hat to her while scanning her with mischievous green eyes, she tensed with embarrassed delight. Still she managed to maintain a poised demeanor until he had dismounted, brushed the dust from his tailored gray pants, and ambled over to join them.

"This is an unexpected surprise. How are you today, Miss Standish?"

"Very well, sir. Did you have a productive morning?"

"I believe that's a fair assessment." He reached down and pulled Janie up into his arms. "As for you, young lady—have you met your first cow yet?"

The little girl giggled. "Miss Standish says I have to wait for you or Mr. Clansky."

"Clancy," Jack corrected her. "And since I'm here, why don't I do the honors?" Turning to his other sister, he asked, "Sweetheart? Care to venture closer?"

"This is fine," Mary assured him.

"The smell is bad enough from here," Louisa agreed cheerfully. "We've brought a picnic, Jack. Are you hungry?"

"Ravenous. But duty before pleasure." He started to lift Janie into the saddle, then, to Trinity's surprise, he announced, "Give me a moment, won't you?" and thrust the little girl into Trinity's arms. Startled, she dutifully cuddled the child against herself while Jack led his stallion over to a group of horses standing in the shadow of the nearby oak tree. Tethering his steed a short distance from the others, he then removed the hobbles from the forefeet of a sturdy-looking brown quarter horse and eased himself into its saddle.

His beautiful stallion must be tired, Trinity decided. *Why else would he trade it for such an ordinary horse? Not that he doesn't look masterful on even an ordinary horse . . .*

She allowed her gaze to wander over him, noting again how relaxed he seemed in a saddle. And how powerful. Memories of their kiss washed over her, along with a familiar tingle that became a sizzle when he pulled up alongside her and bent down toward her. Without thinking, she licked her lips and tilted her face up toward his, then grimaced when he grabbed Janie by the waist and hoisted her onto his lap.

"Save some of that picnic for us," he instructed Trinity; then, with a click of his tongue, he turned the quarter horse toward the herd. In an instant, brother and sister were galloping away.

"Your fiancé is a handsome man," Elena said from behind her.

Trinity turned in time to catch the twinkle in the cook's eye. "Is he? I hadn't noticed. And he's not my fiancé."

"No?"

"No."

Elena arched an eyebrow in disapproval. "Your

grandfather predicted this. He said no man would ever meet your fussy standards, and I defended you. Now you reject a man such as this? A man who is tall and strong and intelligent. A man who values his family above all else. A man—"

"A man who doesn't want to marry *me*." When Elena seemed about to protest, Trinity glared. "Ask him yourself if you don't believe me. He made it very clear last night. And believe me, it's mutual."

"I'll speak to him—"

"Don't you dare." Checking to ensure that Mary and Louisa were out of earshot, Trinity added more gently, "You know full well it wasn't going to be a real marriage. After six months, we would have divorced. Grandpa's will put us in an awkward position, but fortunately, Mr. Ryerson has found a less drastic solution than marriage. He has asked me to defer to his judgment in this matter, and all other matters having to do with the Spur, and I've agreed. I expect you to cooperate just as fully."

Elena sighed. "You should never have worn that ugly black dress. Or argued with him the way you did. He's a gentleman. If you change your ways . . . if you're sweet and charming and flirt with him—"

"Flirt with him?" Trinity bit back a smile. "Should I wear something flattering, and attempt to seduce him?"

"*Si.*"

"I did that last night."

When Elena's eyes popped out of their sockets, Trinity laughed and gave her a quick embrace. "It's for the best, believe me. He's madly in love with another woman—a woman who broke his heart to bits."

"*Verdad*?" The cook sighed again. "I would not want that for you. My husband's heart belonged to another when I married him, and I can still remember how I felt."

"I didn't know that. How awful."

"Over time, he came to appreciate me, but I always knew there was a part of him I could not have. When he died, I told them to bury him with her."

"Elena!" Trinity hugged the cook more warmly. "What a sad story."

"I'm glad you won't be hurt that way."

"Even if I did marry Mr. Ryerson, I'd never be hurt by him, since I don't have romantic expectations. It would only be a temporary marriage. But still, you've made me glad I decided to cooperate with his strategy and avoid the marriage entirely."

"If he doesn't want you, he's not worthy of you."

"Nor I of him," Trinity said with a laugh. "Remember, I had no intention of being a true wife to the poor man. After six months, I would have divorced him and taken off for faraway lands without a backward glance in his direction."

"Unless you were carrying his baby."

Trinity grinned. "That was always *your* strategy, wasn't it?"

"And your grandfather's," Elena admitted. "He knew you'd be stubborn enough to marry for six months, just to satisfy the will. But he said Standish women were so fertile, they always have their first baby before their first wedding anniversary."

Trinity shook her head in disgust. "Now I'm doubly

glad Mr. Ryerson found another way to save the ranch. Grandpa had no right to manipulate my life that way."

"He was worried for you, *m'ija*. He feared you would spend your life wandering the world, searching for something that doesn't exist, when you could be raising babies here on this ranch."

"Searching for something that doesn't exist?" Trinity frowned. "What on earth—oh, never mind. It seems little Jane has had enough of the cows for one day. We'd better finish setting out the food. And after that—" She took a deep breath, then announced, as much to herself as to Elena, "It's time I proved to Mr. Ryerson that I can be a docile and cooperative partner by promising him I'll do anything he asks in exchange for his help saving the ranch."

"Anything?" Elena arched a disapproving eyebrow. "Be careful, *m'ija*. He may be in love with another woman, but he has all the needs of a man. And you are a beautiful girl. A very beautiful, very fertile one. The last thing your family needs is another scandal."

Trinity laughed again. "I don't intend to be *that* docile or cooperative, even if he asks it, which he won't. But—" she squared her shoulders as her prospective partner and his sister rode up to the picnic spot—"I'll do whatever it takes, within reason, to convince him to stay."

Six

Jack felt mildly guilty enjoying the delicious picnic while the ranch hands settled for a quick meal at the branding camp, but Clancy assured him that they'd have a fine supper at sundown, courtesy of a neighboring ranch's chuck wagon. Still, Jack noticed that Clancy himself stayed with the men, except for a quick detour to fetch fresh horses from the gathering under the oak tree.

He also noticed that Trinity seemed restless during their meal, and wondered if she felt uncomfortable over the kiss they had shared the night before. As unfortunate as that might be, it could also be a blessing, since it might help dissuade her from the idea of a marriage of convenience. Of course, it was always possible that she had decided to reject his "loophole" and insist on the temporary marriage, and that her restlessness was based in her concern that that decision would send Jack back to Boston.

Would it? He had to admit he would be disappointed to leave the Lost Spur without having thoroughly explored its investment potential. But the more he thought about it, the more certain he felt that if Trinity insisted on marriage to another man, thus creating a source of friction whenever decisions had to be made, it would render this investment too risky for his further consideration.

So marry her yourself, he told himself mischievously, remembering her luscious, responsive body.

It certainly was a temptation, despite her similarities to Erica. Or perhaps because of those very similarities? *Wouldn't that be the height of irony?* he taunted himself.

It made a certain amount of sense, considering the complete disinterest he'd had in each and every quiet, well-behaved, or levelheaded female he had met since his falling out with Erica. Wasn't that further proof he could only be attracted to women like Erica and Trinity?

And they were attracted to him, too, at least initially. But ultimately, he knew such women could only be satisfied by heroes, rogues, vagabonds, and scoundrels. He had learned that lesson well, and would be a fool to forget it.

When the picnic was drawing to a close, Trinity tapped him on the shoulder and asked him, in a hushed voice, to accompany her for a walk so that they could discuss "several important matters" while Elena and the girls bundled up the uneaten food and placed the dirty dishes into a basket to take back to the ranch.

Taking him by the hand, she led him to the far side of the oak tree where they could talk in relative privacy. Then she bit her lip before admitting, "I've given a lot of thought to last night's discussion, Mr. Ryerson, and I've come to some conclusions, the most important of which is, I will cooperate with your strategy regarding the orphanage."

Relief flooded Jack's exhausted imagination. "You

won't regret this, Miss Standish. Even if I decide against this investment—"

"Oh, but you mustn't! Or rather . . ." She smiled apologetically. "You must do what is best for your investors, of course."

"Either way, you should allow me to negotiate the arrangement with the orphanage. It simplifies matters for you. Don't you see that?"

"I suppose."

Her stubborn frown amused him. "Aren't you relieved, at least slightly, that you won't need to marry a stranger?"

"It's too soon to be relieved. If the orphanage turns down our offer—"

"They won't."

"But if they do? What then?" She stepped closer, her expression troubled. "I've given much thought to this, Mr.—I mean, Jack. Almost the entire night, in fact."

"I'm flattered."

Her violet eyes flashed, warning him against teasing on that particular subject. "I intend to ask Mr. Braddock to find me someone else—someone who will step in if you decide to leave. Of course, since he knows how repulsed you are at the prospect of marrying me, he may already be searching for another bridegroom at this very moment."

When Jack started to protest, she cut him off with a dazzling smile. "I know you see me as hopelessly impetuous, but according to my calculations, I have only seven more weeks in which to marry if I hope to have the full six months completed by the anniversary of Grandpa's death. Do you agree?"

"With what? Your calculations? Yes."

"And so, if the orphanage turns down our offer—"

"They won't."

She glared. "This is a hypothesis, sir."

"I beg your pardon. Continue."

"If I wait two more weeks, and then the orphanage turns down our offer, and you decide to return to Boston, there will be almost no time to find another candidate. So I'm going to write to Mr. Braddock today."

"Fine. As you said, he may well be expecting that letter."

Trinity bit her lip. "Of course . . ."

"Yes?"

"If you decide to *stay*, and the orphanage turns down our offer—which of course they won't—" she paused to smile sweetly, "what shall we do then?"

When Jack hesitated, she took advantage of the silence to add, "Before you answer, please remember that I've compromised to an extraordinary degree already."

He struggled not to smile. "That's true."

Trinity returned his smile. "As you said, the orphanage will almost certainly accept the offer. But on the odd chance that they choose to honor an old man's dying wishes—"

"If that happens—if we become partners, and the trustees thereafter decide to behave irrationally—then I would be honored to become your husband for six months," Jack assured her, confident that such a combination of events would never transpire.

"Truly?" She backed away slightly, her cheeks flushed with what appeared to be a combination of embarrassment and victory. "It's a relief to have that settled."

"Is your mind at ease then?"

Actually—" her flush deepened—"there is one more tiny detail."

He arched an eyebrow. "Russ Braddock described you as an interesting conversationalist. I'm beginning to see what he meant." When she scowled, he prompted more politely, "What is the tiny detail you'd like to discuss?"

"It's odd that you should mention Mr. Braddock," she began, "because this is actually a suggestion *he* made. That we should take advantage of the two-week period while you're evaluating the investment to make certain preparations for our wedding night."

Jack winced and admitted, "I have no idea what that means."

"He's a matchmaker," she reminded him with an apologetic smile. "He has experience with hasty marriages between virtual strangers. He told me some of his couples marry the very day they meet. Is that not a frightening thought?"

Before Jack could respond, she hurried to continue. "Mr. Braddock always advises his couples to wait a week or two, if possible, and to use that time to become better acquainted."

"That makes sense."

"By better acquainted, he's referring to intimacy, not simply an exchange of background information or such. Although of course that's important, too."

"Intimacy?" Jack couldn't help but grin. "My dear Miss Standish—"

"That's quite enough. This constant teasing is a dreadful side to your personality, sir." She eyed him sternly. "Mr. Braddock simply means that we—that any prospective couple—should gradually increase the level of—well, of—"

"Intimacy?"

"Yes. Holding hands, for example. Greeting one another with a kiss or fond embrace. And so on, and so forth, with increasing—well, increasing—"

"Intimacy?"

She backed away from him, her cheeks crimson. "You're being impossibly rude."

Jack burst into laughter. "It's a preposterous concept, Miss Standish. Put forth by Braddock for the sole purpose of manipulating our affections. You can see that, can't you?"

"He was sincerely concerned with *my* welfare, sir. You can't possibly imagine the trepidation a young, inexperienced woman like myself feels at the thought of—well, of sharing a bed with a strange man, to be perfectly blunt. To you, of course, it's simply comical."

Jack adopted a contrite tone. "I apologize for teasing you, Miss Standish. And for impugning the motives of a saint like Russell Braddock. I'd be honored to become more intimate with you over the next two weeks—"

"Be quiet!" Trinity stomped her foot in disgust. "This conversation is finished."

He grinned, unrepentant. "I should return to the herd then. Shall we practice kissing goodbye now?"

"Jack!"

He grabbed her just as she started to storm away. "Do you have any idea how beautiful you look when you're angry and blushing?"

"Do you have any idea what a jackass you're making of yourself?" she countered haughtily. "To think I told Elena you were a gentleman—Oh!" She bit her lip as she inclined her head to a spot directly behind him. "Did you need to speak to your brother, Jane? Or to me?"

He released Trinity and turned in time to see his wide-eyed sister staring in his direction. "Hello, sweetheart." Clearing his throat, he added lamely, "Did you want to visit the cows again?"

"Elena says it's time to go back, so she can start fixing dinner." The little girl took a deep breath, then demanded, "Were you quarrelling again? When *we* quarrel, you tell us it's rude. So why isn't it rude when *you* do it with Miss Standish?"

"Well, for one thing, we weren't quarrelling. Just playing. But from time to time, adults find themselves in disagreement, and sometimes need to talk it through."

"You never quarreled with Erica."

With an exaggerated groan, Jack leapt forward and grabbed the girl up, swinging her playfully in the air. "From this moment onward, every time you mention Erica, you're going to be punished. Did you know that?"

Janie giggled. "Erica, Erica, Erica."

He laughed at the impudent confidence. "All this fresh air seems to be bringing out the brat in you."

"And in you!" the child retorted happily.

Trinity tapped his shoulder, a tentative smile on her lips. "Shall we join the others? Once Elena says it's time to go, one doesn't dare keep her waiting."

"Does this mean we aren't quarrelling any longer?"

"You know exactly what it means, sir. Come along now."

To his surprise, she tucked one hand in the crook of his arm, then offered her other one to Janie, who grabbed it eagerly. Then they strolled back toward Elena and the girls in companionable silence.

When the carriage had finally disappeared from view, Jack swung himself back onto Ranger and headed out to the herd again. His brief ride on the quarter horse when he'd taken Janie to greet the cows had convinced him Clancy was right about Pluto—for all his breeding and majesty, the thoroughbred was simply too nervous around the herd to be useful.

In contrast, Ranger was at home among the restless, complaining steers, and Jack soon learned that the alert cutting horse could teach him as much about this roundup as Clancy could. And so when the horse's attention was grabbed by a renegade steer heading off on his own at a fast clip, Jack clicked his tongue, then urged his steed to "go ahead and show me how it's done." In an instant, the horse sprang into action, overtaking the steer and then planting himself in its path.

The steer slowed his pace, clearly considering whether to simply charge the horse and rider. And given the fact that the animal outweighed Ranger by hundreds of pounds, Jack had a feeling he and his horse would fare badly in such a collision. But Ranger seemed not only confident, but actually cocky, so he decided to trust Clancy's advice, at least for another minute or so.

As the steer grew closer, snorting with disgust,

Ranger whinnied loudly, then bared his teeth in unmistakable warning. The bovine stopped in his tracks, but Ranger wasn't content, and now charged the animal, biting it decisively on its flank. To Jack's amazement, the huge steer turned back toward the herd without further incident, although Ranger followed doggedly, nipping at his prey's hindquarters whenever he sensed any slowing in its pace, until finally the huge animal was back where it belonged.

"Not bad," Clancy congratulated Jack.

"It's as you said. Ranger did all the work."

"Takes some fellas weeks to learn that. Some never learn it at all. You're a natural, son. If I didn't need you to figure out all the dollars and debts, I'd try to convince you to lend a hand out here permanently."

"I'll settle for learning some of those rope tricks you promised to teach me," Jack said with a grin. "But I have to admit, this is fun. Hard work to be sure, but it has its appeal."

"If you want to have some real fun, watch how Ranger handles that big brown fella over yonder. The one with the crown branded on his hide."

"An intruder?" Jack chuckled. "What should I do?"

"Just ease old Ranger up alongside him, and he'll do the rest."

Jack followed the horse trainer's instructions, and once again, Ranger went to work, nipping and bothering the Crowne steer until it had had enough and left the herd. They trailed after the trespasser for a while, until Ranger seemed satisfied that it wouldn't try to come back, then they rejoined Clancy.

"What'd you think?" the foreman asked.

"I'm surprised you don't just set Ranger loose in the herd without a rider."

"It's a temptation," Clancy admitted. "Play around for a while more, then we should head back to the house. I got some chores to do back there."

"And I have some books to examine," Jack said, adding to himself that he also needed time to bathe and dress for dinner. It wouldn't do for his "fiancée" to see him in this dusty condition, especially in light of her precocious suggestion that they become "acquainted" over the next two weeks.

So much like Erica, he reminded himself as he and Ranger patrolled the herd. Pure innocence, combined with a provocative willingness to misbehave. And this time, he didn't intend to resist. Why should he? After all, Trinity had no intention of allowing their "intimacies" to go too far.

And who knows? he told himself jokingly. *Perhaps the trustees at the orphanage really will turn down your offer, and you'll end up in that beautiful girl's bed for six months. The least you can do is spend the next two weeks preparing her for that startling fate.*

He chuckled, knowing that the danger of that happening was virtually nil. The trustees would recognize instantly that their only hope of salvaging something from Abe Standish's bequest was to accept Jack's offer. And if they didn't recognize that, he'd educate them, or advise them to seek legal counsel. Either way, he would see to it that the marriage never took place.

"Too bad," he told Ranger with a philosophical smile. "She's a temptation in many ways, but then again"—his whimsical mood hardened into cool determination—

"so was Erica. I'm not about to blunder into another such mess, temporary or otherwise."

Four hours later, Jack was as tired as he'd ever been in his life, and he had the feeling he would also discover, in the hours to come, that he was as sore as he was tired. But it had been a productive day, familiarizing him with the work that formed the basis for the Lost Spur's once-and-future success.

Clancy had been a good source of information on the ride back to the ranch, especially in regard to the Standish-Crowne feud. When Jack had observed that the split rail fence running between the two ranches didn't seem to be effective in keeping the herds separate—in fact, most of Jack's time on Ranger had been spent rounding up cattle with crowns emblazoned on their hindquarters—Clancy had confirmed that the fence was nothing more than a symbol. It caused more practical problems than it solved, and was expensive to maintain, especially in terms of the labor involved in patrolling and repairing it. But Abe Standish had insisted on it, and Clancy had continued that tradition.

Now, as they approached the corrals, Jack asked the foreman the question that had been on his mind for hours. "Do you believe Walter Crowne murdered Abe?"

Clancy pursed his lips. "Old Walt's got a lot of bad in him—I worked for his family for five years, so I know that for a fact. But is he a murderer? That's not something I'd ever want to say about another fella without knowing for sure."

"My sentiments exactly. And I'm sure you've heard that the sheriff and the doctor feel it was an accident."

"Yeah. I heard all about that."

"Did Abe ever mention any dizzy spells to you?"

Clancy nodded. "They were gitting worse all the time."

"So it's possible the fall was an accident?"

Clancy shrugged. "A man who's been having dizzy spells doesn't usually stand too close to the edge of a cliff now, does he?"

"Not usually."

"I figure he was pushed," the foreman said finally. "I just can't say for sure it was Walt who did the pushing. Can't think of anyone else who'd have a reason to, though. Can you?" He leveled a stare at Jack as if to say, *Draw your own conclusions, but don't ask me to call a man a murderer without proof.*

"Fair enough," Jack said. Then he dismounted from Pluto and turned his attention to Ranger, anxious to liberate the hardworking horse from his saddle and hackamore so he could run free. He had earned it.

"I'll see to the horses," Clancy told him. "You oughta spend some time with your womenfolk. Looks to me like they've been making themselves useful."

Turning to see what had caught the foreman's eye, Jack was charmed by the sight of Louisa and Mary taking down sun-drenched laundry from long lines strung between the kitchen and a storehouse. Strolling over to them, he complimented each girl on her willingness to lend a hand, then asked where Janie was.

"She's in the barn with Trinity," Louisa explained. "All she wants to do is play with the baby pigs. One of the men set up a stall filled with nice clean hay so she could frolic without getting filthy. Speaking of which . . ." His cousin eyed him with mischievous disgust. "You're filthy again."

When Jack slapped a cloud of dirt from his trousers, Mary wailed. "Go away! You'll soil all these nice clean linens."

"Sorry, miss." He grinned and tipped his hat. "I'll just go inside and wash up while you two do all the work."

His sister laughed. "It doesn't feel like work at all. It's been the nicest day. I'm so glad you brought us with you."

"So am I." He turned to Louisa. "Are you glad, too?"

She shrugged her shoulders. "I liked the time we spent in San Francisco better, but this is fine, for a while at least."

"She's bored because all of the men are so old," Mary said impishly.

"All the young boys are busy at the roundup," Jack explained, adding to himself that it was for the best. The last thing he needed was a crowd of buckaroos coaxing Louisa out of her bedroom window every night!

He glanced toward the barn, imagining how much fun it would be to see Janie playing with the piglets, but decided to change into fresh clothes before meeting up with his hostess. Heading for the house by way of the corral, he was surprised to spy three men riding up the long drive that led to the front porch of the ranch house.

"Well I'll be danged," Clancy murmured, slapping Pluto on his rump to send him on his way, then pulling the corral gate closed without taking his eyes off the newcomers.

"I take it you know them?"

"That's Walt Crowne and his two boys."

"Well, in that case, I'll be danged myself," Jack admitted.

"I'll let 'em know they aren't welcome here."

Jack caught the foreman's arm. "Don't be so hasty. For all we know, this could be a good sign. Maybe they're as tired of this damned feud as I am, and they figure this is a good time to start fresh."

"Miss Trinity isn't gonna like them showing up here. And she's surely not gonna like you making them welcome."

"She told me just today that she trusts my judgment when it comes to running this ranch. And," he added with a wink, "she's in the barn with Jane for the time being. So let's just take this one step at a time."

Planting himself in front of the house, his hands on his hips, he waited until the riders were almost upon him before pushing his hat back and nodding in detached greeting. "Welcome to the Lost Spur. I'm Jack Ryerson—a friend of the family. Can I help you?"

"You're the new partner?" The oldest of the three riders grinned as he swung his leg over his horse's back and landed heavily on the ground. Then he stuck out his hand toward Jack. "My name's Walt Crowne. I'm guessing you've heard of me?"

Jack nodded, accepting the brisk handshake. "You own the ranch just south of here."

"That's all you've heard?" Walt Crowne chuckled, then turned to his companions. "These two sour-looking fellas are my sons. Come on down here, boys. Where're your manners?"

The older of the two scowled and made no move to comply with his father's wishes. The younger hesitated also, but only for a moment before jumping to the ground. Then he wiped his hand on his pants and offered it to Jack. "I'm Randy Crowne, sir. Nice to meet you."

"My pleasure." Jack returned the handshake.

"Frank, get your butt down here. *Now.*"

The older son's eyes narrowed, but he finally obeyed his father and joined the group, giving Jack a quick, appraising glance before sticking out his hand. "I'm Frank Crowne."

Jack steeled himself, knowing from the man's expression that he intended to crush rather than shake his hand. Then he met the grip solidly. "Welcome to the Lost Spur, Mr. Crowne."

The father chuckled again, as though knowing the two men were engaged in a painful contest, despite their cool expressions. Finally, they dropped their hands to their sides, each stoic in their discomfort, and Walt observed cheerfully, "We didn't expect a friendly greeting, Ryerson."

Jack locked gazes with him. "Yet you came anyway?"

"You and me got business to discuss."

"Well, then, let's step inside, shall we?"

He noted a flicker of surprise in the patriarch's eyes, and wondered if this would be the first time a Crowne had set foot in Abe Standish's house. From the expression on Frank's face, he guessed the older son didn't care for the idea one bit.

And the younger son? His eyes were wide, and his mouth was hanging open, but it was clear he wasn't thinking about the invitation. His attention was riveted on someone or something behind Jack.

Certain that Trinity had appeared on the scene, Jack turned, prepared for a battle, but instead found that Louisa had stepped noiselessly into view, a tentative smile on her pretty face as she surveyed the new arrivals.

"This is my cousin, Miss Louisa Ryerson. Sweetheart, this gentleman is our new neighbor, Walter Crowne. These are his sons, Frank and Randy."

"Welcome to the Lost Spur," Louisa murmured, wandering closer without taking her gaze off Randy.

Walt tipped his hat. "Good afternoon, Miss Ryerson."

The youngest Crowne edged closer to the girl. "Nice to meet you, miss. I'm Randy. I live over yonder." He gestured behind himself, then gave her a foolish grin. "I'm real pleased to meet you."

Louisa blushed. "I'm pleased to meet you, too."

Walt burst into laughter. "We came here to talk business, Ryerson, but I can see this boy isn't gonna be much use now. We heard you brought some family with you, but no one mentioned how pretty your womenfolk were." To his son, he added dryly, "Why don't you and Miss Ryerson get better acquainted while Frank and I talk to her cousin?"

"Jack?" Louisa gave him a hopeful smile. "He could help us in the yard. Mary and I would love to have someone to talk to while we work. That is," she added hastily to Randy, "if you'd like."

"I'd like it fine," he assured her.

"Well, then." She gestured for him to follow her, and the couple disappeared around the corner of the house.

Still grinning, Crowne turned back to Jack. "Speaking of pretty women, where's the new owner?"

"Why don't you tell me why you're here first? If it's something I think will interest Miss Standish, I'll ask her to join us." Leading the way up the steps, he swung the door wide open and insisted, "We can talk in the study."

The two men followed him into the house, removing their hats as they entered the large foyer. "Never thought I'd see the inside of this place," Crowne murmured.

"I never much wanted to see it," Frank retorted. "Let's just get this over with."

The father's eyes flashed. "I apologize for my son, Ryerson. His ma died when he was three feet tall, and I haven't had much luck teaching him manners since then."

"I treat folks the way they need to be treated," Frank retorted. "We aren't here to socialize. We're here to offer them twice what this place is worth. Isn't that enough? Do we have to make damned fools of ourselves to boot?"

Jack struggled to maintain a cordial expression. "The Spur isn't for sale, Mr. Crowne. Surely you know that."

"And even if it were, you wouldn't sell it to a Crowne?" Walt shrugged. "I figured that pretty little she-cat felt that way, but when I heard she brought in some fancy business advisor from New England, I thought maybe you'd talk some sense into her. It's me or the bank, Ryerson. If they foreclose, you get nothing, and neither does the girl. I'm offering you your only chance for a profit."

"Every payment on the mortgage has been made in

full and on time," Jack informed him quietly. "There's no danger of foreclosure, Mr. Crowne. And I have a feeling we don't agree on what the ranch is worth, so your offer of twice its worth means little at this point. On the other hand," he took a deep breath, "I think it's in both our interests to get to know one another. We're neighbors, after all. And our business interests overlap in certain respects. If you'll step into the study—"

"They'll do no such thing!" Trinity's words of outrage caused the three men to whirl toward the doorway, where the blazing-eyed hostess stood, her hands on her hips, her fury directed toward Jack. "I want them out of here. *Now!*"

"Afternoon, Miss Standish." Walt Crowne gave her a curt nod of his head. "Your partner here invited us in. We'd just as soon've talked outside."

"There's nothing to talk about, outside or anywhere else. I can't believe you had the nerve to step foot on Grandpa's property. Is nothing sacred to you? And as for *you!*" She fixed an icy glare in her prospective partner's direction. "I can't imagine how you intend to justify this presumptuous behavior. Please send your guests on their way immediately. And then please join me in my grandfather's study."

Jack held her stare for a long moment, then turned to Walt Crowne and shrugged. "As I said, the Spur isn't for sale—not even at double the price. But I'd like to speak with you. Not here, apparently—" he arched an eyebrow in Trinity's direction—"but eventually, if I decide to enter into a partnership with Miss Standish, there are matters to discuss. The livestock and the fences, among other things. When the time comes I'll arrange to meet with you in town, if that's convenient."

"Come on out to the ranch," Crowne told him cheerfully. "You're welcome anytime. And don't be so quick to turn down my offer. Once you've had time to find out how things work around these parts, you may find it's the only deal to be had."

Trinity stepped up to the rancher and wagged her finger under his nose. "Don't you dare threaten us, you—you murdering coward!"

Alarmed, Jack pushed his way between the two, then gave Crowne an apologetic wince. "She's understandably distraught over the loss of her only relative."

"Distraught? She's a hellcat through and through. You'll find out soon enough," Crowne muttered. "That stubborn temper of hers is gonna ruin you but good. She got that from her grandpa, and damned if he didn't destroy this place because of it."

Moving toward the door, Walt added over his shoulder, "They say you have a knack for business, Ryerson. Maybe that's so. You seem like a smart fella. But only a fool would invest one penny in this ranch, knowing his partner is a spoiled little female who'd rather see it go to the bank than accept a decent offer from the only fella who has any interest in making one."

"You're forgetting something, Pa," Frank said with a smirk. "It's not just money Ryerson's looking for here. That sassy tongue of hers might just be worth the trouble when he gets her alone on their wedding night."

Jack's hand shot out, grabbing the big man by the throat and driving him against the wall with such force, he thought for a second he had knocked him senseless.

But Frank's eyes were half-open, so Jack assumed he could hear him as he advised in a dry, methodical tone, "Your father was correct about your manners. Until you've learned to act like a gentleman, keep your mouth shut around women—especially *my* women—or I'll shut it for you. Understand?"

There was dead silence for a moment, then Walt Crowne began to chuckle. "My boy had that coming, Ryerson. And I swear, I wouldn't've believed a city fella like you could lay a hand on him and survive. I'm impressed."

"And I'm unimpressed," Jack drawled, pulling his hand away from Frank in disgust. "Take him and go. And if Miss Standish didn't make it clear, allow me to remind you that you and your sons are not welcome on Spur land."

"Fair enough." Crowne slapped his son on the back. "Come on, boy. Let's find your brother and get outta here."

Still bleary-eyed, Frank gave Jack a halfhearted glare, then stumbled toward the door ahead of his father. Once out on the porch, both father and son bellowed Randy's name, and Jack watched from the doorway as the younger son sprinted into sight.

Chagrined with himself for allowing a strange boy to pay court to his cousin, Jack was relieved to see Louisa come around the corner of the house, a sweet smile on her face as she waved goodbye to Randy. The boy in turn was grinning sheepishly as he swung himself onto his horse and tipped his hat in the girl's direction. Then, without further ceremony, the three Crownes galloped away.

Jack glanced over his shoulder at Trinity. "I'll join you in a moment. There's something I need to ask Louisa first."

Trinity bit her lip, then nodded and turned away from him, heading for the study.

He knew she was angry, and wondered if she had any idea that he, too, was vexed. He hadn't traveled thousands of miles to be berated in public. And he certainly wasn't going to allow emotional outbursts and vengeful prejudices to keep him from exploring every means of saving the Lost Spur. Selling the property to Crowne was not an option, of course, but that wasn't the only issue. There was the problem of bringing diseased cattle onto common grazing land, for one. Jack needed to find a way to convince Crowne that such conduct, intentional or otherwise, would not be tolerated. And the expense of maintaining the fences, which had thus far been borne by the Spur, was arguably of mutual benefit and thus should be financed mutually.

But she was correct in her assessment of their character, at least as far as that bastard Frank is concerned, he told himself as he approached Louisa.

The girl was nothing short of starry-eyed as she watched Randy Crowne fade into the distance. Exhaling in a slow, melodramatic sigh, she then seemed to notice her cousin for the first time, and threw her arms around his neck. "Oh, Jack! I adore you for bringing us here."

Startled, he returned the hug, then scanned her expression with anxious thoroughness. "He didn't take any liberties with you, did he?"

"Liberties?" She giggled with delight. "He's as shy as

can be. And the most darling boy I've ever met. He helped me fold the linens, and when our fingers accidentally touched, he stammered and apologized and backed up so quickly, he fell right over the basket."

Jack grinned at the image. "That's a relief. His brother is a boorish lout, and his father is less than civilized, so I was concerned."

"Randy was a perfect gentleman. And did you see those darling blue eyes of his? I melted every time he looked at me." She took Jack's hand in her own and asked sweetly, "Could we invite him to Sunday dinner? I know Trinity doesn't care for his father—"

"She believes he murdered her grandfather, so it's safe to say he's not on her list of potential dinner companions." Jack smiled. "I'm sure there are other blue-eyed boys in the area whom you could invite to dinner. I'd forget about this one if I were you. I doubt you'll ever see him again."

Louisa seemed about to retort, then just shook her head. "I won't allow you to ruin this perfect afternoon with your prejudices, Jack Ryerson. Haven't you somewhere else to be?"

"Actually, I do," he admitted, then he touched his cousin's cheek. "Enjoy your perfect afternoon, sweetheart. And look after Janie and Mary for a while, won't you? Miss Standish and I have something important to discuss."

Seven

As Trinity paced back and forth in her grandfather's study, she fanned herself with his Last Will and Testament, hoping to get her emotions under control before Jack returned. She needed to be calm and objective if she hoped to reassert control over this would-be partnership.

Unfortunately, she didn't even have control over herself! She was obsessed with the image of Jack throttling Frank Crowne. Even now, her heart was pummeling the walls of her chest because of it. She had told him he'd be her hero if he managed to save the ranch, but in that one lightning-quick movement, he had already earned that title, along with her undying gratitude.

Hadn't Janie said it? *Now Jack is here—he'll take care of you.* And Louisa had stated it even more clearly: *You're one of Jack's women now.* And Jack himself had echoed that, warning Frank not to dare speak to "his women" again.

A surge of arousal rumbled through her, and she panicked, fanning herself even more vigorously. If only she hadn't insisted on seeing him right away. If only she had stormed away in a fury, refusing to talk to him for the rest of the day.

Do it now, she advised herself, lunging for the door. *Ask Elena to give him the message that you're indisposed and mustn't be disturbed. He'll assume you're angry, and you should be angry—you would be angry!—if only he weren't so strong and confident and heroic, and—*

Her fingers had barely grazed the handle when there was a sharp knocking sound from the other side; then the door was pulled open and Jack stepped into the room. His expression was everything she wished hers could be: calm, confident, unreadable. Backing away, she mumbled, "I've reconsidered this meeting, sir. We should postpone it, for fear of saying something unpardonable in the heat of anger."

He stepped closer, studying her intently. "If you have something unpardonable to say, I suggest you say it. Be blunt, Miss Standish. I assure you I intend to do the same."

His nearness assaulted her senses, while the image of him vanquishing Frank Crowne blended enticingly with the memory of his kiss the night before. She almost believed she could feel heat radiating from the long, lean muscles of his body—

"Miss Standish?" He rested his hands on her shoulders. "You're furious with me for allowing the Crownes to step foot inside your grandfather's house. Isn't that so?"

She gulped, then nodded.

"Do you suppose I took any pleasure in that? For all I know, the man's a killer. At the very least, he bears some responsibility for the current state of the Lost Spur. And his son . . ." Disgust flashed across his handsome face, but he visibly banished it. "The point is, I had a purpose—a sound business purpose—for speaking with them. That's the reason I'm here, is it not? To infuse some business sense into this enterprise? How can I do that if you refuse to trust me?"

"I trust you. I swear I do." She gulped again, embarrassed by the husky tone to her voice, and insisted more evenly, "I was shocked to see them here. I admit that. Surely you must have known how I'd react. And to invite them into Grandpa's study, of all rooms! Here, where he pored over his accounts, trying to undo the damage that awful man did to his dream."

Jack's hands dropped to his sides. "Perhaps that was excessive. Although I suspect inviting them into the parlor wouldn't have forestalled your public chastisement."

"Pardon?" For the first time, she noticed the hint of annoyance behind his vivid green eyes. "*You're* angry with *me*?"

"Hasn't anyone ever been angry with you, Miss Standish?" he quipped, then he gestured toward the settee. "Please be seated."

"No."

"Pardon?"

"I said 'no.' Hasn't anyone ever said 'no' to you, Mr. Ryerson?" She arched her eyebrow to accentuate the sarcastic tone.

Jack moistened his lips. "Yes, frequently. On the other hand, I haven't been scolded in public since I was ten years old, and I didn't appreciate it. I may one day be your partner, Miss Standish, but I will never be your lackey. In the future, if we disagree, feel free to tell me so, only please do it in private."

She hesitated, then nodded. "You have my word, provided I have your word that you won't allow the Crownes on Grandpa's land again."

"I believe I made that very clear to them, did I not?"

"Yes," she admitted, her voice husky again. "I know you're angry with me, but honestly, won't you let me thank you for that? It was so—and you were so . . ." She felt her cheeks begin to burn. "When you threw Frank against that wall, it was so . . ."

Jack cocked his head to the side. "Go on."

"It was powerful. Brave and powerful. And I was proud to be your partner." Backing away, she added lamely, "I mean, your potential partner."

He stepped up to her again, and again she backed away until she was flush against the wall. Then she tried to smile, to distract him from the sound of her heart beating frantically against her ribs. "I was impressed. And Walt Crowne was, also. And Frank would have been, had he not been in such a stupor." Licking her lips, she insisted, "Everyone's afraid of Frank, you know. When I visited here as a young girl, he bullied the boys constantly, and no one ever stood up to him. But *you* did. You didn't even think about it, you just . . . well, you just dominated him. It must have felt wonderful. For you, I mean. Not for him."

Jack grinned. "I try to solve differences with words, not fisticuffs. But I have to admit, it felt good to put that lout in his place." Dipping his head down so that his face was close to hers, he murmured, "Feel free."

"W-what?"

"You asked my permission to thank me. Please, feel free."

She stared into his laughing green eyes, wondering if

they could see just how flustered and accessible she was at that moment. Her head was swimming. Worse, she was beginning to throb in the most wanton of places.

Despite the tightness in her throat, she managed to demand with feeble outrage, "What are you suggesting?"

"It's Russ Braddock's suggestion, actually."

"Mr. Braddock? Oh!" She felt her cheeks begin to blaze.

"This seems an excellent opportunity to increase our level of intimacy," he said, and while she knew he was half-teasing, the gravelly undertone to his voice told her his body was reacting as strongly as hers to their nearness.

As if in confirmation, Jack pressed closer, covering her mouth with his own, then kissing her with gentle hunger. Without thinking, she slipped her hands behind his neck, then abandoned herself to the warm, salty taste of him. When he parted her lips with his tongue, she welcomed him, and in an instant, waves of dizzying pleasure assaulted her. Swooning against him, she sifted her fingers through his thick hair, grazing his scalp with her nails as she murmured his name.

Jack's hand was busy, too, caressing her breast through the light fabric of her cotton dress, kneading and teasing with gentle thoroughness. Then he pressed his body full against hers, grinding gently but with clear need as he began to swell with arousal.

When his lips moved to her neck, trailing a line of fiery interest, she realized she was moaning his name in soft, unmistakable entreaty. "Jack."

"I agree," he whispered, gathering her against himself

in one last, lingering flood of enjoyment. She heard him draw a deep, steadying breath, and then he released her.

This time, when he grinned down at her, it was with the crooked, apologetic grin of a sometime-rogue who knew he had overstepped. "Do you suppose that's what Braddock had in mind?"

Trinity struggled for a lighthearted tone. "If it was, then you were correct to call him a rascal." Daring to touch his cheek, she added sincerely, "Thank you for throttling Frank Crowne, and for ordering them off my land. It's an image I won't soon forget."

"It was my pleasure, Miss Standish."

"Trinity."

"Trinity," he echoed, his voice raspy once more.

For a moment, she thought he was going to kiss her again, and her body reacted with a jolt of delighted anticipation even as her mind screamed at her to intervene. Then he abruptly turned away and walked to the door, pulling it open and announcing, "I'd better get out of these clothes before Elena scolds me for tracking dirt about the house. I look forward to seeing you again at dinner."

She sighed at the prudent dismissal. "I'll ask Elena to draw a bath for you. Relax and enjoy it, sir. You've earned it today." With one last appreciative smile, she slipped past him into the hall.

Jack waited until she had disappeared from view, then he walked to the desk and sat down in Abe Standish's huge leather chair, wondering at the behavior in which he had engaged that afternoon. Taking advantage of a vulnerable young woman? Throwing a guest against the wall?

Of course, the guest had been rude and disrespectful to a lady, but wouldn't a stern verbal rebuke, coupled with an instruction to leave the premises, have sufficed? And as for the "vulnerable young woman," she had been all too willing to engage in naughty behavior with him. But if willingness were reason enough for a gentleman to take advantage of a female, Jack's love life would have been much more active than it had, in fact, been. In particular, his engagement to Erica—the most willing female he had ever encountered—would have been nothing short of a lusty affair.

No, willingness had never been, and could never be, the sole criterion. Jack had held himself to a higher standard, making love only to women of experience— women who clearly understood all of the ramifications of their behavior. An innocent, unmarried virgin could never properly evaluate the consequences of unbridled passion, even with a discreet and respectful fellow like Jack. He had learned that all too clearly when he had watched his best friend's fiancée retreat in shame when she lost her lover before the wedding night that would have legitimized the baby she carried. The girl had slit her own wrists without ever bothering to read the offer of marriage Jack had sent to her the moment he'd heard of her predicament.

And so Jack had resisted Erica, even to the point of ensuring that their kisses rarely reached a feverish state that might seduce them into making a mistake. But for some reason, he had cheerfully engaged in just such kisses with Trinity twice since they'd met! Why?

Last night, she caught you by surprise, he counseled himself firmly. *And this afternoon—well, she said it herself; there's the remote possibility that the orphanage might turn down your offer, and a few romantic encounters over the next week or two could help prepare her—*

He chuckled under his breath at the feeble attempt to justify his behavior. He knew full well the trustees of the charity would leap at the chance to salvage something from Abe Standish's estate.

Admit it, Jack, he told himself, leaning back in his chair and shaking his head in sheepish self-reproach. *She's a beautiful girl—in some ways, even more beautiful than Erica. You kissed her because you wanted to kiss her, and because you knew that, unlike Erica, she would stop you before it went too far.*

Thus reassured, he reminded himself that a relaxing bath awaited him, and after that, a spicy meal. All in all, a fitting end to a day that had been, as he'd said to his hostess, quite a remarkable one.

Elena had prepared two versions of her *chile colorado,* and Jack chuckled under his breath when little Janie inhaled her full portion of the milder dish. Ordinarily she was a fussy eater, but Clancy had promised to tell a very special story if she cleaned her plate, and she seemed determined to hold him to his word. Between bitefuls, the little girl regaled them with details about "the piggies." She had named each and every member of the litter, and would undoubtedly have brought them to the table had Elena been willing.

When Janie wasn't talking, Clancy stepped in with colorful descriptions of Jack's first day as a *vaquero,* poking fun while also making it clear that he admired the Easterner's gumption and horsemanship.

The little girl and the foreman kept the entire table entertained, although Jack noted that Louisa seemed distant, barely touching the piquant food she had helped prepare. Not that it was too hot for her. In fact, she and Elena were the only diners who tasted the spicy version without having tears spring to their eyes.

She's sulking because there aren't enough boys around here, Jack decided. He remembered how Russell Braddock had slyly assured Louisa that the valley was teeming with unattached cowboys eager to pay court to a pretty girl from Boston. Unfortunately, Braddock hadn't realized that their visit was going to coincide with the roundup.

It was unfortunate that the only boy available to pique her curiosity thus far had been Randy Crowne, but that situation would change over time, as the Spur's hands returned to the bunkhouse. The thought made Jack wince, but after all, one reason for this adventure was to make Louisa happy, and so he would be vigilant but also indulgent to the best of his abilities.

Meanwhile, he was gratified to note that in regard to Mary, at least, the trip seemed an unqualified success. She melted in a heap of laughter each time Janie or Clancy recounted a particularly silly incident, and gobbled up a mixture of the mild and the spicy versions of Elena's scrumptious cooking, piling her food into soft, warm tortillas as though it were the most natural part of her mealtime ritual.

And Trinity? She appeared relaxed and confident, encouraging the storytelling with mischievous delight. But she hardly met Jack's gaze throughout the entire meal, and he was certain he knew why. She was embarrassed over the display of gratitude and arousal that had taken place in the study. Embarrassed, but not ashamed, because it simply was not in her nature to be either prudish or inhibited. In that sense, her similarity to Erica was a relief.

All in all, he thoroughly enjoyed the meal, despite the occasional bout of watery-eyed coughing caused by Elena's fiery cuisine. While a challenge, the food was also delicious, especially as complemented by a bottle of hearty red wine from the private cellar of Charles Castillo, a neighboring rancher. Elena explained that Castillo's land contained what had once been the vineyard for the huge rancho that had encompassed all of the nearby spreads, including Crowne Ranch and the Spur. Most of the old arbors had fallen into disrepair, but the Castillo family tended a few, producing a robust wine for their personal consumption and to give as gifts every Christmas to all their neighbors.

Intrigued by such tidbits of information from Elena and Clancy, Jack could almost visualize how life must have been on a rancho. The quintessential efficient operation, not unlike a medieval manor, where virtually everything one needed to survive and to thrive was produced within one's own boundaries. The huge herds of cattle hadn't been seen as a major source of food in those days, but rather had produced valuable hides, and even more valuable tallow for candles, while hogs and chickens had been raised for eating. Olives for oil and grapes for wine had flourished, as had fruit orchards and fields of corn and wheat.

"It's time, Mr. Clancy," Janie insisted finally. "Tell us the story about the spurs."

"Oh yes, Clancy. Please do." Trinity's eyes sparkled. "It's been ages since I've heard it."

"Well, I reckon a promise is a promise," the foreman said, leaning over to refill his wineglass and Jack's, then settling back and surveying his audience for a long moment before beginning. "You all know that the Spur used to be part of a bigger ranch, owned by a man named Randolph Crowne."

"Randy must be named after him," Louisa interrupted.

"That's right. I remember how old Randolph used to fuss over that baby boy. He didn't show much affection to his son Walt, nor to Frank. But little Randy was the apple of his eye." The foreman shook his head, then continued. "Years and years ago, there was a huge rancho owned by a fancy *Californio* who was famous for the spurs he wore—shiny ones of pure silver, studded with turquoise and onyx. After his land was divided up, a rancher named Ruiz ended up with those spurs. But old Randolph Crowne wanted them real bad. Tried to buy 'em more than once. But Ruiz wouldn't budge, until the year of his daughter's wedding. He planned a grand celebration, called a fiesta, and wanted it to be something to remember forever, so he announced that he was gonna hold a horserace at the end of the fiesta. The prize would be the spurs."

"Oh! Who won?" Janie demanded.

Clancy grinned. "Old Randolph wanted to win, but he had a bad heart, and the doc wouldn't hear of it. And since the old man didn't have confidence in Walt, he made an offer to all of us who worked there, including his foreman, a fella named Abe Standish. Randolph said he'd leave a nice little parcel of land in his will to the man who won those spurs for him.

"You should've seen Abe's face. He'd been wanting his own spread, and now here was a way to git it. So he caught himself a wild stallion—as strong and fast as old Blue Toe out there in the corral—and gentled him quick as can be."

"Did he win?"

"He surely did. Señor Ruiz gave Abe the spurs, and Abe gave 'em to Randolph. That old man was so danged happy he cried tears right there on the spot. Then he drew up a will leaving Abe a nice little corner of Crowne Ranch—not a lot of land, but good pasture with good water.

"Randolph hung those spurs over the door to his parlor so everyone could admire them. He was a happy man, but a dying one. Finally, after a real bad attack, he sent for Walt and told him to bring the spurs to his bedside. When Walt asked why, the old man said he was gonna divide 'em up—one for Walt, one for Abe."

"And Randy's father was jealous?" Louisa asked.

"Powerful jealous. He figured it was the biggest insult his pa could have given him, acting like Abe was just as much a son to him as Walt. So he went down and got those spurs and took 'em out to the smithy and smashed 'em to bits."

"Oh, no!" Janie wailed.

Clancy nodded. "When old Randolph heard about it, he was furious. Sent for a lawyer and re-drew his will. Said if he couldn't give the spur to Abe, he'd give him half his ranch instead. Two weeks later, Randolph Crowne died. And Abe Standish became a rancher."

"No wonder they feuded," Louisa murmured.

"Bad blood from there on out," Clancy confirmed. "Walt hired a fancy San Francisco lawyer to say his pa wasn't right in the head when he changed his will, but Abe won, just like he'd won the race. It stuck in Walt's craw, believe me."

"And Mr. Standish named his ranch after the spur that he should have received. It's a lovely story, Mr. Clancy," Mary said with a sigh.

"I've always loved it, too," Trinity echoed.

Jack had to admit he felt inspired as well, and couldn't wait to excuse himself and head for the study, knowing that he could find even more valuable information in Abe Standish's journals, which covered the period of time from Randolph Crowne's death to Abe's last week of life.

Jack believed there must have been an earlier journal as well. If Abe had known Crowne was going to leave him a ranch in his will, he would have been making plans for how best to approach the daunting task of creating a cattle empire.

Where is it? he asked himself, scanning the shelves of the study for one more tattered red volume. Finally, good sense dictated that he concentrate on the resources he had at hand, and he settled into Abe's leather chair, chuckling at the protests of his sore muscles. As much as he had enjoyed his day as a buckaroo, he decided he'd best confine his efforts from there on out to more cerebral pursuits. And as much as he had enjoyed his amorous encounters with Trinity, he needed to avoid those as well, and return to the "boring," methodical habits that had made him a success.

Less than an hour had passed when he heard a light knock on the study door, and he winced to think that his hostess might have plans of her own. Vowing to resist her, he strode to the door and pulled it open, then chuckled to see that his prediction had been wrong after all. It was Mary, not Trinity, who stood smiling up at him.

"I wanted to say good night," she explained.

"Come in for a minute." Jack took her by the hand and led her over to sit with him on a soft leather sofa. "It's nice to see you looking so happy, sweetheart."

"I love it here," she said with a sigh, adding quickly, "I love Boston, too. And I miss my friends, and Margaret and Mr. O'Shea and Uncle Owen, but—" Her blue eyes began to sparkle. "I thought it would be strange and scary here, but I felt at home right from the start. And there are so many interesting things to learn."

"I agree."

"Janie loves it, too. But Louisa . . ." She bit her lip.

"She's cross with me, because I ordered Randy Crowne's family off the ranch?"

Mary nodded. "Randy was very sweet to us, Jack. I know his father and brother are horrid, but he didn't seem to be."

"I'm not judging him, sweetheart. He could be a prince, for all I know, but there's bad blood between these two families, and at the very least, he was raised by a boorish lout, which is reason enough to keep him at a distance. His loyalties are to his family, don't you suppose? And his family hates the Standishes. And the older brother treated Trinity disrespectfully."

When Mary sighed, Jack chuckled. "Randy wouldn't have time to visit, even if we did welcome him. You've seen how all the hands here are busy, haven't you? That's because the Spur and some of the neighboring ranches have begun their yearly roundup. Clancy tells me the Crowne family and the Ruiz family will be starting a similar effort tomorrow. I'm sure that will occupy all of Randy's time for the next few weeks."

"Louisa will be disappointed. She was hoping—"

Jack noted his sister's wince, and arched an eyebrow. "She was hoping you'd be able to change my mind?"

Mary nodded. "But if Randy is going off to round up cows anyway . . ."

"Tragic, isn't it?" Jack drawled. "She'll have to find some way to survive until the Spur hands come home. Assuming we're still here by then, of course."

"I keep forgetting we might decide not to help Trinity."

"We'll help her," Jack corrected his sister. "Even if I can't offer financial assistance, I intend to leave detailed advice for her and Clancy. And they can contact me for further advice as needed. We won't just turn our backs on them."

"Good." Mary studied him curiously. "If you decide to stay, who will the investor be? Uncle Owen?"

Jack hesitated, then remembered the lecture she had given him weeks earlier as they'd waited for Louisa to come back through the bedroom window. It was time to acknowledge that she was slowly leaving childhood behind.

Settling back, he asked, "Are you interested in the details of my business? That's good, considering that my financial situation intersects with your own."

Her eyes widened. "I have a financial situation?"

He tried not to grin. "A very comfortable one. When Father died, he left a sizeable estate to his three children in equal shares. Since I was an adult, he left my share to me outright. Yours and Jane's are in trust. Do you know what that means?"

She shook her head.

"It means it is being managed by someone else on your behalf. Yours truly, in fact. I am the trustee, which means I watch over your funds and invest them for you."

"Like you invest Uncle Owen's?"

"No. Owen is willing to take a certain amount of risk. I take no risks with your assets, nor with Jane's. The funds are safe and growing. One day, they will be distributed to you."

"When?"

He took a deep breath. "Once you've attained nineteen years of age, provided you're married. Married or not, it will be finally distributed at age twenty-two."

"But what if I need it sooner?"

"If there's something you want, you have only to ask. You know that. Fortunately, I am able to provide for you out of my own accounts. That's why I'm so very careful with my own money, sweetheart," he explained. "You've heard Uncle Owen urge me to make the sort of risky investments he enjoys. But I never do."

"Because of me and Janie?"

"Because Father entrusted you girls to me, and I'd never do anything to jeopardize that. However . . ." He took her delicate hand in his own. "I'll share something with you in confidence. I am considering using my own funds—not yours or Jane's, but my own—for this investment in the Lost Spur."

"How exciting! Uncle Owen is always so pleased when you do it for him. I'm glad you're going to keep all of the profit for yourself this time."

"Are you?" He studied her fondly. "I haven't decided for certain yet. I might offer the opportunity to Owen, but if the risk seems modest enough, I might take this one for myself. Or it may prove too risky even for Owen, in which case we'll return to Boston."

"I hope we stay. I don't want Trinity to lose her ranch."

"Nor do I." He patted her hand. "I haven't told her I'm considering using my own money in this enterprise, so don't mention it to her. If I decide to pass the opportunity along to Owen, I don't want Miss Standish to see it as a lack of confidence."

"I won't say anything." Mary cocked her head to the side. "Does Louisa have a trust fund?"

"Yes."

"And are you her trustee, too?"

"Yes."

"Does she know about it?"

Jack nodded. "To her credit, she never badgers me about it. For all her impetuousness, she hasn't a greedy or acquisitive bone in her body."

Mary smiled. "If Janie knew about hers, she'd want to spend it all on candy and dolls."

"A natural reaction for a child," Jack said with a chuckle. "Which is why children aren't allowed to manage their own affairs. But as you grow older, I'll involve you in yours, if you'd like."

"Couldn't we invest *my* trust fund in the Lost Spur?"

Startled, Jack asked carefully, "Why would you want to do that?"

His sister's blue eyes began to twinkle. "I believe it will be your most successful project ever."

"I have a good feeling about it myself," he admitted. "But investing your money is out of the question. You'll have to be content with profiting through your relationship with me."

"I will, Jack." Without warning, she gave him an effusive hug. "Thank you for taking care of us."

"My pleasure," he murmured, embracing her tightly. "You and Jane—and Louisa—are my whole world. I'd be lost and lonely without you. Did you know that?"

Mary nodded against his chest. "Especially since Erica left?"

"That was for the best. She and I were not a good match, as Russell Braddock would say. For one thing, I could never have a rational conversation with her about my business, as I've just done with you. I've enjoyed this, Mary."

She pulled free and smiled up at him, clearly flattered. "I want to learn everything, so I can manage my own money if I don't have a husband by the time I'm twenty-two."

"And even if you have one, he might not have an aptitude for business. He'll be fortunate to have a wife like you, either way. Now, it's time for you to go to bed. I'm going to turn in early myself."

Mary giggled. "You're tired from riding Ranger? Are

you going to do that again tomorrow? It was so much fun listening to Mr. Clancy's stories at dinner."

He laughed. "My career as a buckaroo was a one-day affair. But Clancy promised to teach me to swing a lasso, so there will undoubtedly be more hilarity at my expense." Planting a kiss on her cheek, he stood up and offered his hand to assist her to her feet. "Run on up to bed now, sweetheart. I'll look in on you after a while."

"Good night, Jack." She hugged him one last time, then sprinted from the room, leaving him to marvel at how quickly she was changing, and how proud he was of her. To think that she actually enjoyed discussing business! After his experience with Erica, it hadn't occurred to him that any female in his life would ever be so inclined.

As happened so frequently since his arrival at the Lost Spur, thoughts of Erica turned quickly to thoughts of another headstrong, tempestuous beauty, whom he suspected was also not "inclined" toward business. He imagined her in her bedroom—or rather, out on her balcony—dreaming of adventures in far-off lands. Yet within a matter of weeks she could find herself running a ranch alone. Wasn't it time Jack started preparing her for such an eventuality?

Trinity sat in front of the fireplace in her bedroom, her maps spread all around her, and tried to focus on her well-plotted future. Once the Spur was safe from the Crownes, she would begin her travels, tracing her father's footsteps as recorded in the countless letters he had sent to her over the years.

First, Morocco, she reminded herself with a melancholy smile. *That's where he was when you were born, so it's a fitting place to start. Remember the letter he wrote to Mother that day? He didn't even know he was a father, although he was so clearly enamored with the idea. Of course*—she paused to sniff—*he thought you were going to be a boy. But the letter he sent after he heard otherwise was so joyful, I'm sure his disappointment was only fleeting.*

She turned next to the map of Cairo. He'd been there six years later, when Trinity's mother had succumbed to a cruel case of consumption, dying before he had a chance to see her one last time. Trinity didn't remember much from those days—only her mother, frail and wracked with coughing spells; and her father weeping in the graveyard, bemoaning her loss.

A crisp knocking on her door made her jump, and she hastily dabbed at the tears in her eyes, knowing instinctively that the visitor was Jack. The last thing she needed was for him to see her this way. He already believed she was too temperamental and sentimental.

"Even though *he's* the one who kissed *you,*" she reminded herself aloud, annoyed at the unfairness of it all. "And wasn't he temperamental this afternoon when he threw Frank across the room? That's hardly the behavior of a rational accountant. And now here he is at your bedroom door in the middle of the night! What could be so important that it can't wait for a more proper time and place?"

The thought startled her. Had he come to her room with plans to kiss her again? If so, he would be sorely disappointed. And she would be within her rights to be indignant—to take the opportunity to inform him coolly that she no longer wished to follow Russell Braddock's advice in regard to becoming accustomed to one another, if Jack saw that as permission to come to her bedroom at any hour!

Summoning a haughty expression, she threw open the door. "Is something wrong, Mr. Ryerson?"

"There's a hairless, squirming creature in my baby sister's bed," he said with a grin. "But other than that, all is well."

"A hairless . . . ? Oh!" She laughed in spite of herself. "How darling!"

"Elena assures me that as soon as Janie is asleep, she'll sneak in and return the little intruder to his littermates." His green eyes warmed. "I know it's late, but I was hoping we might talk for just a moment."

"Of course. I'll join you in the study, unless . . ." She gestured toward the balcony. "It's a beautiful night. See how the mountains are silhouetted against the sky?"

"Inspiring," he admitted. "But this will just take a minute. I wanted you to know I plan on riding out to the orphanage tomorrow morning—"

"Oh!" She clapped her hands, amazed and delighted. "Does this mean you've decided to stay? So quickly?"

He grimaced as he stepped into the room. "We agreed that whether I stayed or not, I would negotiate the agreement with the Delta Valley trustees."

"Oh, of course."

"Would you like to accompany me?"

"Accompany you?"

"To the orphanage." He eyed her sternly. "I thought you might want to keep abreast of the details."

"In case you leave?" she murmured, deflated at the prospect of trying to run a ranch on her own.

"Even if I stay, you will be an equal partner with me in this enterprise, will you not? I appreciate your trust, but it's in your best interest to understand the situation yourself. It may not be intrinsically interesting—"

"I'm sure it's fascinating, Jack. And I'm pleased that you'd want me to come with you tomorrow. I only wonder if my presence might not create some doubt in the trustees' minds."

"Pardon?"

Trinity smiled. "Come and sit with me for a moment." Leading the way onto the balcony, she seated herself on a narrow bench, motioning for him to take the larger, more comfortable wooden rocking chair. "If you go alone, you will clearly seem to be managing my affairs, which will indicate to them that you are staying, and that you fully intend to marry me if they're foolish enough to reject your generous offer. If I come along, they may perceive that our relationship is—well, undefined, for lack of a better word."

"It's an excellent word, and an excellent point," he admitted. "You seem to have more of a head for business matters than I supposed." He began to nod in vigorous agreement. "Until this matter of the orphanage is settled, we must present an unassailable front."

"Then it's doubly wonderful that you beat Frank senseless this afternoon," Trinity said, teasing. "Perhaps they will see it as a sign you'd do anything for this cause, even if it means marrying me."

Jack chuckled.

"I've been meaning to apologize for calling Walt

Crowne a murderer to his face this afternoon after I promised to stop making such accusations," she added ruefully. "Do you suppose they'll sue us over it?"

"I don't imagine they'll want to recite the details of that meeting in open court," Jack reassured her. "Just try not to let them anger you. And I'll do the same."

"I'll try. And I'll try to learn as much as I can about running the ranch, too. I already know a little, from the lawyer Mr. Braddock hired to handle the first mortgage payment."

Jack's gaze softened. "Russ told me you sold some jewels to make that payment. That's unfortunate, and I hope to avoid any recurrence. Even if I don't stay, I'll leave a list of the ranch's assets that you should sell, so you don't liquidate any more personal valuables."

"That's doubly fortunate, because I don't *have* any more personal valuables." When he winced again, she assured him quickly, "I have all I need. And a firm offer of employment from the Porters, so don't be concerned."

He studied her for a moment, then asked, "Have you read any of your grandfather's journals?"

"No. He wrote me letters, and I've read them all dozens of times, but not his journals. Not yet."

"They're more or less primers on running a successful ranch. He was a genius at business—did you know that? He kept meticulous records, anticipating every possible eventuality."

"Why does that sound familiar?"

"Pardon? Oh." He flushed. "I appreciate the comparison."

"He would have loved to have a son like you. His own

son—my father—was impulsive and completely undisciplined."

"Why does *that* sound familiar?"

She drew back, startled and offended. "How am I undisciplined?"

"I didn't mean it as an insult," he assured her. "You're adventuresome, like your father. Of course, so was Abe, but he tempered it with cool, rational analysis."

"So? I'm irrational as well as undisciplined?"

Jack leaned forward, his green eyes twinkling. "You're embroiled in the most irrational form of human interaction—a feud. You would personally tie the noose around Walter Crowne's neck if the sheriff would only allow it. You're willing to marry a total stranger to save a ranch you don't even want. And you're hellbent on travelling to exotic places unescorted."

"Oh." She struggled not to smile. "I thought this was just another unfair comparison to your former fiancée."

"Well, there's that, too," he said with a grin. Then he coughed and added, "I was teasing."

"Were you?" She arched an eyebrow in disgust. "Perhaps we should change the subject. Or better still—" she jumped to her feet—"perhaps you should go. You'll need your rest if you're to convince the trustees to accept your offer tomorrow."

"Trinity." He stood and took her hands in his own. "You're an irresistibly beautiful girl who loves to travel and who finds fault with every word I utter. Admit it," he urged, a tentative grin lighting his face. "You find my attitude maddening, my attention to detail boring, and my preoccupation with business stifling. Forgive me if I see a fleeting resemblance to Erica in all that."

"Do I look like her?"

"Huh?" He shook his head. "No, not at all. Her hair is reddish and her eyes are golden brown. You're as beautiful as she—in some ways, even prettier—but that's where the physical resemblance ends."

Her jealousy faded into sincere sympathy for his brokenhearted condition. "I'm sorry she hurt you, Jack. Were you devastated for months?"

"Hardly devastated," he murmured. "More disappointed than anything. And perplexed. And determined not to repeat the mistake."

Trinity scowled. "It's true. You really *are* maddeningly analytical."

"Exactly." His eyes twinkled. "Now that that's settled, shall we return to the subject of your business education?"

"I'd love to read Grandpa's journals. Especially the first one, where he tells the story of the spurs just as Clancy did at dinner."

Jack licked his lips, then demanded, "What makes you think there's a journal from those days?"

"I beg your pardon? Didn't you yourself suggest—"

"Yes, I suggested you read the journals that I've been studying in the library. But I've been unable to locate one from the time Abe was foreman at Crowne Ranch. I had begun to think it didn't exist, but you sound as though you're certain it does."

"It exists, or at least, it did at one time." Trinity swept back into her bedroom and located the ledger into which she had pasted each of her grandfather's letters, starting from when she'd been a small child. Leafing quickly, she found the one he'd written to her the day she left for

Europe with the Porters. "Here, do you see? He was planning a surprise for me, he says. He intended to hide a brooch here at the ranch, and if I found its hiding place during my next visit, I could have it."

She smiled sadly. "He was always doing such things. Trying to lure me here. To spark my imagination about the Spur. But the truth is, I knew he would have given me that brooch anyway. It was my grandmother's and had been in our family for four generations. Who else would he have given it to?"

"That's a charming story," Jack admitted. "But what has it to do with a journal?"

"Oh." She grimaced in apology. "Do you see this paragraph, where he promises to place the brooch and a few other valuables into a strongbox, which he would then hide? One of the other valuables was that first journal—the one he most wanted me to read, so that I'd understand his love for this ranch."

"So it's here somewhere?"

She smiled at the excitement in his voice. "If that first journal is indeed missing, then yes, I suppose so. When I heard about his death, and learned the details of his financial situation—particularly the mortgage—I just assumed he had abandoned this game, and sold the brooch to help save the Spur. But perhaps he didn't. Wouldn't that be odd? It's worth quite a bit, Jack. Not as much as the mortgage, of course, but it's studded with diamonds, and . . ."

She broke off, mesmerized by the sparkle in his emerald eyes. "Would you like me to find it for you, Jack?"

He flushed but nodded. "I'd love to get my hands on

it. The journal," he added hastily, "not the brooch. I'm not suggesting for a moment—"

"It's fine," she said, pleased by his distress. "The girls and I will begin our hunt for the box tomorrow, leaving no floorboard or brick unturned. With any luck, we'll find it before you return from the orphanage."

"Well, then . . ." He was clearly embarrassed, and turned his attention to the rest of Abe's letters. "Fascinating."

"Would you like to take this and read it?"

"What? Oh, yes, eventually. For now, though . . ." He turned the pages carefully. "You've done a remarkable job preserving these. And annotating them, I see."

It was Trinity's turn to blush. "It's a silly habit I started with Father's correspondence—keeping track of his travels by pasting each letter to a ledger page, and then making notes at the bottom of the page, summarizing where he'd been, and what he'd seen. It was a way of having him close to me, I suppose."

Conscious of the compassion in his green eyes, she laughed lightly and gestured toward the maps on the floor. "Do you see from whence my wanderlust was born? More proof of your theory, I suppose, that I am Erica's kindred spirit, despite my protests to the contrary."

Jack pursed his lips, nodding slowly. "I suppose."

"You have a long ride ahead of you tomorrow," she reminded him. "And there's a hairless creature in your baby sister's bed that should be removed without further delay. But first . . ." She moistened her lips and suggested softly, "Shouldn't you kiss me good night? If the orphanage turns down your offer, we'll be glad of the practice. And if they accept it, it will be our last."

He studied her for a moment, then smiled and lowered his mouth to hers, tasting her gently, with no hint of the lust that had invaded their earlier encounters. "Sleep well, Trinity. I'll be back before dark, hopefully with good news. Or at least," he amended huskily, "with prudent news."

Seduced by the gracious remark, she stared at the door for a long while after he had disappeared through it. "If not good news, then prudent news," she murmured, knowing that he was correct—that as much as they might find one another attractive, it would be a devastating blow to their partnership—and to their friendship—should the orphanage do anything but accept Jack's offer. And soon.

Eight

Jack enjoyed the two-hour ride from the Spur to the Delta Valley Home for Boys, knowing that his girls were in good hands. Janie had been up at dawn, helping Elena feed the baby animals. Mary had still been asleep, but had appeared serene when he'd peeked his head into her bedroom to check on her. And Trinity had a treasure hunt on which to spend her day.

Even Louisa had seemed happy, appearing at the pre-dawn breakfast table to ask Jack's permission to ride out to the roundup with Clancy. Before he could object, she had explained that she was bringing a book to read, and intended to stay up on the rise, with the extra horses, on the exact spot where they'd picnicked the prior afternoon.

"I just want to look at the boys," she told him sweetly. "Mr. Clancy said I could use his spyglass, and he promises to keep the ranch hands away from where I'm sitting. I just want to see them."

Jack had struggled not to grin at the heartrending lament, and after receiving assurances from Clancy that the hands would be too busy to bother Louisa, and Louisa in turn would be no bother, he cheerfully agreed to the arrangement.

As the orphanage came into view, a small boy who

had been sitting on the fence jumped off of his perch and began to wave and run toward Jack. Sobered by the knowledge that this poor lad was all alone in the world, Jack reined Pluto to a slow walk and raised his hand in greeting, calling out, "Hello, there."

The boy stared for a moment, then his shoulders slumped, but he continued walking toward Jack until he was within a few yards. "Morning, mister. That's a fast-looking horse."

"You have a good eye." Jack studied the boy's tall, underfed form. He appeared to be close in age to Janie, or perhaps a year or two older.

"My pa knows horses."

"And he taught you? That's good." Swinging down from his saddle, he offered, "Would you like to ride him back to the orphanage? My legs could use some walking."

"I need to stay here, in case my pa comes. He'll be in a hurry to get outta here, and I want to be ready."

Jack pursed his lips. So, the boy's father wasn't dead after all? But he'd be in a hurry? Did that mean he was some sort of fugitive from justice? In some ways, he imagined that was just as hard on the boy as losing the man entirely. "You're expecting him today?"

"Soon as he knows I'm here."

"I see. How long *have* you been here?"

The boy shrugged. "I don't know. A couple of weeks, I reckon."

"And you sit out here every day? Waiting?"

The boy nodded.

"What's your name?"

"Nicholas Holloway, sir. Pleased to meet you," he

added, thrusting his hand upward as though anticipating Jack's handshake.

Amused, Jack returned the gesture briskly. "I'm Jack Ryerson."

"If you're here looking for help for the roundup, they're mostly all gone."

"The orphanage hires boys out?"

"The real big ones. Not my size. But I wouldn't go anyway, 'cause I might miss Pa."

"Right." Jack rumpled the boy's dark brown hair. "Have you had breakfast, Nicholas?"

"Sure. They make me have it, even if I'm not hungry."

Jack chuckled. "I have a sister your age, and I must admit, I apply the same policy to her."

"Huh?"

"She doesn't always want to eat when we eat, but I usually insist she at least have a piece of toast."

"I like toast. She's my age?"

"More or less."

"I'm seven."

"Janie is six."

"Is she taller'n me?"

"Much shorter."

The boy nodded, a faraway look in his eyes. "My sisters were littler than me, too. I haven't seen a girl since I haven't seen them. There aren't any girls here."

"So I'm told. That must seem strange."

"Yeah."

Jack wanted to ask about the boy's sisters, but wasn't sure just what to say. Something in the boy's statement had been fundamentally ominous. "I need to go and meet with the headmaster, Nicholas. Are you sure you don't want to get out of the sun for a while?"

"You should call me Nicky, mister. No one calls me Nicholas, except when they're yelling at me."

"Nicky it is, then. So?"

"I'll stay here. Just in case."

"Well, then . . ." The thought of leaving him there tugged at Jack's heart. "I'll bring you something cool to drink when I come back by. How does that sound?"

"That sounds good, mister."

"Jack."

Nicky bit his lip, then nodded. "That sounds good, Jack."

"Mr. Everett will see you now, Mr. Ryerson."

Jack thanked the servant who had greeted him at the door, then proceeded into the office of Joseph Everett, headmaster of the Delta Valley Home for Boys. As with everything else in the place, the office was sparsely furnished, almost austere. So far, Jack hadn't seen any of the boys other than Nicky, although the workers bustling about the place seemed young enough—and downtrodden enough—to be recent orphans themselves.

"Mr. Ryerson! My apologies for keeping you waiting." A large, heavyset man with a bushy headful of graying hair bustled from behind his desk to shake Jack's hand. "My assistant tells me you're here about the Standish estate. Sad business, that. Were you a close friend of Abraham?"

"No. I'm a business associate—and friend—of his granddaughter."

"Ah, the lovely Miss Trinity. I haven't had the pleasure, but I've heard only lavish praise. She was vacationing in Europe when the accident took place, wasn't she?"

Jack scowled. "She was in Paris on business."

"Well, of course. I meant no disrespect."

Settle down, Jack, he cautioned himself, surprised at his visceral reaction to such words as "vacation" and "accident." If he wasn't careful, he was going to become as embroiled in this feud, and the concomitant illogic, as Trinity!

"Please have a seat, Mr. Ryerson. Can I offer you some refreshment? Lemonade? Something stronger?"

"Your assistant already gave me a glass of water, thank you. I did make a request, though. That someone make sure little Nicky—the boy out by the gate—gets something to drink. The sun's going to be hot today, and he looked a little bedraggled."

The headmaster's eyes narrowed. "We do our best with that boy, but he insists on sitting out there all day long, rain or shine. If he told you any differently—"

"He didn't complain, and I'm not suggesting he's been mistreated." Jack took another deep breath, disturbed by the negative tone the discussion was taking. Tact and charm—his traditional negotiating tactics—seemed to be failing him, and he needed to correct that if he wanted to put his offer forward in the best light.

"I've heard nothing but praise concerning your establishment, sir," he assured Everett finally. "The mere fact that Abe Standish chose to make yearly donations is testament to your solid reputation."

The headmaster visibly relaxed. "Little Nicky is a particularly sad case, Mr. Ryerson. Believe me, we have all reacted to him the same way you have. One wishes to help, but the child makes it almost impossible."

"Is there any real prospect for his father's return?"

"Return?" Everett frowned. "His father is dead, sir. Oh!" He chuckled and shook his head. "He told you he was waiting for him? That's what he tells everyone, because that's what the poor child believes. The truth is too horrible, you see, for him to accept."

"And what is the truth?"

"Gregory Holloway shot his wife and two daughters in the head, then turned the pistol on himself, two months ago."

"My God."

Everett nodded. "It was a miracle Nicky wasn't home that night. He was visiting with friends in town."

"That was fortunate," Jack murmured. "These friends . . .?"

"You're wondering why he's here, rather than with them? Can you imagine anyone trying to deal with the boy, when he keeps insisting his father is alive and innocent of any wrongdoing? The mere suggestion of his father's guilt agitates the child."

"But there is no doubt?"

"I beg your pardon?"

Jack arched an eyebrow. "You said the man turned the pistol on himself. If the blast obscured his features in any way, perhaps the identification was incorrect."

"Oh, I see what you're saying. No, his face was not blown away. In fact," he added, his voice oddly accusatory, "it was Nicky himself who identified the body."

Jack's stomach knotted. "You can't be serious."

"Who else was there? The wife was dead. The people of Stockton barely knew Holloway. He accompanied his family to town last year, but as soon as they were settled in, he left for Mexico, on some scheme to get rich overnight. Apparently it didn't pan out. He returned, disgruntled, and killed himself and his family. Nicky's survival is a miracle. We only hope one day the boy realizes that." The headmaster grimaced. "I'm a busy man, Mr. Ryerson. If you're here to discuss Mr. Standish's devise—"

"That's exactly why I'm here," Jack agreed. "Under the will, the orphanage receives nothing if Trinity Standish lives on the ranch with her husband for six months before the anniversary of Abe's death. I'm here to give notice that Miss Standish has every intention of doing just that unless some other arrangement can be made."

"Other arrangement?"

Jack adopted a reassuring tone. "Surely you can sympathize with Miss Standish's plight. She's in mourning for a beloved relative. It's an awkward time to contemplate marriage. However, she is determined to keep the ranch. I've suggested, and she agrees, that we offer you—or rather, the trustees—a substantial sum of money in exchange for your promise not to enforce the provisions of the will. Here are the details," he added, reaching into his vest and proffering the document he had prepared the night before.

Everett frowned. "The Lost Spur Ranch is worth many times this amount."

"Is it?" Jack shrugged. "There's a mortgage. That would have to be satisfied even if Delta Valley took title under the will, which I assure you will never happen."

"Miss Standish has a suitor?"

"Yes."

"Can I assume it's you?"

"Yes." Jack leaned forward in his chair. "Don't doubt my resolve, sir. I will gladly marry her, and she I. In fact, it is her preference, since she believes it's what her grandfather wanted."

The headmaster exhaled loudly. "It's not my decision, in any case. I'll present it to the trustees, although I should warn you, they were very fond of Mr. Standish. They may feel, as does his granddaughter, that the terms of his will should be enforced verbatim."

"As trustees, they have a fiduciary duty to the orphanage, not to Abe Standish. If they honor that duty, they'll have no choice but to accept my terms."

Everett grinned. "You're very persuasive. Shall I arrange a meeting, so you can present your offer yourself? Say two weeks from today, at noon?"

Jack nodded, relieved. "Feel free to share our conversation, and this document, with them in the meantime. I look forward to meeting them, and seeing you again." He shook the man's hand briskly.

"Stay for lunch," Everett urged. "It will give you a chance to visit with young Nicky."

"I'd like that," Jack admitted. "And I'm glad to hear he comes in for meals, at least."

"He follows our rules, I'll say that for him. And when it's his turn for chores, he does them without complaint, which is more than I can say for most of my charges."

"He's clearly a fine boy," Jack agreed. "What are the chances he'll be adopted?"

"Frankly? He would be an ideal candidate if it

weren't for his morbid vigil. He's a fine looking, strong, intelligent boy. Young enough that someone could still hope to raise him as their own, but old enough to be useful around the house right away. Aside from new-born babies, Nicky is just the sort most people come here looking for."

"But once a prospective parent talks to him, they're discouraged by his 'morbid vigil,' as you call it?" Jack shook his head. "Perhaps I can find a way to reason with him over lunch."

"He'd make a fine son for a patient man like yourself."

"I'm already raising two sisters and an orphaned cousin," Jack said with a chuckle. "That's more than enough responsibility for a bachelor such as I."

"And if you and Miss Standish marry, you'll be having babies of your own?"

Reminding himself that the trustees might ask Everett for an assessment of Jack's willingness to marry Trinity, he responded with a casual nod. "She'll make a fine mother. I know that from the way she has quickly endeared herself to my little sisters. And to me." He flashed a confident smile. "I'm sorry she couldn't join us today. You would have seen firsthand how attractive she is. And how determined she is to keep the Lost Spur in the family."

"You've done a commendable job of communicating that to me. And by extension to the trustees. I'm sure we'll reach a mutually profitable and agreeable resolution to this matter on your next visit. For now, let's join the children in the dining hall, shall we?"

* * *

"It isn't here, either. It isn't anywhere," lamented Janie as she stretched out on the oak floor of Abe Standish's study and stared up into Trinity's laughing face, a picture of frustration.

"It has to be somewhere. And I never really thought Grandpa would hide it here. It's too unimaginative."

"Then why are we looking here?"

"Trinity didn't want to disturb Jack," Mary reminded her, pulling out a large book from the shelf and checking diligently behind it, as she'd been doing for most of the afternoon. "So we're searching this room while he's at the orphanage."

Trinity resumed tapping on the paneled wall behind her grandfather's desk. "That's right. Tomorrow, we'll search the attic. That's a much more likely hiding place for a treasure box."

Janie sighed. "I wish Jack would come home so we could stop."

"You can stop right now if you'd like. You checked every inch of the floor for loose boards, didn't you?"

"Some inches I checked twice," the girl confirmed, jumping to her feet and stretching her arms before moving to the window and peering out anxiously. "Oh! He's here, he's here! *And he brought one of the boys with him!*"

"He what?" Trinity began, but Janie had already bounded from the room.

"He wouldn't do that, would he?" Mary asked.

Trinity crossed to the window in time to see Jack assisting a young boy down from Pluto's back. "What can he be thinking?" she murmured.

"Do you mind if I go out and see them?"

"What? Oh, of course. We'll both go." Trinity tried to smile. "I'm certain there must be an interesting reason why he'd make this sort of decision without consulting me." Realizing too late that Jack's perceptive sister was growing uneasy, she was quick to add, "It looks like Janie's asking them a dozen questions. Shouldn't we hurry so we can hear the answers?"

Mary nodded, then bounded out into the hall. Within seconds, Trinity could see the girl run out onto the porch and down the steps to join Jack, and while Trinity knew she should be out there, too, she remained at the window, watching wistfully.

It all comes so naturally to him, she told herself as she watched his interaction with the children. *I suppose you would have been the same way if you'd had any brothers or sisters, or even cousins, to grow up with. Jack probably took one look at that darling boy and just knew he'd be a wonderful addition to his family. All you see is a strange little child with intimidating needs.*

At that moment, Jack looked up at the window and flashed her a sheepish smile. She waved in return, hoping her expression was a cheerful one. But still she couldn't bring herself to join the warmhearted gathering. Instead, she wandered over to the bookcase and stroked the spines of Abe Standish's journals.

What an odd family tradition you passed along to me, Grandpa. You were an only child, as was Father. As was I. It's a wonder the Standishes have survived at all with such tepid dedication to procreation.

"Is something wrong?"

She spun toward Jack and gave him an apologetic

smile. "Not at all. Welcome back. Was your mission successful?"

"It was inconclusive, which is another way of saying we have two more weeks of practicing our intimacy before we know for certain what will happen." His green eyes twinkled as he crossed the room to plant a kiss on her cheek. "How's my beautiful fiancée today?"

She felt her cheeks redden. "You're in a frightfully good mood. I suppose that's how most men react when they have their first son?"

"First son? Oh, do you mean Nicky?" Jack grimaced. "Is that what you think? No wonder you stared at me as though I'd lost my mind."

"You went to an orphanage and came home with a strange little boy. What else was I to think?"

He closed his eyes and stretched the muscles of his back, as though saddle-weary to the bone. "It's nothing like that. He's just a guest for the next few weeks. I should have consulted you, I suppose—"

"Nonsense. You can invite any guest, and adopt any child, you wish. Come and sit for a minute. You've been spending too many hours in the saddle, then staying up half the night with the ledgers. Here." She urged him into the desk chair, then began to massage his neck with her fingertips. "Is that better?"

"Infinitely," he admitted, rolling his head from side to side to accommodate her touch.

"Have you eaten?"

"I had a meal at the orphanage."

"Oh dear. Gruel?"

Jack chuckled. "They eat well there, courtesy of donations from the Cattlemen's Association." Swiveling in his seat, he looked her in the eye. "Nicky's entire family was murdered a few months back. The perpetrator was his father. He shot his wife and two daughters, then turned the pistol on himself."

Trinity gasped in horror. "The poor boy! And how cruel to be sent to an orphanage so quickly. Were there no neighbors or family friends to take him in, at least for a while?"

"It's complicated." Jack took her by her hands and urged her to sit in a chair directly across from him. "His mind won't accept the truth about his father. He's convinced someone else committed the murders. He's also somewhat obsessed with the idea that his father will appear at any moment and clear up the whole misunderstanding. It's sad, and it also makes people uncomfortable. The neighbors didn't know how to handle his—well, his fantasy, so they sent him straight off to Delta Valley."

Touched, Trinity patted Jack's forearm. "How wonderful of you to help him. You put me to shame, Jack Ryerson."

"In what way?"

"The truth?" She folded her hands in her lap, then stared at them soberly. "I have no maternal instinct at all. None. And here you are, instinctively taking this strange little child into your heart. How I wish I could be more like you."

"If you had been there today, hearing what I heard, you would have had the same reaction. The same instinctive need to help him."

"No, Jack. It's something lacking in me."

"That's ridiculous," he told her. "I've seen you with

the girls. Janie in particular. There's nothing wrong with
your maternal instinct."

"Janie is adorable and I enjoy her. But I have no desire to mother her. Nor to mother anyone else. I envy her
when I watch her with the piglets, in fact. She responds
so naturally to their needs, where I just shy away." Before he could continue his protest, she challenged him
softly. "Did you ever wonder what would happen if we
complied with the terms of the will, and I conceived
your child during the six-month marriage?"

Jack winced. "Since I always planned on circumventing the will, I never really considered the possibility. It's an interesting question, though. What was *your*
plan for dealing with such a development?"

"I would have allowed you to take the child to Boston
and to raise it with no further involvement on my part."
She noted the flicker of shock in his eyes and nodded
coolly. "Do you see? You find it appalling, as you should.
I am unnaturally devoid of any maternal instinct."

He licked his lips, as though searching for something
to say, and finally murmured, "The first time we spoke,
you said you intended to marry one day, after you'd
done some travelling. Obviously, you want to marry a
man who enjoys an adventurous lifestyle, but isn't it
likely you'll have a child eventually?"

"I'm resigned to it," she admitted. "Most men will
eventually want a son. But there are nannies, and governesses, and tutors—"

"And boarding schools?"

"Never!" She flushed when she saw that he had ma-
nipulated her. "Oh, for heaven's sake."

"It appears you have some trace of maternal instinct

after all," he said teasingly. Then he grabbed her by the waist and pulled her to her feet at the same time that he himself rose from the chair. "Come and meet Nicky. I defy you to resist him."

"I have no intention of resisting him. I'm just relieved you're not expecting me to raise him," she quipped, pulling away from him and arching an eyebrow in feigned reproach. Then she abandoned the teasing to ask, "Is there any possibility at all that Nicky's right? That his father didn't shoot his family?"

Jack sobered visibly. "No possibility at all. That's one of the reasons I brought him here. So that he and I could talk it through, again and again, until he's finally ready to face the truth. For now, he candidly admits that he himself identified his father's dead body. Yet in the same breath, he says it couldn't have been his father. When you ask him how he can be so sure, he says, 'Because my pa would never shoot my ma. And he'd never shoot himself and leave me all alone in the world.'"

"And the sheriff is sure the man killed himself?"

"The coroner says there's no doubt."

Trinity sniffed. "They can be wrong. Just like they say Grandpa fell when I know he was pushed."

Jack's expression darkened. "You're not going to say that to Nicky, are you? He doesn't need that kind of talk, Trinity. Trust me—in this case, the authorities have absolutely no doubt. A neighbor saw Gregory Holloway ride up to the house at twilight, and within minutes, heard three shots ring out. The neighbor raced over to the scene and found the woman and two little girls, shot in their hearts. And in the corner was Holloway with the gun still grasped in his fingers. Before the neighbor could intervene, Holloway shot himself in the head. The coroner verified that the wound was certainly self-inflicted."

"Oh, Jack."

He nodded. "One of the daughters was still alive. She died in the neighbor's arms. Before she died, she said, 'Papa shot me.'"

Trinity's eyes filled with tears. "How horrible."

"Nicky was spending a few days at a neighboring farm. They brought him to the undertaker's to identify Holloway's body."

"How cruel!"

"The neighbors didn't know Holloway well. He had brought his family to Stockton, settled them into a little cottage, and then left immediately for some sort of lucrative business opportunity in Mexico. The town came to know and love the family, but not the father. Messages came from time to time, promising that he'd be home soon, but apparently, the business venture had failed. He was apparently trying to find a way to salvage some of their savings, but without success."

She could see the pain in Jack's eyes, and knew he was wondering if he might have been able to help. Touching his cheek, she murmured, "So? Is that what the sheriff decided? That Mr. Holloway was despondent over his failed business, and that's why he killed his family?"

"It's the only theory they have. Mrs. Holloway's reputation in the community was sterling, and she spoke with great love and respect of her husband, so it's doubtful her behavior provoked the outburst. And it's just as you said—he must have been despondent. It's just a blessing that Nicky wasn't there, or he almost certainly would have died, too."

"You did a wonderful thing bringing him here, Jack Ryerson. Forgive me for reacting so selfishly."

Jack smiled. "It's just for two weeks. You should have heard the argument *he* put up. He's convinced his father will come home from Mexico and go to the orphanage to find him. We had to stop in Stockton and make certain the sheriff knew to direct him here instead."

"It's so sad."

"He'll want to sit out by the gate all day, waiting. That's what he did each day at the orphanage. But he's willing to do some chores. And since he's completely impressed by Pluto, I thought I'd have him exercise him every day. And he can help Janie with the baby pigs—that should be distracting. With any luck, he'll start to realize that he can't spend the rest of his life waiting for something that is never going to occur."

"It's a wonderful plan. And if two weeks isn't long enough, he can stay as long as he likes. Even if you decide to go back to Boston," she added carefully. "I'm sure Elena and Clancy would be happy to help me take care of him."

Jack chuckled. "You could handle it fine on your own, but frankly, the sooner I bring him back to the orphanage, the better. The headmaster seems to think that once Nicky stops living in the past, he'll be a prime candidate for a quick adoption. That's what the boy really needs." He took her by the arm and coaxed, "Come and meet him. I guarantee you'll fall in love with him, maternal instinct or not."

"Fine." She allowed him to pilot her out into the hall and onto the porch, where the children had been joined by Clancy and Louisa, who had apparently just returned themselves. Louisa in particular was gushing over little Nicky, hugging him and making him flush with gratitude and happiness.

"Do you see?" Trinity whispered to Jack. "Louisa will make a wonderful mother. She knows instinctively what to do."

"You're not going to yell at him or poke him with sticks or anything, are you?" he demanded in mock dismay.

"Be quiet."

He chuckled and announced in a loud, cheery voice, "Hey, Nick? Do you remember the beautiful ranch owner I told you about? This is she—Miss Trinity Standish. Come and make her acquaintance."

The little boy gave Trinity a tentative smile, then to her delight, he strode over to her and bowed at the waist. "Pleased to meet you, Miss Standish. I'm honored."

"Welcome to the Lost Spur," Trinity murmured, dropping to one knee and searching his eyes anxiously. "I'm so glad you've come to help us."

"I'm real strong," the boy said, nodding. "Jack says I'm gonna exercise his horse, but I can do other things, too."

"We can always use another hand with the horses," Clancy said. "Speaking of which, I'd better get back to work. Come on by the corral later, Nicky, and we'll have us a nice, long talk."

Nicky watched the foreman amble away. "Everyone's nice here."

"We're all glad to have you," Trinity replied. "To help us, but also as our guest."

"I don't need to be a guest. I like to work horses. As long as I don't go too far from the house. My pa's gonna be here soon, and I want to be easy to find."

She bit her lip. "I don't want you going too far from the house either, so that's settled. Are you hungry?"

Nicky nodded. "It smells real good here."

"That's because Elena's making tortillas," Janie explained to him. "If we wash our hands and stand where she can see us, she'll give us some hot off the griddle, with butter all over them. Want to try them with us?"

"Sure," he said, then he glanced up and asked quickly, "Can I, Jack?"

"You can do whatever you want," Jack replied.

The three children bolted away, and Louisa started to follow at a more judicious pace, but Jack stopped her with a cheerful, "How was the roundup, Louisa? Did you spy any handsome *vaqueros?*"

She blushed. "Quite a few. You were right, Jack. That's where all the boys are. And Mr. Clancy promised to introduce me to each one of them soon."

"So? No more sulking over the Crowne boy?"

Louisa bristled. "Whenever I dare have an opinion, you label it 'sulking.' So I suppose I just won't dare have a thought of my own for the next month. Is that better?"

"Go have a tortilla," he advised dryly. When she had exited in a huff, he added to Trinity, "I may have a better maternal instinct than you, but my paternal instinct fails me when it comes to that girl."

"She's a woman, Jack. Not a child. Perhaps you shouldn't try to father her. Concentrate on little Nicky. I'll see if I can help with Louisa. After all, there's less than three years' difference in our ages."

"I suppose that's true. She'll always seem like a bratty little girl to me. Of course," his eyes began to twinkle, "so do you sometimes."

"Watch yourself," she warned. "I still haven't quite forgiven you for inviting guests to Grandpa's ranch without *my* permission." When he winced, she gave him a triumphant smile. "There, do you see how it feels to be teased? Now stop your foolishness and tell me all about your conversation with the headmaster. And then—" she sat down on the step and beamed up at him—"I'll tell you about the first day of my treasure hunt."

The next two weeks were a blur for Trinity as she juggled myriad new and charming responsibilities, ranging from helping Janie with the piglets; trying to coax Louisa into revealing what she was thinking; searching every room, from the attic to the bedrooms to the parlor, for the strongbox that held her grandfather's keepsakes; keeping a watchful eye on Nicky as Jack patiently attempted to convince him that spending his every free minute perched on the Spur's front gate was a futile pursuit; and, most importantly, trying to please Jack, so he would decide to become her partner. And short of that, at least to discern his mood so she could prepare herself for his leaving, if that was how it had to be.

Nicky proved to be a pure delight. Although he steadfastly clung to his belief that his father would come for him, he brought a ray of unexpected sunshine to the ranch with his crooked smile and painfully sweet desire to please. If nothing else, Trinity knew she would always remember the hilarious moment during that first night when Janie had announced, "The new boy wants to sleep on the porch, but he's afraid to ask you."

Jack had clearly been taken aback, but had murmured, "I don't see why not, Nicky, as long as you're warm enough."

To which Janie had responded, "I want to sleep on the porch, too. I'll be warm."

Jack had scowled. "Why do *you* want to sleep on the porch?"

"Because it's outside. My room," she had reminded him haughtily, "is inside."

"So it is. Fine. Sleep on the porch. But the mosquitoes may change your mind."

Then Mary had asked softly, "May I also, Jack?"

Thoroughly perplexed, he had demanded, "Why?" to which Janie had responded impatiently, "*Her* room is inside, too."

Trinity had laughed so hard, she thought she'd hiccup at the expression on Jack's face. And then, as though it weren't comical enough, Louisa had offered to sleep with the children "so they don't get into mischief."

Jack had snorted and turned to Trinity. "I suppose you want to sleep on the porch, too?"

"If I did, I'd do so. I wouldn't need to ask your permission," she had reminded him cheerfully. To everyone's amusement, he had then predictably excused himself with some mumbled explanation about "accounts to review."

As much as Trinity loved to tease him, she had come to adore his attention to every detail of the ranch. More importantly, she appreciated his habit of involving her in those details. Every evening they met in the study so Jack could explain some aspect of the ranch's workings, and while it alarmed her on one level—was he prepar-

ing her for his imminent departure?—it was also fascinating.

Of course he was still Jack, and so he teased her by
insisting upon greeting her with a playful kiss—and dis-
missing her just as mischievously, as long as no one else
in the household witnessed the behavior. But these were
simply brushes of his lips across her cheeks. Otherwise,
he never once repeated the intimacies that had charac-
terized their first three days together, despite the opportunities presented by their sessions in the study, when
his mouth would sometimes come so close to her ear
that she could feel the heat of his breath. At such moments she wanted to scream, *Kiss me! Kiss me while we
can still indulge the fantasy that the orphanage will turn
down your offer!*

She knew, of course, why he refused to mix finances
with pleasure, and knew further that he was absolutely
correct to prepare her for the worst. If that happened—
if he took his lovely family and departed—there was
still a chance that she could muddle through and save
her grandfather's ranch, thanks to Jack's painstaking
lessons.

It would be a relief, she decided, when the orphanage
finally accepted their offer. That, combined with Jack's
enthusiastic interest in every aspect of the ranch's operation, would almost certainly convince him to stay.

It would be a relief, but also a disappointment. And
before she knew it, it was just one day away.

Nine

It hadn't taken many days for Jack to realize that he was indeed going to stay in California and restore the Spur to all its glory. It was just the sort of challenge he loved, made even more irresistible by the raucous, untamed atmosphere that permeated the ranch. Not that he spent as much time in that milieu as he might have liked, but even when he was sequestered in the study, he had Abe Standish's riveting accounts of springtimes past to inspire him.

He hadn't yet told his prospective partner the good news, even though he knew she was anxious. For reasons he hadn't bothered to explore, it was important to him to make another decision first: whether it would be Owen Talbot's money, or Jack's own funds, that would finance the ranch's recovery. The latter prospect excited and concerned him, but by the time two weeks had passed, he faced the inevitable—that he wanted this particular project for his own, win or lose.

With that decision came a rush of exhilaration so intense, he couldn't bear to spend another moment indoors, and while the sun was still high in the afternoon sky, he headed for the corral to inveigle another roping lesson from Clancy.

The foreman was busy with Nicky, and Jack watched them for a while, hoping for some sign that the child was abandoning his "morbid vigil." He had been cooperative these last two weeks, but always, at the end of the day, one would find him sitting on the front porch, staring off into the distance, waiting for Greg Holloway. And as often as not, Louisa would be with him, her arm draped around his slender shoulders, her soothing voice assuring him that "this might be the day." And as much as Jack disapproved of encouraging the boy, he also knew these were the most treasured moments of the child's lonely life, and so he didn't scold his cousin for keeping the tragic fantasy alive.

Sobered, Jack picked up a rope and began to practice, conscious of Clancy's advice from their last lesson. *You spend too much time making a show of it for the ladies,* the foreman had scolded him. *Just throw the danged thing and be done with it.*

But half the fun of this new activity was hearing the soft whir of the lariat as it circled around and around overhead, so he began his practicing as he'd done before, "making a show of it," but also successfully landing the noose time after time. He was definitely ready for a moving target, and grinned when Janie bounded into view, her green eyes twinkling with mischief.

For a moment, he was captivated, not only by the healthy glow on her suntanned features, but the radiance that shone from within her. She had been this way almost since their arrival, and whether it was the piglets, or the enjoyment she found playing with Nicky, or the hours she spent treasure hunting and conspiring with

Trinity, Jack almost couldn't remember how she'd been back in Boston.

"Run away, but not too quickly," he suggested, twirling the rope above his head with a slow, steady motion. "I'll try to catch you."

His sister began to giggle as she backed away, then shrieked with delight when he finally sent the lasso toward her. And missed.

"You can't catch me!" she exclaimed breathlessly. "Trinity, look! Jack can't catch me."

Out of the corner of his eye he saw his hostess strolling toward the corral, and a familiar wave of hunger gripped him. There was something so easy and beguiling about the way she carried herself, and thanks to the evening in his study when she'd come to him in revealing satin and lace, he could barely look at her without imagining the long, lean legs and full, high breasts that her light summer frock tried unsuccessfully to hide.

"It's not like you to come out and play so early in the day, Jack Ryerson," she said with a mischievous smile. Then her tone turned hopeful. "Have you finished your review? The timing would be convenient."

"Because I'll be visiting the orphanage again tomorrow?"

Trinity nodded. "And because the next payment on the mortgage is almost due. We haven't discussed it specifically—"

I was planning to go over that with you tonight, if you're willing."

"I'm always willing."

Jack grinned. "There's a frightening thought."

"Rope me again," Janie interrupted, an impish grin on her face. When he began to twirl the lasso slowly over his head, she turned and dashed away, and he sent the loop flying, ensnaring her expertly.

She shrieked in mock dismay while struggling to free her arms, which were now tightly bound to her body. "Let me go! Trinity, save me!"

Trinity's laughter filled the air. "Don't be such a bully, Jack Ryerson."

"Watch yourself, or you'll be next," he warned, hauling Janie back toward himself, then carefully extricating her from her bonds.

"Yes," Janie said, clapping her newly freed hands in delight. "Rope Trinity."

"Don't be silly, you two." Trinity gave Jack an ominous glare.

He held her gaze as he gathered the loose rope up; then, with a wink in his little sister's direction, he began to twirl the lasso above his head with a leisurely yet subtly threatening air.

"You wouldn't dare." Trinity's tone was confident, but he noticed that she had glanced toward the open barn door, planning her escape just in case. He continued to bait her, whirling the loop faster and faster, until finally she broke into a run. At that same moment, he sent the noose flying, and it dropped perfectly, tying her arms against her sides without causing her to fall.

"Yay!" Janie crowed.

"You're a traitor, Jane Ryerson," Trinity told her with a grin; then she gave Jack a haughty look. "Nice throw, cowboy. Now release me immediately."

Elena's voice, calling from the kitchen yard, interrupted them. *"M'ijita! Donde esta?"*

"I'm here!" Janie yelled back.

"Ya estan listas las tortillas!"

"Oh!" Janie ducked under the line between Jack and Trinity and began to dash toward the voice. "The tortillas are ready, Jack. Hurry before the boy eats them all!"

Jack caught his sister's arm with his free hand. "Why do you insist on calling him 'the boy'?"

"He *is* a boy," Janie retorted. "We have to hurry, Jack. Didn't you hear what Elena said? *Las tortillas estan listas.* They're best when they're fresh from the grill. The butter melts all over them, and they're so warm and soft and *delicioso.*"

"We'll join you in a moment." He grinned toward Trinity as his sister rushed away. "Her French tutor's not going to know what to do with her."

"She's right, you know. They'll all be gone if we don't hurry." His hostess smiled sweetly. "Untie me, won't you?"

Jack ambled toward her, gathering up the slack in the rope. "I want to talk to you first."

Her cheeks reddened. "Fine. Untie me."

"I want to talk to you in private," he said, tugging lightly at the line so she was forced to follow him in the direction of the barn.

"That's enough, Jack Ryerson. What if someone sees you behaving this way?"

"Didn't you hear? *Estan listas las tortillas.* No one's going to notice us." He pulled her into the dimly illuminated building, then over to a vacant stall lined with fresh straw. Taking a seat, he stretched his legs, then patted the hay invitingly. "Join me."

"Untie me."

Jack exhaled loudly, then gave the rope a yank, pulling her right into his lap. When she wriggled, laughing but also clearly determined to get away, he wrestled her onto her back in the straw, then loomed over her, entranced by the sheer beauty of her face.

She stared back, her violet eyes filled with confusion. "What are you doing?"

"You asked me if I've completed my review of the ranch's finances. The answer is yes. And if your partnership offer is still open, I would be honored to accept it."

"Oh, Jack." She bit her lip, then whispered, "Untie me so I can show my appreciation."

"That's not necessary," he murmured, loosening the knot and then slipping the noose from around her. "I intend to make a tidy profit for both of us in the coming months."

"I don't care about the money." She twined her arms around his neck. "I'm just so grateful to you for keeping this place out of Walter Crowne's hands." Lacing her fingers in his hair, she urged his head down toward hers. "Kiss me, Jack."

He hesitated, knowing that they needed to talk, not kiss, but she was too beautiful to resist, so he moistened his lips, then covered her mouth with his own, tasting her first lightly, and then with hungry insistence. To his amazed delight, her tongue sparred with his until they were devouring one another, their bodies writhing in appreciation of the sensations each movement provoked.

As their kisses deepened, he swelled against her, and she slowly began to grind her pelvis against him, clearly conscious of the pleasure she was giving him. Stunned, he dared to paw at her skirts, edging them up her legs and insinuating his hand between her thighs. He was certain she'd try to stop him, but instead, she allowed his fingertips to edge closer and closer, until he could almost graze the soft, wet folds.

"Jack," she moaned, gripping her thighs together in a halfhearted show of resistance.

"Trust me," he whispered, stroking her gently, desperate now to penetrate her defenses. Her hand slipped down immediately to restrain his wrist, and he dutifully withdrew.

Still inflamed, he turned his attentions to her breasts, fumbling at her bodice with his free hand, teasing her nipples through the thin cotton fabric while also working a row of small pink buttons until he was able to push aside the dress, revealing a sheer, silky camisole. Quickly trailing kisses down her neck until his lips could tease her nipples, he shuddered with arousal, then slipped his free hand under her buttocks and began again to grind his swollen manhood against her.

Trinity's breath became short, shallow gasps, and the legs that had resisted him now wrapped themselves around his thigh in a hedonistic burst of fevered abandon. He knew at that moment he could have her, despite her earlier protestations that she was saving herself for her wedding night. She was his for the taking, even knowing that the orphanage would accept their offer—

"Marry me," she pleaded, as though reading his mind. "It would only be for six months, and it would be glorious."

"It would be a disaster," he corrected, struggling to control his raging need.

"But a glorious one," Trinity repeated, pulsing stubbornly against him.

Jack sat up and pulled her into his lap, then looked directly into her eyes. "It would be a mistake. As tempting as it is—and I can honestly say I've never been as tempted, by anyone or anything—we would regret it one day."

Lowering her gaze, she murmured, "You're correct, of course."

He nuzzled her neck, still aroused despite himself. "You want a husband who will sail with you around the world. And when you meet him, you'll want to tell him you waited for him."

"And you want a girl who doesn't remind you of Erica."

"That's an oversimplification," he protested. "But it does make the point, doesn't it?"

She nodded, then scooted out of his lap and knelt before him, sandwiching his face between her hands. "I wish it could be otherwise. You're the finest man I've ever met. And you're my hero for saving the Spur."

"I haven't saved it yet."

"You will. I know it in my bones, and I'm so very grateful." Smoothing her skirts back into place with prim thoroughness, she settled back into a seated position a few feet away from him. "How long do you suppose you'll need to stay?"

He shrugged. "A few months at the least. Three at the outside, or, at least, that's what I'm hoping. *You* needn't stay at all," he added quickly. "But it will be a while before we'll see a profit, so you won't be able to travel extensively."

"I'll stay, unless you think I'll be in the way."

An unexpected lump formed in Jack's throat, and he cleared it hastily. "The girls and I would love it."

"But not Nicky? Will you really be taking him back with you tomorrow?"

"No. I'm going to ask Headmaster Everett for a few more weeks. Our talks about his father haven't gone well."

"I know. He always says the same thing: his father could never hurt his mother, so the man who hurt his mother couldn't possibly be his father. It has an unassailable logic to it."

"Except he himself identified the man as his father."

"That's where the logic fails," she agreed, flashing him a sympathetic smile. "I'm sure Nicky knows that, deep inside. You'll find a way to convince him."

Jack shrugged. "I don't want to keep him here for too long. The right couple might be at the orphanage at this very moment, and I don't want him to miss them."

"I agree. I think that's why Janie calls him 'the boy,' by the way."

"Pardon?"

"It's her way of reminding herself that he isn't a permanent part of her life. She'll miss him, as will Mary. But it's Louisa who will be heartbroken. Did you know that?"

Jack nodded. "I've never seen her as happy as she's

been these last two weeks. Almost radiant, wouldn't you say?"

"Because she has a strong maternal instinct."

Her woeful tone amused Jack. "That again?"

"You know it's true. It's the strongest reason against our marrying, in fact. You were meant to have dozens of sons and daughters, and I'd prefer to have none." She jumped to her feet. "We'd best join the others. *Estan listas las tortillas*, as you know."

Jack laughed and stood to face her. "Hot and warm, with butter drizzled in every fold. Why do I feel as though I've already had my treat?"

Her cheeks flamed. "How ungallant. Another reason we should never marry. You're making it rather too easy to end our engagement, Mr. Ryerson."

"Good. The last thing I need is a beautiful brat pestering me while I try to restore this broken-down ranch." He caught her by the arm as she pretended to retreat in disgust, then he pulled her close and murmured, "I didn't deserve this afternoon with you, but I'll always cherish it."

"Don't be romantic," she protested softly. "It will just make it more difficult. Here." She raised herself on her tiptoes and kissed his cheek. "One last intimacy, courtesy of Mr. Braddock's seditious suggestion."

"One last intimacy," he agreed, then he tipped her face up toward his and kissed her lips gently. When he released her, her violet eyes were shining with gratitude. Then she turned and walked out of the stall, leaving him to stare after her, knowing that it was just infatuation— the same sort of infatuation that had almost caused him to marry the wrong girl once before.

Six glorious months . . . And then what? A divorce?
It was unthinkable, but the alternative—an unhappy, unfulfilled wife yearning for excitement that he simply
couldn't provide—would be even worse. And *he* would
be unfulfilled, too, because what she'd said was true—
he wanted sons and daughters. Not dozens, perhaps, but
a lively, loving brood, and a companion who found joy
and contentment in raising them, knowing Jack was always nearby, in his office, poring over his ubiquitous
accounts.

Squaring his shoulders, he assured himself that the
morrow could not come soon enough, then headed for
Abe Standish's study for one final review of the documents he'd prepared to cement his contract with the orphanage.

Clancy had sent one of the hands into town earlier
that week to inform the bank that Jack would be paying a call, so the investor wasn't surprised when he was
greeted by name and with great enthusiasm. He suspected the manager—a slender young man named Bill
Carver—was relieved that the matter of the Standish
mortgage was going to be resolved. After all, it was undoubtedly Mr. Carver who had decided not to exercise
the bank's option to call the entire loan due upon Abe's
death—an option clearly detailed in the mortgage itself.
Whether out of respect for Trinity, hope that she might
be able to reverse the ranch's fortunes, or just a greedy
desire to wring another payment or two out of her before an eventual foreclosure, Carver had already accepted one timely quarterly payment from Trinity, and

had done so cheerfully if her version of that meeting was accurate.

Ushering Jack into his office, Carver closed the door, then motioned toward a pair of handsome leather chairs. "I've been looking forward to this meeting, Mr. Ryerson. Your reputation precedes you."

"Oh?" Jack settled into his seat. "Do we have mutual acquaintances?"

Carver smiled. "Stockton is still a small town in many ways. News of your arrival spread quickly, and your visit to the orphanage confirmed rumors that you were here to assist our prettiest lady in distress."

Jack frowned. "I see."

"We're a curious lot, and most of us have contacts in San Francisco and in the East. It didn't take long to discover that you routinely save failing businesses, making quite a handsome profit for a select group of investors. It's fascinating that you see such potential in the Lost Spur. Most of us view it as something of an albatross."

"Is that so?" Jack feigned confusion. "I would think prime grazing land and abundant water would be the hallmarks of an excellent investment hereabouts."

"Walt Crowne would be the first to agree with you," Carver said with a smirk.

Jack's patience began to evaporate. "I have an another appointment today, so I'm afraid we'll need to forgo further pleasantries and complete our business transaction."

Carver shrugged. "Whatever you say."

"I've arranged payment through a bank in San Francisco, although the funds will be coming from a Boston investor. But of course," Jack added dryly, "you already knew that."

"When can we expect the money?"

"I'm told within a week. That's more than reasonable, wouldn't you say?"

Carver nodded. "It's impressive that you can muster such a large sum so easily."

Jack was about to assure him that it wasn't so large a sum in his line of business, but something in the banker's twinkling eyes made him hesitate.

"Miss Standish must have been grateful when you told her she'd own the Lost Spur free and clear by the end of the day. She must be itching to find a way to thank you. I figure that makes you about the luckiest man in the county, Mr. Ryerson."

Jack pursed his lips, conscious that he was being baited, and that he needed to consider his next move carefully. "I'm here to make the next quarterly payment, Carver, using my investor's funds. Those funds will be repaid by future profits from the ranch. Miss Standish has no reason to be grateful—it's a simple business arrangement. And—" he took a sharp, steadying breath—"one payment will hardly clear title, although I assure you, each future payment will be timely until title is indeed clear. Your bank will have profited along with myself and my associates. All in all, an excellent arrangement."

Carver leaned forward, his eyes shining with anticipation. "Unfortunately, we've decided to call the entire balance due and payable. That's our right under the agreement, and we're exercising it, effective immediately."

"Why?" Jack demanded, hoping he didn't sound as shocked as he felt. "Why now?"

Carver shrugged. "It's a business decision. You, better than anyone, should understand that."

"But I don't. It makes no sense. You didn't call it due when Miss Standish made the first payment. But now that she has a seasoned investment advisor to guide her, and to protect the bank's investment in the process, you shift your strategy?" Jack sprang to his feet and began to pace. "I'm not as prepared as I'd like to be, but I guarantee you, I can prove to you that you're making a mistake."

"The only mistake we made was not calling the balance due the day Abe was pronounced dead. This nasty business would have been over by now—"

"What nasty business?"

"The bad blood between you and the Crownes."

Jack stared in dismay. "The feud? That has nothing to do with me." A wave of optimism swept over him. "Is that what prompted this decision? Let me assure you, Carver, I'm as appalled by the feud as you are. I'd never allow such an irrational phenomenon to play any part in my business decisions. If that's your only concern, be reassured. My investment strategy for the Lost Spur will be based on solid, rational principles. We'll all make a profit."

"The feud won't influence your decisions?"

"Absolutely not."

"Does that mean you're willing to sell a portion of the ranch to Walt Crowne?" Carver grinned. "If so, you have no problem. With the proceeds of that sale, you can pay the bank every dime you owe without delay. Good business all around, just as you've promised."

Before Jack could argue, the banker added dryly, "If you wanted to convince folks you weren't involved in the feud, you shouldn't have tangled with Frank Crowne."

"I beg your pardon?"

"We heard all about it," Carver told him with a sneer. "You're lucky to be alive, Ryerson. Be grateful you caught him off his guard. Be grateful all you'll lose in this deal is Trinity Standish's gratitude. Go on back to Boston, and think twice before you take a swing at a man like Frank again."

"That's what this is all about?"

Carver shrugged. "At first, we were just giving the Standish girl time to grieve. We heard she was hiring some sort of advisor, and we figured you'd come here and advise her to sell to Crowne. Instead, you went and made a personal enemy of Frank. That wasn't very smart. The Crownes are a powerful family, not to mention this bank's best customer."

"I can guarantee you each and every payment will be timely. It's to the bank's advantage to wait. To earn interest every quarter, knowing that the investment is safe and secured. And if you're unhappy with the terms, we can renegotiate—"

"It's not just about money, Ryerson. Like I said, the Crownes are our most valued customers." He stood to glare at Jack. "We don't need some fancy investment fellow from the East coming to give us advice. In fact, I'm the one who has some advice for you, and if you're smart, you'll take it."

Jack met his gaze calmly. "And what is that?"

"Take your fancy Eastern investment money and go on home. We'll handle the eviction respectfully. You have my word on that."

"Your word? That's supposed to mean something to me?" Jack growled, springing to his feet. "You'll have your money—every goddamned dime of it—within a week."

"What?" Carver blanched. "Don't be a fool, Ryerson. The Crownes aren't going to let you make a success of the Spur."

"I'll send instructions to San Francisco immediately. Good day, sir."

"Wait!" Carver grabbed Jack's sleeve, then released it quickly when his eyes narrowed in warning. Backing away, the banker insisted, "Sooner or later, you'll sell to them, and when you do, you won't get back half what you've put into the place. Walt would've paid you well for it—that was his plan. But then you went and clobbered his boy. Don't make another mistake, Ryerson. Crowne'll break you if you stay."

"Apparently, he has already broken *you*," Jack retorted. "How does that feel, Carver? You can't earn the gratitude of a beautiful girl, or gain a reputation based on smart banking decisions, so you settle for being Crowne's lackey? Are you proud, threatening to evict a helpless female from the ranch her grandfather built for her? Unfortunately, you miscalculated. Trinity Standish isn't helpless. And she isn't alone. Tell that to the Crownes. And tell them to stay out of my way, or *I'll* break *them*." Grabbing his hat, he added with mock respect, "Good day, sir."

Striding from the office, he could hear his own blood roaring in his ears. Never in his life had he been so furious—or so furiously out of control. He had placed his entire life's savings at risk in a moment of blind rage. If he didn't force himself to think, quickly and clearly, it would be too late to salvage the situation—to make a counter offer that was impressive enough to force Carver to reconsider, while still preserving logical options.

And a part of him knew that if that failed, he had to go back to Trinity and insist that she sell a portion of the ranch to Crowne. She would be angry and brokenhearted, but he had learned over the last two weeks that she had a fair head for business, and in time perhaps he could persuade her to trust him this one final time.

Anything, even seeing that hurt in her eyes, would be better than losing every penny he had ever earned over something so odious and absurd as the Standish-Crowne feud.

He strode out into the fresh spring air and inhaled deeply. It might have helped settle his frayed emotions, had Frank Crowne not been there, lounging against a railing, a triumphant grin on his face.

"Something wrong, Ryerson?"

Jack's hands clenched into fists at his sides, but he managed not to otherwise react.

Frank chuckled. "Don't tell me Abe's granddaughter hasn't been putting a smile on your face. I guarantee you, if I had two weeks alone with her, I'd be grinning from ear to ear."

"You appear to be doing just that," Jack drawled. "Have you been taking liberties with those cows you've been rounding up? Is that what put that disgusting smile on your face?"

"We both know why I'm smiling," Frank retorted. "Once the bank forecloses, I'll be the owner of the Spur and you'll be running back to Boston with your tail between your legs."

Jack stepped closer, noting with satisfaction the flash of fear in Frank's eyes. "I've decided to stay."

"What?" Frank cocked his head to the side, then slowly shook his head. "Pa said you'd never be fool enough to let a female ruin you, but I knew it. That day at the ranch, I knew she had you by the ballocks."

"That day at the ranch?" Jack grinned. "I had *you* by the ballocks that day, Crowne, if I remember correctly."

Frank's countenance darkened. "Out here, a fella doesn't attack a guest in his own home. That's how you caught me by surprise that day, or I'd of killed you where you stood."

"Kill me now," Jack suggested. "I have a few minutes to spare before my next appointment. That should be plenty of time to settle this."

"All right now, boys. That's enough," said a voice from behind Jack. "I don't allow fighting on the streets of Stockton, even over a girl as pretty as Miss Trinity."

Jack turned to eye the sheriff with disdain. "Interesting timing."

"Nothing interesting about it," the sheriff admitted. "Walt Crowne warned me there might be trouble out here this morning. I don't know how he knew, and I don't want to know. I just want you both to go about your business."

Jack studied the sheriff's face and decided the man

probably didn't have an inkling what the Crownes had just done to Trinity—and to Jack. And even if he knew, there was nothing illegal about it. Immoral, yes, but not illegal.

"I need to send a telegram, sheriff. After that, I assure you, I have no desire to stay in this town one minute longer."

"Be quick about it, then. And Frank? Your pa said you're to go on home. Right away. Or there'll be trouble."

It was Jack's turn to chuckle. "I hope you appreciate that father of yours, Crowne. This is the second time he's saved your life this month."

"That's enough, fellas." The sheriff moved quickly to stand between Jack and an enraged Frank. "I don't imagine either one of you wants to spend the rest of the day in a cell. Settle down, Frank," he added under his breath.

Frank seemed about to protest, then he shrugged instead. "I already got what I wanted out of this day—I got the Spur. It's just a matter of time now. So go on like the sheriff says, Ryerson. Run on back to that little whore and tell her you lost her ranch for her. And give her a message from me. Tell her—"

Jack's left hand shot out, grabbing Frank by the collar and forcing him hard against the railing while his right hand landed a bone-cracking punch on Frank's jaw. The cowboy toppled over the rail and onto the dirt road, where he rapidly regained his footing, snarled, and motioned for his opponent to join him. But the sheriff grabbed Jack's arm and warned, "You've got two choices, Ryerson. Leave quickly and quietly, or spend twenty-four hours in a cell. I'm sure Miss Standish would be worried—maybe even scared—if you weren't home by suppertime."

"Miss Standish would be delighted to know that I

taught this mongrel another lesson in manners," Jack assured him, his stare fixed on Frank.

"That won't be necessary." Walter Crowne had appeared out of nowhere, his leathered face twisted with displeasure. "My son apologizes, Ryerson. Don't you, Frank?"

"Dammit, Pa—"

"I said apologize!" Without waiting, Walt turned his attention to Jack. "It's nothing personal, Ryerson. You stepped into the middle of something that's needed settling for a long time. You should've left when you had your chance, but you didn't, so now you're part of it, too—there's no denying that. But it's nothing personal against you and yours."

"Nothing personal?" Jack shook his head in slow, disbelieving disgust. "How does it feel, Crowne? Trying to steal an innocent girl's inheritance."

"I tried to buy it, fair and square. You gave her bad advice about that, Ryerson. Or, more likely, the little she-cat didn't listen to you." An amused grin lit Walt's face for a moment, then his expression hardened. "Like I said, you should've left when you had the chance. Now you're gonna lose money—a powerful lot of money— and your fancy reputation will be spoilt. But I'll have my land back. That's how it's gotta be. All one ranch, just like it was when I was a boy."

Jack fixed him with a carefully leveled glare. "If I were you, I'd spend less time trying to steal the Lost Spur, and more time protecting your own land."

"Huh?"

"From what I've seen, your business tactics are as primitive as your son's fighting ability. Once the Spur is running smoothly again, I might just go after Crowne Ranch for myself. Like you said—" he flashed the man a disrespectful grin—"it sure would be nice to see those two parcels reunited again."

"God damn you, Ryerson!" Frank roared, flying at Jack with fists raised, but his father and the sheriff each grabbed an arm to restrain the wild-eyed son.

"You're making a damned fool out of yourself, Frank," Walt muttered. "Sheriff? Take him over to the saloon and cool him off."

"Sure, Walt." The sheriff yanked on Frank's elbow. "Let's go."

"There'll be another time for this," Frank assured Jack over his shoulder, but he followed the sheriff without further protest.

Walt watched them depart, then took a deep breath. "I said it to Frank, and now I'm telling you, son: You're making a damned fool out of yourself."

"Just keep that mongrel out of my way," Jack advised him, his voice close to a growl. Then he strode down the steps, freed Pluto from the hitching post, and swung himself into the saddle, riding toward the outskirts of town without a backward glance.

You're making a damned fool out of yourself . . .

Even at a full run, Pluto's hooves could not make enough noise to drown Walt Crowne's words from Jack's mind. Instead, he taunted himself with them, knowing they were true.

He was conservative by nature, but had become even more prudent following the deaths of his parents, out of

respect for the need to become a stable guardian for his
sisters. The results had been excellent, producing a
comfortable return on his own safe investments, as well
as generous commissions on the more risky ventures of
his clients.

Now he had jeopardized every penny, not to mention his own livelihood. After all, who would retain him
to manage their affairs when they heard how he'd decimated his own?

It was only when the orphanage came into view that
he reined Pluto to a walk and forced himself to take a
few deep breaths and rethink the situation rationally.
Yes, this was a much more risky endeavor than he had
anticipated. So risky, in fact, that he couldn't dare involve Owen, or any of the other investors who had
trusted him in the past. Jack's own funds were in jeopardy, but only if the ranch failed. And hadn't he decided,
coolly and calmly over the past few weeks, that the
ranch's fortunes could be restored?

Nothing had changed except the level of investment,
and while that was a daunting consideration, it was not
insurmountable, assuming no further unanticipated
costs presented themselves. His calculations had allowed for a certain margin of monthly expenses, along
with the mortgage payments. With careful budgeting,
Jack could still cover such demands from his meager re-
serves.

Which wouldn't be quite so meager if it weren't for
the need to pay the orphanage . . .

Jack took another, deeper breath, stunned at the im-
plications of that dangerous notion. He could save
money—money he now desperately needed—by mar-

rying Trinity. It would be so easy. So sinfully easy. How had she phrased it? *Six glorious months...*

The passion they had shared in the barn rushed back to seduce him with memories of her fragrant, silky tresses; her hungry kisses; their throbbing needs— needs he hadn't dared allow them to satisfy for one another. But for six glorious months he could make love to her. The prospect made him shudder with desire so strong, he nearly groaned aloud. She was so beautiful. So inspiring. So enticing, with her sweet mix of intelligence and whimsy. Learning about the ranch; hunting for her grandfather's treasure box; sashaying around in her lacy dresses, always with a cheerful smile and a warm embrace for Jack and the girls, despite the fact that she longed to be thousands of miles from that dusty ranch, pursuing grand adventures—

Just like Erica.

Jack nodded slowly, amazed at the mistake he had almost been willing to make a second time. And this time, it would have been worse, because this time, he had been forewarned.

"Concentrate, Jack," he advised himself grimly. "You could save money by marrying Trinity, but at what cost? Do you want your sisters to witness a sham marriage? Do you dare risk having a child with a woman who has no interest in raising it? Do you want to hold her in your arms at night, knowing her dreams are filled with other, less practical fellows? At best, you will have betrayed your principles, and at worst—well, at worst, there would be heartache and humiliation despite everyone's best intentions."

He shook his head, clearing away the hurtful images,

then forced himself to be sensible. "You're panicking unnecessarily. The ranch was a sound investment yesterday and it remains sound today. Riskier, yes, but the strategy for restoring profitability hasn't changed. And a linchpin of that strategy is this deal with the trustees, so why keep them waiting one moment longer?"

"Mr. Ryerson!" The headmaster greeted Jack with an enthusiastic handshake. "It's good to see you again. The trustees are waiting for you in the courtyard."

"Thank you." Jack arched an eyebrow. "Do I sense a favorable outcome to my proposal?"

"I've no way of knowing for sure," Everett said. "But their initial reaction when I presented the concept last week was positive. And speaking of favorable outcomes . . ." He reached for a pitcher that had been set on a hall table and poured Jack a glass of water. "Have you decided to make young Nicky a permanent part of your household?"

Jack took a quick gulp before assuring him, "He's a fine boy, but he needs a mother as well as a father. Unfortunately, I haven't quite convinced *him* of that fact yet, so I thought I'd keep him with us for another week or so. I hope that doesn't inconvenience you."

"Not at all." The headmaster sighed. "When I saw the two of you riding off that afternoon—well, never mind all that. You have more pressing matters to attend to. Right this way."

He ushered Jack through a set of doors and onto a shady veranda where three well-dressed men sat in wicker chairs around a glass-topped table. Even before the introductions began, Jack was able to match the faces to the names he had learned through his research the preceding weeks, knowing that the two younger men were local farmers, while the eldest and most distinguished of the three was a successful mercantile entrepreneur from Sacramento named Robert Wolcott.

It was Wolcott who took the lead thereafter, motioning for Jack to join them at the table, and offering whiskey, which Jack declined.

"Well, then . . ." The spokesman sat directly across from the visitor. "I suppose we ought to get right down to it."

"I'd appreciate that, sir."

Wolcott glanced at each of his fellow trustees, then cleared his throat. "I don't mind telling you, Mr. Ryerson, you've presented us with something of a moral dilemma."

Jack nodded respectfully. "I understand you had a long and rewarding relationship with Abraham Standish, sir. You would like to honor the terms of his will, as would his granddaughter. I've managed to convince her that we can honor the spirit of those terms, if not their letter, by ensuring that the Lost Spur stays in the Standish family without the need for her to marry while in mourning—a circumstance Abe certainly didn't contemplate when he drew up his will.

"However—" Jack took a moment to look directly into the eyes of each trustee in turn—"our respect for Abe Standish notwithstanding, your fiduciary duty as trustees of Delta Valley is clear. Whatever moral dilemma my proposition may create for you, you really have only one choice. You must do whatever is most beneficial financially for the orphanage, within the bounds of the law. And I assure you, gentlemen, the arrangement I've proposed is quite legal."

Wolcott moistened his lips. "It's not that simple, Mr. Ryerson."

"I'm afraid it is," Jack responded firmly. "With all due respect, sir, you simply have no choice but to maximize the profit to the orphanage. It's your solemn duty to the orphans, and there's simply no way around it."

"In that case—" Wolcott leaned across the table toward Jack and murmured apologetically—"I'm afraid I have bad news for you, son."

Ten

"Honestly, Grandpa, where *did* you hide that darned box?" Trinity sat back on her heels, grinning in frustration. She had made up her mind that she'd find the "treasure" before her handsome partner returned from the orphanage, so that he wouldn't be the only one with good news to share. But only three rooms had remained unsearched—the three guest bedrooms—and she had spent the entire day combing them from floor to ceiling without success.

Suppose Jack's news is no better than your own, she teased herself. *Suppose the orphanage refused his offer, and you're forced to surrender to his lusty advances every night for six wonderful months?*

She laughed, knowing that she only dared have such naughty thoughts because there was no danger of their proving accurate. If she honestly believed she might find herself in his bed within the month, she knew she would be confused. Intrigued and excited, but also frightened, not only by the prospect of surrendering her virginity, but also by the sobering reality of being someone's wife for six whole months. And if they weren't careful, she'd be someone's *mother,* too, and that would be for quite a bit longer!

Jack was right about all that from the start, she admitted as she carefully tapped a loose floorboard back into place. *Grandpa would never want you to marry a stranger—even a darling, intelligent stranger like Jack—for just six months. Or to give birth to a little Standish grandbaby just to abandon it. Or to marry a man who was hopelessly in love with another woman . . .*

She scowled, knowing that this last fact would truly have haunted them both had they followed the terms of the will to the letter. Poor, brokenhearted Jack. He was a cheerful man by nature, and so he rarely showed his pain, but she knew he thought of Erica often. And she suspected she hadn't made it any easier for him, flirting with him the way she'd done over the last few weeks. But all of that was about to stop, and in her heart, she knew it was for the best.

"Trinity?"

"Oh!" She jumped to her feet, brushing her hands on her apron, then laughed in embarrassed delight. "Goodness, Jack, I didn't even realize you were home!"

"Forgive me for startling you. But it's imperative that we speak. Immediately."

Amused by his formal tone, she stroked his jaw with her fingertips. "So? Is our business partnership official?"

"Yes, although there will be documents for you to sign."

"And I assume our engagement is officially ended?" she asked, teasing. "You must at least pretend to be disappointed, or I will feel horribly insulted."

He scowled and motioned toward the bed. "Have a seat, won't you?"

She didn't follow his instruction. Instead, she took a moment to contemplate his uncharacteristic behavior. Either he was exhausted from his long ride, or something had gone terribly wrong. But what? Had they demanded more money? More time? Or perhaps it was something else entirely. Perhaps they had demanded Nicky's immediate return. "You should rest first, Jack. Or at least have something to eat or drink. You've been gone for hours—"

"The orphanage rejected my offer. Now would you please sit down so we can discuss alternatives?"

She winced at the harsh tone, but decided to cooperate, at least for the moment, so she sat on the edge of the bed, folding her hands in her lap. "How much do they want?"

"Excuse me?"

"You said they rejected your offer. What was their counteroffer?"

"There was no counteroffer."

Trinity wanted to ask another question—*any* question—but her throat was too dry, and so she gulped, then forced herself to whisper, "I don't understand."

For the first time, his mood softened, and he dropped to one knee in front of her. "I don't blame you for being horrified. I still can't quite believe it myself. I see now I should have anticipated it, but I swear, I didn't comprehend the depth of irrationality that pervades this mess."

"It isn't irrationality, it's loyalty," she corrected him with an uncertain smile. "They want to honor Grandpa's wishes—"

"*No.*" His green eyes flashed as he stood up and

backed away from her, his manner once again cold and distant. "It's not honor, it's insanity. It's the damned feud, and if we're not careful, it's going to ruin us all."

"The feud?"

Jack gave her a curt nod. "Walter Crowne made the trustees an offer—double that of mine—in exchange for their promise to vigorously enforce the terms of the will."

A gasp escaped her throat before she could stifle it, and Jack responded by insisting, in a voice that was more like a growl, "You're shocked? *You?* The woman who would strangle Crowne with her bare hands if given half the chance? I would have thought this would make perfect sense to you."

"They doubled your offer," she repeated, ignoring his diatribe. "Can't we counteroffer?"

"To what end? Everything Crowne offers will be applied toward his eventual purchase of title from them, which means he can afford to offer the full value of the ranch if necessary."

"Applied toward his purchase? But he can't purchase it from them if they never own it, and they'll never own it if I marry in the next five weeks. And," she squared her shoulders, "that's exactly what I intend to do."

"You're an excellent feuder," Jack drawled.

This time, she noted the insult with a glare. "You act as though I'm the cause of all this. Oh!" She grimaced. "*Am* I? Did my taunting of Crowne provoke him?"

"No more than did my pummeling of his son," Jack admitted, his scowl relaxing into a self-mocking smile. "But I suspect he would have done this even if we'd both behaved impeccably. The seeds of this insanity were

sown long ago, Trinity, although it is we who will be
forced to pay the price."

"Don't be silly." She slid to her feet and approached
him. "You've done all you could do, Jack. Now it's my
turn. I'll send a telegram to Mr. Braddock immediately.
With any luck, he'll send someone right away, but even
if I have to make poor Clancy marry me, title *will* be secured in time."

"It's not that simple."

"Of course it is," she told him, although inside she
wasn't so sure. The notion of marrying a stranger had
chilled her for so many weeks, and then she had been
given a blessed reprieve by Jack's loophole. Suddenly,
it loomed again in her future, complicated in the most
confounding of ways by the intimacies she had shared
with Jack in the interim.

All of the anger in his eyes had disappeared, replaced
by anguish that tore at her conscience. He had never
wanted to be a part of this. He had made it clear more
than once that he would never have come to California
had he thought the marriage clause might be enforced.
The entire concept offended him, both as a businessman
and as a romantic.

Because Jack Ryerson *was* a romantic. He had given
his heart to Erica, and even after she broke it to bits, he
still wanted to impress upon his sisters the certainty that
they would marry for love. Never for profit, or out of
any sense of desperation.

Taking his hand in her own, she murmured, "I'm sorry
I made a jest about marrying Clancy. I know you're concerned with what the girls will think when I marry a complete stranger for pecuniary reasons, but I swear, we'll

think of some plausible explanation. We'll tell them that the man is someone from my past—a long-lost love, or some such thing. Janie at least will believe us. Louisa, and perhaps Mary, will see the truth, but it won't reflect on *your* character. Only on mine. I'll see to that."

"Your character is not the issue," he protested. "And the truth is, I can't afford for you to marry a stranger."

"Pardon?"

"It would complicate things, Trinity. I can't agree to it. Not now. The investment has already been made, and I owe it to my—to my investor—to protect it."

She felt her cheeks begin to blaze. "What are you suggesting?"

"It isn't a suggestion. It is the only possible solution, unless you're willing to forfeit the ranch to Crowne." He grimaced. "Again, I apologize."

"It's the only possible solution," she reminded him carefully. "And it's only for six months, Jack."

"Listen to me." He squeezed her shoulders gently. "If our marriage is a sham, in any sense, Crowne will win. He will force the orphanage to challenge it in court, and they will prevail. If we marry—and we must marry—we must intend it to last forever. Do you understand that?"

"Jack . . ."

"I know," he said, growling again. "One day you may well choose to divorce me, or simply to leave me. Every marriage has that possibility. But we cannot go into this one with that understanding. If we do, and you are called to testify on that issue, you will be forced either to lie, or to risk proving Crowne's case."

"And what about you?" she asked, her voice trembling. "If they challenge us in court, and ask you if you're in love with another woman—?"

"I'm not in love with anyone! Do you think I'm a complete fool?"

"Certainly not." She jutted her chin forward in proud disdain. "Tell me what you want me to do and I'll do it."

Jack rested his hands on her shoulders again. "Forgive me for raising my voice. It's been a frustrating day."

"I don't blame you," she told him, and to her relief, she realized it was true. "I blame Walter Crowne."

Jack nodded. "He's a despicable man. You were right about that. The whole lot of them disgust me."

"So?" She managed a wistful smile. "What now?"

His jaw tightened visibly. "You said we have five weeks, but I'd like to have the wedding as soon as possible. And I'd like it to be as—well, as convincing as possible, which means there should be guests."

"I'll speak with Elena. In the meantime . . ." She winced. "What shall we tell the girls?"

"I'll take care of that at dinner tonight."

"I see." She scanned his expression, hungry for any sign of the old Jack, but no compassion or humor seemed to have survived the day. "Go and rest, Jack. I'll come and wake you at dinnertime."

"I'll be in the study," he told her, his tone flat and beleaguered. "There's so much at stake, Trinity. I need to do everything with utmost care. There will be documents for you to sign—"

"Don't be silly. I trust you."

"These documents will protect me as well as you."

"Oh. Well, then, of course. I'll sign whatever you ask."

"You can't just sign whatever I tell you to sign," he

corrected her sharply. "You have to read each document carefully."

She bit her lip, conscious of the fact that "the old Jack" would never have snapped at her the way this man was doing. All because he was being forced to marry her. It was unbearable, and she wanted to throw it all back in his face. To refuse to sign anything. To reject his coarse, ungallant marriage proposal, promising instead to sell the ranch to Walter Crowne so they could repay "Uncle Owen" for the damned mortgage payment.

But she couldn't do it. Her pride, while fiercely offended by Jack, was ultimately more insistent on thwarting Crowne.

"Go and rest," she repeated finally. "You've had a frustrating day."

"I'll be in the study." He hesitated, then gave her a weary smile. "Are you furious with me?"

"No. I'm furious with Walter Crowne. And I'm cross with Grandpa and Mr. Braddock. But you?" She took his hand and kissed it lightly. "You are my hero, sir. Have you forgotten?"

She had hoped it would bring a smile to his face, if not peace to his heart, but instead, she saw it crush the last vestiges of his resolve. Murmuring only, "You deserve better," he turned and strode from the room, leaving her to wonder how either of them would survive this ill-fated liaison.

She dressed simply for dinner, intent upon cooperating with Jack's plan, whatever that might be. She had meant what she'd said to him: he *was* her hero for refusing to allow Walter Crowne to triumph. He was giving her so much more than investment advice and funds, all because he could not allow a brute like Crowne to take advantage of a female.

And he was her hero for another reason: for marrying her, rather than allowing her to send to Braddock for another, lesser stranger. They each had their reasons for dreading this match, but at least they had mutual respect, coupled with a healthy physical attraction for one another. Because of that, she dared yet to believe that their wedding night, while awkward, would also be endurable.

As always, Janie chattered happily all through dinner, her stories punctuated by teasing remarks from her older sister. Louisa was quiet but seemed content, while Nicky ate in complete silence, his gaze rarely leaving his plate. No one seemed to notice Jack's somber mood, or if they did, they apparently attributed it to weariness from his long ride and didn't comment on it. For her part, Trinity followed Nicky's example and prayed that the meal and the evening as a whole would end quickly.

"May I be excused? It's time to feed my babies," Janie said, half out of her chair before the words were out of her mouth.

"Stay for a moment." Jack cleared his throat and met his family's inquiring gaze. "I have something to tell you. Something that I believe will please each of you greatly."

"You found the treasure box?" Janie demanded. "Where was it? We looked everywhere! Even in places we aren't allowed to go."

"It can't be that," Mary told her. "He hasn't even been home all day. It's something he learned in town."

"Or at the orphanage," Louisa continued. Then she

flushed and slipped her arm around Nicky's shoulders. "Oh, dear! Jack?"

Trinity cringed at the spark of hope in the little boy's eyes and blurted out, "No, no. It's nothing like that."

"*You* already know?" Janie scowled. "Jack never tells *me* secrets first."

"That's because you can't keep a secret," Mary said with a laugh.

"I can too!"

"*That's enough*!" Jack eyed his sisters sternly. "Rather than speculate, shouldn't you just be quiet and listen?"

The girls stared at him as though he'd grown a second head, then Louisa muttered, "At least now we know it isn't *good* news. It was cruel of you to raise poor Nicky's hopes unnecessarily, Jack."

He seemed about to snap at her, then took a deep breath and insisted, "If I did that, I apologize." He gave Nicky a pained smile. "Mr. Everett sends his regards."

The boy nodded, his expression stoic.

"Go on, Jack," Trinity urged him softly. "Everyone's listening."

He cleared his throat again. "As I said, it's good news. We've all become very fond of Trinity these last few weeks—"

"We're staying!" Janie sprang from her chair and cat-apulted herself into Jack's lap. Hugging him effusively, she insisted, "That's the best surprise! I didn't want to leave my piggies. Or," she sent a polite smile in Trinity's direction, "you, either."

Trinity bit back a smile. "I'm very pleased also. I've had dozens of reasons for hoping you'd all stay, and one of them is these charming dinners. I would miss them terribly if you left."

"Go on back to your seat, Jane," Jack said, setting her down onto the floor. When she'd complied, he arched an eyebrow in playful warning. "I should have said I have two announcements. Yes, we're going to stay here, for the rest of the year at least."

Janie squealed with renewed delight, while Mary smiled and insisted, "I'm glad, too, Jack. I didn't want to leave Trinity alone with those wretched Crownes trying to steal her ranch."

"They aren't *all* wretched," Louisa reminded her, then turned to her cousin. "It's wonderful news, Jack. What's the other announcement?"

He grimaced, then raised his half-empty wineglass and locked gazes with Trinity. "Miss Trinity Standish has done me the great honor of accepting my proposal of marriage."

Mary and Louisa gasped in unison, while Janie demanded, "What does it mean?"

"It means Jack and I are going to be married, honey," Trinity told her.

The little girl frowned. "I already knew that."

"You did?"

Janie nodded. "Mr. Braddock *makes* people marry each other, even if they don't want to. That's why Erica went away."

"This has nothing to do with Erica. Or with Russell Braddock," Jack told her sharply. "I came here to find an investment, not a bride. But I've been fortunate enough to find both. Is that clear?"

Once again, the girls and Nicky stared at him in

shocked silence, until finally Trinity reached across the table and patted her fiancé's hand. "Jack and I hope you're all as happy about this as we are."

"You're happy to marry a grouch who raises his voice at the table?" Louisa muttered. "I'd never do that. Not to save a thousand ranches."

"Hush," Trinity warned her quickly, not daring to look at Jack's reaction. "You're wrong to say such things, Louisa."

"Do you love him?"

"Yes." Trinity felt her cheeks redden. "More than you can possibly understand."

"I knew that, too," Janie whispered to Mary. "I saw them kissing lots of times."

Trinity winced. "In the barn?"

"In your grandpapa's study," Janie replied, then her green eyes narrowed. "Did you kiss him in the barn, too?"

Relieved, Trinity laughed lightly. "I'm afraid so. He's very handsome, you know."

"Jack?" Louisa flashed her cousin a warm smile. "Forgive me. I didn't know."

"That's fine," he murmured. "Are you pleased?"

"It's so utterly romantic." She reached around Mary to squeeze Trinity's shoulder. "Will there be a huge wedding? With guests and dancing?"

Trinity eyed Jack, who nodded and said, "It will be a nice wedding, but subdued. After all, it's been less than six months since Trinity lost her grandfather."

"But there will be guests?"

"Yes. Some of the neighbors."

"May I invite Randy Crowne?" When Jack's jaw

dropped open, Louisa hastened to add, "I know his father and brother have been horrid. I doubt they'd come, even if you invited them. But Randy's sweet and gentle—"

"I know he made a good first impression on you, Louisa, but inviting him is out of the question," Trinity interrupted, all too aware of Jack's displeasure. "On the other hand, we'll be sure the buckaroos are in attendance, so if it's a dance partner you want—"

"I want to dance with Randy." She drew back from Jack's annoyed snort, turning her full attention to Trinity instead. "He's nothing like his family. I've spent some time with him lately—"

Trinity gasped. "When? Where? Oh, Louisa—what were you thinking?"

"I was perfectly safe," Louisa retorted. "I had to beg him just to kiss me the first time—"

"Trinity asked you when and where this took place," Jack interrupted, his expression murderous. "I'd like to hear the answer."

His cousin bit her lip. "When he came here that first day, I told him about the picnic we'd had, up on the ridge overlooking the cows. I said I'd try to convince Trinity to take us there again the next afternoon, and he promised to meet me. Then—well, then you and his brother had that awful fight, so I didn't dare ask, but I didn't want to disappoint him . . ."

"So you convinced Clancy you wanted to go and watch the roundup through the spyglass. In other words, you lied."

Louisa started to reply, then just shrugged her shoulders instead.

"And since then?"

"He visits me, when everyone's asleep. Just to talk," she added quickly.

"How convenient that you've been sleeping on the porch," Jack drawled. "That arrangement ends tonight. For everyone."

Janie frowned. "Where will the boy sleep?"

Jack spun on her, his eyes flashing. "His name is Nicky. And he'll sleep in one of the guestrooms. You and Mary will share a room. Is that clear?"

"You're horrid and we all hate you!" Louisa jumped out of her seat and ran for the stairs in tears.

Jack's mouth was drawn into a tight, unforgiving line. "Jane, you may go and visit the pigs for a few minutes, if your sister will accompany you. Nicky?"

"Yes, sir?"

Would you go along with them, to make certain they're safe?"

"Yes, sir."

"Thank you."

He waited until the children had departed, then drawled, "That went well, don't you think?"

"I think you're tired. And in your defense, Louisa's behavior has been indiscreet, if not fully dangerous."

"Thank you for that. And—" he gave her a half-hearted smile, "for saying what you did, when she asked if you loved me."

"I love all of you," Trinity replied lightly. "Even Louisa, although I must say, she's a trial. Won't you go upstairs and sleep now, Jack? I'll make sure everyone goes safely to bed."

He backed his chair away from the table. "I'll be in

the study. When Jane comes back, will you ask her to join me?"

"May I ask why?"

He chuckled softly. "There's no need to protect her. I just want to apologize in private. I have so many apologies to make," he added, more to himself than to Trinity.

She wanted to tell him he needn't apologize for being human, nor for resenting the position in which he'd been placed by Abe Standish, Russell Braddock, the Crownes, Louisa, and last but not least, by Trinity herself. But she knew he didn't really need reassurance. Just rest. With the morning, the old Jack would return. And if he did not, if this mood persisted, she would send him away, for his own good as well as for the sake of her own pride.

Because she suspected it wasn't the investment money, or even Louisa's innocent indiscretions, that were weighing so heavily on him. It was the prospect of marrying a woman he didn't love—a woman who reminded him in all the worst ways of the beautiful, willful girl who had broken his heart. And while Trinity could sympathize with his misery, she wasn't willing to take the blame for it, even to save her grandfather's ranch. Better to marry a stranger . . .

"Jack?" Janie peeked her head into the study and murmured cautiously, "Trinity made me interrupt you."

"Come here." He patted his knee, and was pleased when her face lit up and she bounded across the room and into his lap.

Embracing him with all the might in her slender

arms, she announced solemnly, "I'll never call Nicky a boy again."

Jack welcomed the burst of laughter that seemed to cleanse his heart of the day's confusion. "He *is* a boy, after all. I'd just prefer you call him by his name. I'm going to tell you why, but it's a secret, so you must promise not to repeat it."

"A secret?" she repeated, her green eyes wide with amazement.

"At dinner, you said I never tell you secrets first. So I thought we'd give it a try."

"I won't tell anyone. I promise."

"Fine." He brushed a tendril of golden brown hair from her cheek. "First, I'd like to apologize for my behavior at dinner."

Janie eyed him fondly. "You were very cross."

"Yes, I was. But not with you."

"With Louisa?"

"With myself more than anyone. I haven't been myself today, Jane. I've said and done things—well, things I frankly can't quite believe. Making rash decisions, imperiling my finances, brawling in the streets, browbeating my family . . ." He smiled into her sympathetic green eyes. "One of the rash decisions I made is the very secret I've decided to share with you. It's about Nicky."

Janie squirmed with anticipation. "About his father?"

"His father is dead. But I've made arrangements to adopt him. That means *I'm* going to be his new father."

She cocked her head to one side. "Will I be his sister?"

"His aunt, actually."

"His aunt?" She grinned in delight. "Does he have to do what I say?"

"No. But he will respect you, and you he. That's why it's important for you to start calling him by name. Do you see?"

Jane pursed her lips, as though considering the information carefully. "When you marry Trinity, will she be his mother?"

"That's an excellent question. The answer is, she'll either be his mother or his stepmother."

"If she's his stepmother, can Louisa be his real mother? That's better, I think."

The statement perplexed Jack. "You don't think Trinity would be a good mother? Why not? She's very loving to you, isn't she?"

Janie nodded. "But not like a mamma."

He hesitated, wondering whether to pursue the subject, then shook his head. Janie was only six years old, after all—hardly a proper judge of a woman's fitness for motherhood.

On the other hand, Trinity was a full-grown woman, and had judged herself to be lacking in such capacity. Had Janie sensed the same lack of interest? If he and Trinity had a child, would that child sense it?

He shook off the absurd thought, attributing it to the strain of the day. "I didn't really think through my decision. I was angry with the management of the orphanage, and couldn't stomach the idea of ever returning Nicky to them. But I should have discussed it with Trinity first. And with Nicky himself."

"You haven't told either of them?"

"No."

"Then I'm *really* the only one who knows?"

Jack smiled. "Yes. I'll speak to each of them tomorrow, but until then, I'd appreciate it if you wouldn't say a word to anyone."

"I won't. I promise."

"Thank you, sweetheart." He kissed her cheek, then set her onto her feet. "Run on up to bed now, won't you?"

"Good night, Jack." She bounded toward the door, then turned to ask, "Jack?"

"Yes?"

"May I tell Mary? I'll make her promise not to tell anyone else."

He groaned in amused defeat. "Fine. But tell her first that I expect her not to repeat it."

Janie clapped her hands. "Secrets are more wonderful when you can tell them, aren't they?"

"I suppose so. Good night, sweetheart."

"Good night, Jack."

Trinity waited in vain for the return of "the old Jack," but saw only a grim-faced, determined man who had apparently decided to avoid marriage by killing himself with work before the blissful moment arrived. He was up before dawn, riding out to join the hands, where, according to Clancy's reports, he single-handedly attempted to cut, rope, and brand anything that dared cross his path. Then he returned to the ranch in the late afternoon, only to begin another full day of poring over accounts and drafting endless papers for Trinity to sign.

His fanatical behavior continued for three days

straight, and while Trinity wanted to find a way to either
soothe him or strangle him, she was too busy with her
own flurry of absurd assignments. Elena, an unforgiving taskmistress where hospitality was concerned, was
determined to turn the small wedding into the social
event of the season.

"When they talk about this year, they will remember
this beautiful fiesta most of all," Elena assured the
bride. "I'll make sure of that. You'll wear the dress my
tia made—"

"I can't!" Trinity wailed. "It's beautiful, but honestly,
Elena, what will Jack think? It's too revealing, and even
if it weren't, I'm supposed to be in mourning—"

"Your grandfather would want you to wear it, and so
you will."

Trinity groaned. "I've stopped trying to guess what
Grandpa would have wanted."

"There's no need to guess," Elena told her. "He
wanted you to marry a good man, and to produce grand-
sons to run this ranch. He wanted all the neighbors to
see how beautiful you are. He wanted the Lost Spur
Ranch to have a reputation for hospitality that was the
envy of everyone for miles around."

Trinity had to admit it sounded accurate. Terrifyingly
accurate, since she might indeed produce a grandson to
run the ranch if she wasn't careful. And the outrageous
off-the-shoulder, waltz-length creation of white cotton
ruffles that Elena's aunt had crafted in traditional fiesta
style was not the outfit of a woman who was trying to
be careful.

Jack probably won't even notice, she reassured herself on the evening before the wedding as she stood in

front of the mirror and surveyed her bare shoulders and calves with a wistful smile. *And it truly is the most beautiful dress in the world.*

A knock at the door interrupted her self-inspection, then Mary and Janie peeked their heads into the room. "Oo-h, you look so beautiful," Janie said, cooing. "Do you want to see ours? Elena's auntie just finished them."

"Come in. Oh! Oh, my word. Wait until Jack sees you." She stared in delight at their sassy fiesta dresses, styled much like her own, but from vibrant blue cotton trimmed with multi-colored ribbons. "If this doesn't melt his heart, nothing will."

"Is Jack's heart cold?" Janie asked.

"Of course not. It's just an expression. It means you two are absolutely breathtaking."

"And you're so beautiful," Mary repeated. "Don't worry, Trinity. Jack told Jane he hasn't been himself—"

"Hush!" Janie glared. "It's a secret."

"That's not the secret part," Mary replied evenly. Then she told Trinity, "He said he's been hitting men and making bad decisions and yelling at us, but only because he's cross with the orphanage."

"I believe that's true." Trinity hesitated, then prodded lightly, asking, "There's a secret?"

Janie nodded, her green eyes twinkling. "Jack told me first. Even before he told you or Nicky."

"Shh!" Janie elbowed her sister. "That's enough."

Intrigued, Trinity arched an eyebrow. "It has something to do with Nicky? It's not about his father, is it?"

Janie shuffled her feet, then murmured, "Not about his *old* father."

"Jane!" Mary grabbed Trinity by the hand. "Don't tell Jack. Please? He'll be cross at the wedding if you do."

"His old father?" Trinity struggled to understand, then gasped. "Are you saying Jack adopted him?"

The roses drained from Janie's cheeks. "I didn't say that."

"But that's what you meant?" She dropped to one knee and hugged the grim-faced child. "Don't worry. I won't repeat it to anyone."

"My first secret, and I didn't keep it very well."

"You did a fine job. Please don't worry. Tomorrow is my wedding day, and I want everyone to be smiling and happy." She hugged her again, then stood up to give Mary a fond embrace. "After tomorrow, I'll have two wonderful sisters-in-law."

Mary smiled. "I can hardly wait."

"Is Louisa trying on her dress, too?"

"She's crying," Janie said. "Because Jack won't let that boy—I mean, *Randy*—come tomorrow."

"She says it's just like Romeo and Juliet," Mary added. "She says it's romantic and tragic."

Trinity sighed. "She barely knows Randy. She can't possibly be in love with him. It's just infatuation."

"She's known him just as long as you've known Jack," Mary reminded her, then she blanched. "I didn't mean you don't love Jack. I just meant—"

"I know what you meant." Trinity gave her a reassuring smile. "When Louisa sees all the handsome *vaqueros* at the wedding tomorrow, she'll be glad she has a beautiful dress to wear so she can dance with all of them. But for me, there is only one handsome *vaquero* in the whole world."

"Who?" Janie asked, breathless with delight.

Mary giggled. "She's talking about Jack, you goose." To Trinity, she added, "Do you really feel that way about him?"

"I'll tell you a secret. That's how I first saw Jack—as a handsome cowboy, riding up on his stallion to save my ranch. I'll always feel that way about him."

"It's so romantic." Mary wrapped her arms around herself. "I'm so glad you really love him. Erica thought she did, but she didn't. But you sound so sure."

Trinity felt the beauty of the moment slip away at the mention of Erica's name. Worse, she realized this would happen again and again throughout her marriage, casting a shadow over even the loveliest moments, and dooming it to ultimate failure.

Embracing the girls, she murmured, "Give me a good night kiss now, then go take off those dresses so they'll be fresh for tomorrow."

Once they had scampered happily away, she closed the door behind them, then wriggled out of her wedding dress and into a demure quilted dressing gown, knowing there was something she had to do—for herself *and* for Jack—without delay.

"Jack?"

She waited in the doorway for a moment, uncertain of how to proceed. But when he turned his bloodshot eyes in her direction and gave her a weary smile, she almost flew to his side. "Look at you! You're exhausting yourself with all this paperwork." Cupping his chin in her hand, she scolded him with a playful, "Have you forgotten you're getting married tomorrow?"

"You're in such good spirits," he murmured. "I thought you'd be—"

"Yes?"

He shrugged and moved to sit on the edge of his desk. "You once told me I couldn't possibly understand how intimidating a wedding night was for an innocent girl."

"I'm intimidated," she agreed, "but not horrified. I believe you're dreading it more than I."

He chuckled softly. "That's an odd choice of words. I regret the necessity of imposing on you, but I hardly dread it."

"The necessity of imposing on me?" She sighed as she sank into a chair. "It only seems necessary because I refused to consider your other options. I'm ready to consider them now."

"I beg your pardon?"

She gave him her most confident smile. "The other options. You once suggested I sell a portion of my land to Crowne. Enough to pay off the mortgage. I'm ready to do that now, in exchange for his signing over his agreement with the orphanage to us."

Jack looked down at the floor. "I'm surprised. And impressed with your grasp of business matters."

"I've had a good teacher."

"So?" He raised his gaze to hers. "The prospect of a wedding night is worse than the thought of selling your land to Crowne?" Before she could answer, he leaned toward her, grasping her by the shoulders. "Do you think I haven't been racking my brain these last few days, trying to find a solution to this? The truth is, Walter Crowne's offer to buy a portion of your land was just a trap—a way to divest you of partial title while waiting for an opportunity to steal the rest."

Trinity bit her lip. "How can you know that?"

"I had an ugly but informative encounter with him a few days ago. He made it very clear that he won't rest until every inch of the Lost Spur is back under Crowne ownership."

"Oh, dear." She wriggled free of his hands. "He was at the orphanage?"

"At the bank." Jack raked his hand through his tousled hair, then jumped up and began to pace. "I didn't want to tell you this—didn't want to burden you with it—but our situation is rather more desperate than you know."

"Tell me," she pleaded, springing to her feet as he had done. "It's been clear for days that something's gone awfully wrong. If we're partners, you need to share every detail with me, good or bad."

He stopped in his tracks, a few feet from where she stood, and nodded grimly. "You have a right to know. The bank called the entire balance of the mortgage payable immediately."

Stunned, Trinity sank back into her chair. "I don't understand. Are you saying—did you *pay* it? Oh my God, Jack. No wonder you've been so concerned. There's so much more at risk now. Such a huge sum of money. And even if your investor can withstand the loss, your reputation will be damaged if you—if we fail." Overwhelmed, she buried her face in her hands. "I can't believe you did this."

His hand grazed her shoulder. "Can you forgive me?"

"Forgive you?" She stood and wrapped her arms around his waist, then leaned her cheek on his chest. "You did this for me? It's unbelievable, Jack. How will I ever thank you. You really are a hero—"

"Stop saying that!" He wrenched free, glaring. "We all have our fantasies, Trinity, and I understand your need to be swept off your feet by some dashing hero. But I don't need these constant reminders, any more than you need to be reminded of *my* fantasies."

"*Jack Ryerson!*"

His tone turned cool. "We have only two options. We can admit defeat, lose everything, and allow that bastard Crowne to win. Or we can try to forget our fantasies and marry tomorrow."

"For six months." Tears welled in her eyes. "Not forever, Jack. I can't bear to see you miserable forever. To be the cause of it—"

"Crowne is the cause of it. How I *loathe* him. Whether or not he killed your grandfather—and I'm beginning to believe he did—he definitely set out to destroy him. And by God, I won't let him get away with it."

"*We* won't let him get away with it," Trinity corrected him, wiping the tears from her eyes.

He nodded, his green eyes blazing. "Good. I need your complete cooperation in this. Not just tomorrow, or for six months, but indefinitely. I meant what I said— if either of us views this marriage as temporary— Crowne will find a way to discredit it. When we take those vows tomorrow, it must be forever."

"I understand."

He rubbed his bloodshot eyes before continuing. "In time, as our financial situation permits, you'll be able to travel. I can't promise it will be as extensive or luxurious as you've dreamed—"

"It doesn't matter, Jack."

"It doesn't matter *now*," he corrected. "But one day it will. I'll try to accommodate you as much as possible. The last thing I will ever wish is a divorce. Or to drive you into another man's arms—"

"Jack! I swear—"

"Don't! Don't make promises you can't keep. Neither of us should do that."

She could see the pain in his eyes, and knew he was remembering his last engagement. Did he honestly believe he had "driven" Erica into her sea captain's arms? And did he truly believe Trinity would be unfaithful to him, after all he was willing to sacrifice for her?

She had to find a way to prove to him that she wasn't like Erica. In a perverse way, he enjoyed finding similarities, because it made him feel closer to the love he had lost. But it also made it impossible for him to trust her. To see that while she might not be the great love of his life, she could be a good partner if only he'd let her.

And suddenly, she knew how to begin. "I think we should adopt Nicky."

He stared, clearly thunderstruck.

"It would be good for him, Jack, to have a mother and a father. And it would demonstrate to the town—and to a judge, if it ever came to that—that our marriage is a permanent one. It makes sense, doesn't it?"

"Janie told you?" He shook his head in amused disgust. "It's bad enough we're *marrying* for the wrong reasons. I don't think we should adopt a child just to strengthen our legal position."

Trinity turned away quickly, unwilling to let him see the tears that were flooding her eyes again. It all felt so hopeless. So unfair. And even this one bright spot—this chance to do something wonderful for a poor little orphan—was tainted by Jack's certainty that their marriage would be a permanent failure. How could they dare consummate such a union, knowing that more children might result?

He stepped up behind her and rested his hands on her waist. "Will you ever be able to forgive me?"

She turned, no longer crying, and asked quietly, "Will *you* ever be able to forgive *me*?"

"You've done nothing wrong."

"That's why this is so unfair," she told him, backing away toward the door. "Neither of us has. It's Crowne. And to a lesser extent, Grandpa and Mr. Braddock. But the price will be paid by you and me. And by your family. But not by your investor," she added, squaring her shoulders and locking gazes with her fiancé. "Let the orphanage dare try to discredit this marriage. They will find that our partnership is unassailable."

Jack was nodding, his expression softer than she'd seen it since his return from his fateful trip. "As I said before, you deserve better."

"As do you, sir," she said. Then she turned and walked proudly out of the room.

Eleven

Trinity's first impulse when she awoke on the morning of her wedding day was to bundle up the ruffled fiesta dress and throw it off the balcony in favor of the severe black outfit she had been wearing when Jack first rode into her life.

It struck her as ironic that she had hoped the black dress would cool any awkward romantic or lustful feelings her prospective husband might otherwise develop, so that the relationship would remain as businesslike as possible. Now, given Jack's attitude, there was no need for severe black. He already saw the marriage as a mournful development! And if his attitude these last few days was any indication, there was no need to worry about lustful feelings, so pulling back her hair and hiding her curves were no longer necessary tactics. He'd probably be as curt and aloof during their wedding night as he'd been for every other encounter since his return from the orphanage.

She felt a rush of anger at the man who insisted on reminding her that this marriage was forever—that she'd never again have a chance to be a bride; to dress in a gorgeous gown, hear the oohs and aahs of the guests, feel the warmth of her bridegroom's love on her face as

he beamed down at her during the ceremony, then be
swept up into a passionate embrace that would last a
lifetime . . .

Hugging the ruffled dress close, she promised herself
not to allow Jack to ruin this, her one moment as a
bride. She hadn't spent much time craving it—had, in
fact, planned on avoiding it for as long as possible—but
still, a part of her had always believed that one day, she
would have her moment.

*And I will have it, in spite of your gloomy mood, Jack
Ryerson,* she announced with a haughty toss of her
head. Then she stepped out onto the balcony to see what
all the commotion below was about, and melted with
delight. The air was crisp, the sky a dazzling clear blue,
and the shady yard had literally been transformed,
thanks to rows of tables covered with pure white linens
and laden with flowers. Dozens of chairs had been
arranged to provide a graceful aisle leading to a low
platform covered by a canopy.

Elena, who was busy directing the ranch hands as
they strung colorful lanterns around the wedding stage,
spied Trinity and called out cheerfully, "It's a beautiful
day for a wedding, *m'ija!*"

"I agree." Trinity swallowed a lump of disappointment, then forced herself to embrace this—the most important day of her life, Jack Ryerson notwithstanding.
"Come and help me with my hair, Elena. I want everything to be perfect for my wedding day."

To her surprise, once she'd made up her mind, the
morning became a glorious one. Elena praised and
pampered and generally made her feel like a princess,
dousing her with fragrant powders after her bath, then

skillfully working her long, pale tresses into a profusion of curls that cascaded down her back and would have dominated her face as well had silver combs and pink roses not held them at bay.

"Everyone wants to see your beautiful face," Elena explained, tinting her lips to a soft, sensuous pink, then carefully layering her long, black lashes with an inky emulsion that made them appear even thicker and more luxurious. "The color of your eyes is so special. Like violets. If only you'd given me more time to prepare, I could have used violets for your hair and bouquet—"

"I love the roses," Trinity insisted. "Everything's so perfect, Elena. How will I ever thank you?"

"If you cry, your eyelids will turn black. And if I start to cry, I won't be able to stop, and soon the guests will arrive, and nothing will be ready." Wiping away a tear that belied her stern tone, Elena stepped back and surveyed her handiwork proudly. "When he sees you, he will be overpowered with love and desire."

Trinity gave the housekeeper a sympathetic smile. "Don't be disappointed if he isn't. He's preoccupied, and probably won't notice what a wonderful party you've planned with such little notice. But *I'll* always remember it as the most beautiful day of my life."

"Well, then . . ." The woman dabbed at a new rush of tears. "It's time to set out the tamales. And I have to watch that little one, or she'll wear her dress into the pigsty." She sighed, then asked, "Do you plan on waiting up here until it's time for the ceremony? My uncle and his friends will play a romantic song for you as you walk down the aisle. Or if you'd prefer—"

"That sounds perfect. The girls will walk with me,

won't they? Do we have enough roses for Janie to—
well, to perhaps sprinkle them ahead on the path? I
know it sounds silly—"

"It sounds lovely, *m'ija*. I'll see to it. You just rest.
And try to eat something so you don't faint. We don't
want anyone thinking you are *embarazada*."

"What? Oh!" Trinity flushed. "Actually, Jack would
probably love that. It would save him the trouble of having to impregnate me tonight."

"*M'ija!*"

She grinned mischievously. "Just to be safe, I'll have
a tamale. Could I eat up here, please? I don't want anyone to see me ahead of time."

"Of course. I'll send enough for you and for Louisa."

"She's still in her room? Do you suppose she'd dare
not come to the wedding?"

"She'll be there," Elena assured her. "She's a good
girl, and she understands family loyalties. Don't worry
about that, *m'ijita*. Don't worry about anything. This is
your day. Let us make it perfect for you."

"I will," Trinity said softly. "Thank you, Elena. For
everything, but especially, for reminding me of that."

There was so much to be done—schedules to be met,
documents to be drawn, orders to be filled—but Jack
knew it was also important to appear confident and relaxed as the guests began to arrive for the wedding.
Aside from the melee with the Crownes, this was his
first opportunity to play host at the Lost Spur Ranch—
to demonstrate to the neighbors that by virtue of his

marriage to Trinity, he was not simply a business advisor, but Abe Standish's successor.

Elena had done a masterful job, creating an impression of wealth and abundance with her lavish spread of food and the endless profusion of fragrant pink roses. Mary and Jane were doing their part also, looking adorable in their frilly, calf-length dresses as they alternatively served the adult guests and giggled and ran with the younger ones.

Even Louisa, while subdued, had deigned to join a gathering of young women.

Everyone's behaving but you, he chastised himself. *Thanks to your brutish performance in the study last night, the bride hasn't dared show her face, which is undoubtedly swollen and blotchy from crying herself to sleep. If she needed one more reason to dread this day— or more specifically, this night—you certainly managed to provide it.*

If he thought he could put her mind at ease, even a little, he would have gone up to her room, but he had a feeling he was the last person on earth, other than a Crowne, she wanted to see at the moment. And it might just set off another crying jag.

And so, with a deep breath, he stepped out of the shadows and strode into the middle of the festivities, introducing himself to each neighbor in turn, and extending every hospitality to them with as cheerful a manner as he could muster. The ranchers plied him with questions about the future of the ranch, and Jack fielded them all with an ease he only wished he actually felt.

Then Janie was tugging him by the arm, back into the shadows, where Elena breathlessly instructed him on the upcoming ceremony. It was time, she insisted. Her uncle was ready to serenade the bride; the guests had all had more than enough to drink; and the sun was just beginning to dip behind the long row of oak trees that provided a backdrop for the stage. All that was left was for Jack to take his place on the stage with Father Corona.

"In just a moment," he promised, shooing the housekeeper and his sisters away, then shaking his head in annoyed amusement. He'd been so busy thinking about the ranch, he'd forgotten to prepare himself for this moment on a personal level. He was giving up his bachelorhood—over that he had no regrets. And he was marrying a beautiful, virtuous, intelligent woman—a woman who could drive him wild with arousal in a way no other female, not even Erica, had ever done.

Just don't allow her to see that. Not today, and definitely not tonight, he instructed himself sternly. *If she even senses it, it'll frighten her to death. Don't send her running back to her room in tears before the marriage has even begun!*

Squaring his shoulders, he skirted the edge of the audience, then climbed up on the platform and introduced himself to a thin old priest with a grip of iron, who proceeded to give him a brief but intense lecture on the responsibilities of a bridegroom.

Thoroughly shaken by the priest's ominous words, Jack scanned the guests for a reassuring face, but his sisters and Louisa had disappeared, as had Elena and Clancy. Then a murmur of delight rippled through the audience, whose eyes were fixed on the second floor of the house, and Jack turned his gaze upward as well.

A blow to his chest could not have winded him any

more forcefully than the sight of Trinity, standing on the balcony in all the glory of an angel, waving shyly to the crowd, and beaming as Elena's uncle strummed his guitar and sang to her.

She was nothing short of luminous in her provocative blend of ruffles and roses, her head piled with curls, her smile brilliant and confident. Even when the song had ended and the bride disappeared back into her room, Jack could imagine her, sweeping down the stairs, a vision of beauty and grace, headed in his direction.

His heart thundered in his chest, and might have burst through its walls had Janie not appeared at the far end of the aisle, allowing him to focus on her sweet, juvenile antics as she tossed handfuls of rose petals along the pathway. Then Mary was there, solemn and serious, and prettier than he'd ever seen her.

He hadn't expected Louisa to participate, and was humbled when she not only walked proudly toward the stage, but also took a moment to look him directly in the face, and to smile a smile so warm and forgiving, it almost brought tears to his eyes. Consumed with gratitude and relief, he nodded and smiled, and was pleased when she bit her lip, as though she, too, was overcome by the simple reunion.

And then Trinity stepped into view, so tall and graceful and beautiful beyond belief that Jack shuddered with anticipation. She was clearly relaxed, gracing each guest with a dazzling smile as she passed each row of chairs, while never once glancing, even for a moment, at her future husband. Even when she approached the single step onto the platform, and he reached his hand down to assist her, she accepted his help without truly acknowledging him, then graced the priest with one of her priceless smiles and a nod of her head to indicate that he could, in fact, begin.

Jack had seen her shoulders before, thanks to the revealing nightgown she'd worn that first night in the study, but it didn't matter. These might as well have been the first bare female shoulders he'd ever seen, and they were exquisite—graceful, sensuous, fragrant. He wanted to brush his lips over her, nipping at her soft, warm skin. He wanted to pull the dress lower, so that the playful ruffles no longer hid her full, firm breasts from him. He wanted—

"Señor Ryerson?"

He stared blankly at the priest.

"For heaven's sake, Jack," Trinity whispered, her gaze cast downward on the bouquet in her hands. "At least *pretend* to be at peace with this. What will the girls think?"

"The girls?" he repeated, confused by the question.

"Do you take this woman for your wife, Señor?" Father Corona interrupted helpfully.

"Yes. Yes. Absolutely."

"And you, Trinity Catherine Standish? Do you take this man for your husband? To love, honor, and obey without question, for as long as you both shall live?"

"Yes, Father, I do," she murmured.

Confusion pounded at Jack's temples, blurring all realities except one: he was going to be able to kiss her now. To pull her into his arms and engulf her in the passion that was consuming him.

But to his chagrin, Father Corona launched into a fiery sermon on the importance of fidelity and loyalty in a marriage. It might have been bearable had Trinity been willing to share Jack's frustration, but she continued to ignore him, concentrating with rapt attention on every word the priest uttered.

The restless bridegroom was about to growl, "Get on with it, man!" when Father Corona finally ended his diatribe, invoking in its place a moment of contemplation. Jack watched Trinity bow her head, and knew he should do likewise, but instead he licked his lips, praying only that the kiss would be the next item on the agenda.

Jack was fairly certain, from the twinkle in Father Corona's hazel eyes, that the priest knew exactly how torturous these last few minutes had been. Then the old man confirmed it by arching an eyebrow and saying, "Patience, my son, is a virtue every husband must master." Then he grinned and added, "Isn't it time you gave your beautiful new wife a kiss? A *respectful* one."

Jack glared, then turned to look down at his bride. She had tilted her face up toward his, but her expression, while lovely, was also distant. Resting his hands on her slender waist, he pulled her toward himself, resisted an urge to nibble on her shoulder, and instead covered her mouth with his own, kissing her deeply.

She allowed the kiss, but didn't encourage it. Didn't slide her hands behind his head and run her fingers through his hair, as she'd always done in the past. Under any other circumstances, he would have tried to coax a response from her, but he knew Father Corona's admonition about respect had been a wise one. So he stopped kissing his bride, but still held her, scanning her expression for some indication of what she was feeling for him at that moment.

Unfortunately, the end of the kiss signaled a wild outburst from the guests, who literally rushed the stage in their eagerness to congratulate the new couple. Before Jack could prevent it, Trinity had been swept away by a crowd of females cooing and gushing over the beauty of the ceremony. And men were pumping Jack's hand and stating the obvious—that he had married a rare and exquisite beauty, and was the envy of every man there.

At the first opportunity, Trinity escaped back into the house and flew up the stairs to the safety of her bedroom. *Her* bedroom—not the one she'd be sharing with Jack that night. She needed a few moments alone, to savor her beautiful wedding. The sights, the sounds, the darling little girls and charming priest and haunting strains of the serenade—it couldn't have been more perfect. Except, of course, for Jack.

He had been handsome, as always, but clearly uncomfortable with the entire event and anxious to get back to running the ranch. Even during the ceremony itself he had been a smoldering cauldron of impatience, so much so that Father Corona had even found it necessary to chastise him!

"Wait until we go to court and the judge hears about *that*," Trinity told herself with wry chagrin. "How can we convince anyone that this marriage is real when the bridegroom couldn't even spare the time to take his vows?"

Still, except for Jack, it had been perfect. And the kiss itself had been somewhat more than she had expected.

Apparently he knew enough about weddings to make sure that element was handled adroitly.

She laughed in spite of herself, acknowledging that she had enjoyed it, just a bit. And she intended to try and enjoy the wedding night, too—again, in spite of Jack. Of course, if he approached it with the same mix of impatience and thoroughness, it would be over quickly and she'd be a mother in nine months.

Laughing again, she crept onto the balcony, hoping to catch another glimpse of her perfect wedding without attracting attention to the fact that she had deserted the festivities. What she saw made her sigh with contentment. Louisa, surrounded by attentive males. Mary with her own pair of youthful admirers. Elena—radiant despite her exhausting, three-day effort—dancing with Clancy to the strains of her uncle's guitar. And, of course, Janie, running wild, her carefully sculpted curls long since loosened from their bonds as she urged Nicky to join her in plundering the trays of delicious food.

Closing her eyes, Trinity imagined herself for just a moment dancing with her new husband. That would have been a nice touch. In fact, she was half-tempted to send Janie to him to suggest it. *More evidence of our unassailable union,* she teased herself as she swayed to the music.

When she opened her eyes, she was embarrassed to find that all eyes were on her, and she waved in half-hearted apology. The guests seemed so shocked, or, at least, so transfixed by the sight of her on the balcony, she wondered if perhaps leaving her own wedding wasn't a more serious gaffe than she had realized.

Then she felt a rough, warm hand on her shoulder and knew, before she spun to face him, that it hadn't been the sight of a bride standing alone that had mesmerized the crowd. "Jack . . ."

He grasped her by her waist, then pulled her close, as he'd done at the end of the ceremony.

She didn't dare resist—not with so many witnesses. And even if she could have, she didn't want to do anything but melt into his arms, so she slipped her hands behind his head and whispered, "Let's give the judge one last bit of unassailable proof."

Predictably, he scowled—did he have any other expression these days?—but only for a second, then his mouth crushed down over hers, robbing her of both breath and reason. Gasping, she laced her fingers in his thick hair, desperate for the kiss to last forever. Then his mouth was on her neck, consuming her, devouring her earlobe and shoulder while she moaned with delight.

A cheer rose up from the crowd, and while it was muffled due to Jack's feverish enjoyment of her earlobe, she knew enough to be mortified, and halfheartedly pushed against his chest. To her amazement, he flashed her a grin reminiscent of their tryst in the barn, then he scooped her up into his arms, provoking another, lustier outburst from the guests.

"Jack, that's enough," she said, scolding.

"Enough? I don't think I'll ever have enough of you," he said, his voice thick with desire.

"What? Jack, be reasonable! Oh!" She shrieked in embarrassed delight as he carried her into her room and threw her down onto the bed; then she stared through disbelieving eyes as he began to strip off his coat and shirt.

"Are you insane? Mary or Jane could walk in—"

"I locked the door," he assured her, his green eyes sparkling with mischief.

"Why? Oh, no!" She covered her face as he pulled off his trousers and threw them to the ground, then she scrambled for the far side of the bed, but he caught her by the waist and pinned her beneath himself before staring down with such hunger that she shrank into the pillow, terrified and aroused.

"You're so beautiful," he repeated. "This dress—it's incredible." He tugged at the top of the bodice, forcing it further down on her shoulders, then he grinned, apparently noticing the knotted ribbon that held it in place. Before she could stop him, he had untied the bow, and the ruffles slid lower of their own accord.

Not satisfied, he pushed the fabric down to her waist, then stared in clear adoration at her firm, pink-tipped breasts. "My God . . ."

"That's enough, Jack. Wait until tonight—"

"Why?" He chuckled sympathetically, then lowered his mouth to her nipple, tugging at it with his lips. The resulting jolt of pleasure confused Trinity, and she tried to wriggle free, then groaned in abject encouragement when he restrained her by lowering his body onto hers again and gently thrusting his engorged manhood against her.

Then he began to kiss her, his tongue plundering deeply, evoking further confusion and pleasure. Her hands began to explore the taut muscles of his back, enjoying the heat from his skin, and the nearness of the powerful, bare buttocks that continued to work their hypnotic magic on her.

"You're so beautiful," he crooned again and again, caressing her breasts, then moving his hand down to her leg, working it between her thighs as he'd done in the barn. Then his litany changed, slowly and seductively. "You're so soft. So warm. So drenched."

"Jack . . ."

"It's fine," he said, his voice soothing and desperate. "Feel this, darling." His finger slid into her, then out, then in again.

"I can't! Oh, Jack, it feels so wrong. So . . . oh, Jack. It's so-o-o wrong." She arched in blissful enjoyment.

"It's not wrong. It's right. It's all so right, darling." He fumbled with her skirts until his manhood could maneuver itself between her slippery thighs. "It's time, darling. I've never wanted anything the way I want this. You. Now."

Caught up in his passion, she dared to coil her hand around his shaft, then wailed. "I'm not ready for *this*."

"You're ready." His finger toyed inside her expertly. You trust me, don't you?"

"Yes. Yes." Gulping, she whispered, "Tell me what to do."

"It's easy." He forced her thighs apart, then gave her an encouraging smile. "The first minute or two may be uncomfortable, but after that I swear you'll enjoy it."

Trembling, she nodded for him to continue.

Then with another, wider grin, he descended upon her, kissing her deeply while pressing her thighs apart, then slowly, methodically thrusting himself into her.

For one raw moment, as she felt her virginity give way, she thought her trust had been misplaced after all. Then he began to soothe her with gentle strokes, deep kisses, and lavish praise that combined to warm her, while new and more resonant waves of pleasure caught her in their spell and she began to move her hips to their rhythm.

Tighter and tighter grew the circles of pleasure, their centers growing denser until they became a throbbing core that enslaved her, tightening and heightening until finally, it exploded, causing her to gasp Jack's name against his chest as she squirmed and wriggled, capturing every bit of ecstasy her greedy body could demand.

While she focused on her own release, Jack's movements grew more heated, as though having seen to Trinity's needs, he could now fully satisfy his own. He began to thrust rapidly, and with more desperation, and then he, too, was exploding, and she clung to him in happy, satisfied disbelief.

After a long, luxurious silence, he murmured, "You enjoyed yourself? I didn't hurt you too much?"

She cuddled against his chest. "I scarcely remember the part that hurt."

"Good." He stroked her hair. "There are a hundred things I need to say to you, but for the moment—" he grimaced in apology—"we should really return to our guests."

"Hmm? Oh!" She sat up, shocked that she'd forgotten a yard filled with inquisitive minds. "What will they think of us?"

"They'll think we're a healthy, lusty couple," Jack said with a grin. "We allowed them to witness the ceremony. Why not the consummation?"

"More evidence for the trial? How convenient." Rolling free of him, she struggled to restore her dress to its previous condition.

"That's not what I meant."

"Even if you did, I don't want to quarrel."

"Nor do I." He reached across the bed and pulled her back into his arms. "Can I tell you something?" When she nodded, he stroked her cheek and murmured, "You're the finest, most beautiful, most intelligent woman I've ever met. One of the reasons I decided to accept this project was the prospect of being your partner. It's gotten a bit more complicated than that—a marriage rather than a simple partnership—but if we follow that long-winded priest's advice and are patient and respectful with one another, I believe it can be a limited success."

"A limited success?" To Trinity, that sounded like a death sentence.

"Limited in some respects," he corrected with a wink. "In at least one arena, it is an unqualified success."

Flustered, she scrambled away from him. "I can't imagine what you mean. Put your trousers on and go entertain our guests while I fix my hair."

"Leave it loose like that."

"More evidence of our consummation?" she scoffed. "I'd rather leave something to their imaginations."

Jack pulled on his clothes, then walked over to her, tipping her face up toward his. "I have time for one dance before I get back to work, if you'd do me the honor."

"Oh, Jack, you aren't really going to work on our wedding night, are you?"

"Believe me, I'd like nothing better than to spend the entire night making love to you—"

"That's not what I meant." She shook her head in embarrassed reproach. "Your family will want to spend some time with you. Louisa in particular. And there's the matter of Nicky. Have you broached the subject of adoption with him at all?"

"I tried yesterday, when we were out with the herd. I told him I'd like to be his father, and he thanked me but reminded me he already had one."

"Poor dear."

Jack nodded. "He's been talking more, though. Telling me stories about his father. If half of them are true, the man was fairly amazing. Hard to imagine he could have done what he did."

Trinity winced, remembering that the headmaster had told Jack the murders and suicide were prompted by a failed business venture. It had sounded incredible at the time, but over the last few days, she had seen a disquieting example of how seriously a man could take such things.

On impulse, she kissed her bridegroom's cheek, then waved him toward the door. "Go on. I'll join you for our dance in a moment."

"More evidence?" he said teasingly.

"Why else would I dance with the likes of you?"

He grinned, gave her a sweeping bow, then disappeared into the hall, leaving her to repair her hairstyle while savoring every detail of their lovemaking. *An unqualified success.*

And the rest could be equally as successful, if Trinity simply gave up her dreams of travelling, became more enthusiastic at the prospect of motherhood, and resigned herself to the fact that her husband was in love with another woman.

So that's just what she was going to do.

* * *

Jack sat atop Ranger, surveying the Standish-Crowne fence from a nearby rise. The damned thing was an expensive nuisance, but he had come to understand why Abe had maintained it so religiously. The idea of a Crowne stepping foot on Standish land, or even Crowne cattle mingling freely with his, infuriated Jack. He had only to think of Louisa's flirtation with the younger son to want to erect a solid, ten-foot barrier rather than this low, split rail contraption built on eight-foot centers.

As he studied the fence he stretched, conscious of every bone in his battered, sleep-starved body. Not that he was complaining. The work felt good. And the lack of sleep felt even better, considering its source: his sassy, golden-haired bride.

She had single-handedly kept his spirits high since their wedding day, never complaining about his long hours or exhausted condition. She catered to his sisters during the day, teaching them geography by means of her collection of hand-drawn maps, and piquing their imaginations with her never-ending treasure hunt, which had now extended into the barn.

She had even accompanied him on a ride to Charles Castillo's ranch, accepting an invitation that had been extended to Jack at the wedding after he complimented the rancher's wines. A tour of the vineyard and cellar had convinced Jack that the rancher's avocation could become a profitable enterprise with a minimum investment and some sophisticated management. He hadn't discussed his idea with Castillo yet, nor with Trinity. In fact, he had tried his best not to give it any thought at all, since he had no funds to invest and no time to devote to another enterprise.

Still, the excursion had taught him two valuable lessons. The first was that even if he failed miserably at saving the ranch, there would be other projects with which he could begin to rebuild his fortune and his reputation. The second lesson was even more valuable: he sincerely loved spending time with his new bride. He was even beginning to enjoy the prospect of being dragged to Morocco and Egypt by the pretty temptress.

His wandering mind was pulled back to business when he noticed one particular section of the fence that was sagging. Urging Ranger forward to inspect it more closely, he realized it subtly defied the pattern of the rest of the fence. Section after section had been built on eight-foot centers—in fact, their measurements appeared to coincide exactly to the inch. But the sagging section was a good nine feet in length, while the one immediately to its right was short—just about seven feet long, if Jack's eye was correct.

"That's not like you, Abe," Jack told the absent patriarch cheerfully. "If you and I have nothing else in common, it's precision to the point of obsession. How did you make such an odd mistake? And why didn't you notice it over eighteen long months?"

If Abe had noticed it, he would have fixed it. Jack knew that because he himself couldn't tolerate the aberration now that he had discovered it. His only question to himself was whether to come back with a shovel right away, or wait until the next day.

"Or have Little Bob do it," he advised himself, then he chuckled to think how the burly buckaroo would react to fixing a fence that wasn't even broken. Better to do it himself, so he touched Ranger's sides with his heels and instructed, "Let's get home, boy. You can rest after that. Old Blue Toe can bring me back out here."

When the horse whinnied, Jack burst out laughing. "Hear that, Abe? Ranger and I are trying to save your ranch. You could cooperate by not making us dig holes out in the middle of nowhere for no good reason."

His smile faded and he pulled up gently, then turned Ranger back so he could again survey the fence. Digging holes for no good reason? That *really* didn't sound like Abe Standish. So why had the old man arranged for Jack to do just that?

Trinity was helping Louisa take down the wash when they heard the sound of a horse approaching at a gallop. Hurrying to get a better view, she gasped at the sight of her husband, more handsome than ever, riding right toward her. Jumping off his horse, he instructed her, "Go and change into something sturdier. We have work to do."

"Work?" She eyed him with amused suspicion. "What's this all about?"

"Go take off that pretty dress, or I'll do it for you. In fact . . ."

She flushed and batted his hands away. "Tell me where we're going."

"You're as stubborn as your grandfather, do you know that? Wait here." He strode into the barn, returning with a pick and shovel, which he fastened to his horse's saddle. "Come on, you can ride up here with me." Before she could object, he was back in his saddle.

Then he leaned down to half-drag her up behind him. "Ready?"

"For what?" she demanded, laughing as they took off at a gallop that forced her to cling to his waist. Not that she minded. She had barely touched him in the daytime since their wedding tryst, although the nights had more than made up for that neglect.

"Where are we going?" she shouted into the wind.

"Didn't Father Corona tell you to be patient?"

"I believe he was speaking to you, not to me." Snuggling against his back, she resigned herself to playing along with his mysterious behavior.

Finally, he pulled to a halt on the top of a rise, then gestured toward the low fence that marked the Spur's boundary. "Tell me what you see."

"I see a fence."

"Your grandfather built it with his own two hands."

"I know." She sighed with contentment. "It's part of my legacy."

"In more ways than one, if my suspicions are correct."

"Oh?"

"I only have limited time for nonsense today, Mrs. Ryerson, so I suggest you take a closer look."

She narrowed her eyes, trying to see what her husband saw, then threw up her hands in disgust. "It's a fence. Like any other fence. Except, of course, since Grandpa built it, it's more perfect than it has to be. He was like you that way, Jack, did you know that?" She snuggled against him. "Now that I've seen the fence—"

"You said it's more perfect than it has to be. How perfect *is* it?"

"It goes on for miles, but only has one little saggy section. I'd say that's fairly perfect." She frowned, noting for the first time that the "saggy section" was out of proportion to the rest of the fence. "It's a good thing Grandpa never noticed this. He always prided himself on measuring everything precisely."

"Right. He never once noticed it over eighteen long months. I suppose that means he wasn't very observant."

"Grandpa? He was the most observant man in the world." She moistened her lips, mesmerized by her husband's laughing green eyes. "If you're trying to seduce me, Mr. Ryerson, you're doing a masterful job."

"Later. For now, don't you think we should fix that fence? Abe would have wanted us to, wouldn't he?"

"I doubt he would want his granddaughter digging holes—" Trinity began, then she cocked her head to the side. "Is that what you're saying? He wanted me to notice this? And dig there?"

Jack shrugged. "It does sounds farfetched. Let's just go back to the ranch—"

"Jack Ryerson!" She laughed in frustration. "What are you and Grandpa trying to tell me? To dig a hole—oh! He wants me to dig a hole there? On that very spot?"

"Evidently."

"You found the treasure!" She threw her arms around his and kissed him happily. "I'd call you my hero if it didn't annoy you so."

He grinned fondly. "You do love adventure, don't you?"

"Yes," she admitted. "So let's hurry, shall we?"

Twelve

Ranger carried them quickly to the sagging section, where Jack measured out the spot where the original posthole should have been dug. Then, while his bride watched in breathless anticipation, he broke the ground with the pick, once and then again, until they heard the sound of metal on metal.

"Stop!" She dropped to her knees and began to rake the dirt out with her hands. "Oh, Jack! Look!"

"Here, be careful." He yanked a small strongbox from its resting place, then set it away from the fence. "Stand back and I'll break the lock."

One quick blow made the lid spring open, and then Trinity was on her knees again, sifting through myriad mysterious objects wrapped in oilcloth. The first was a journal, which she hugged to her heart for a moment, then turned over to Jack, who accepted it eagerly.

Unwrapping the next object more carefully, she found herself holding a dainty gold brooch set with sparkling emeralds. "They're almost as beautiful as your eyes," she gushed. "Do you think it's worth enough to pay back your investor?"

Jack cupped her chin in his hand. "Is that why you've

been so anxious to find this? Poor darling. I'd never dream of allowing you to sell this."

"But Jack—"

"Look at me." He pulled her up gently, so they were kneeling directly before one another. "The ranch is going to be fine. And as for the investor—well, I am he. And I'm confident my investment is quite safe."

"What are you saying?" She bit her lip. "Mr. Braddock told me you're too cautious ever to use your own money. Oh! It's because you didn't dare risk someone else's?" Before he could answer, she added forcefully, "I can't allow it, Jack. Grandpa would never have wanted you to take such a risk."

"Hush now." He silenced her with a kiss, then admitted, "This is why I didn't tell you. But the truth is, in the last day or two, I've begun to see some encouraging progress. And now that I have the first journal, I'm even more confident. I can retrace the very steps Abe himself took when he first established the ranch. Promise me you won't worry."

"You sound so sure."

"It's just the sort of challenge I love," he told her with a grin.

"I believe you. You should see how your eyes are shining."

"And you should see yours. The lingering effects of the treasure hunt."

She threw her arms around his neck. "You make me feel so alive, Jack Ryerson."

"Do I?" He nuzzled her neck. "What would you say if I told you your adventure hasn't yet ended?"

Trinity laughed and tried to pull away. "Here, where

anyone can see us? If it's adventure you want, I've been wondering what it would have been like, that day in the barn, if I had let you do all the things you wanted to do to me."

"I have a fantasy of my own," he admitted, his voice husky. "It involves a certain silky nightdress and a midnight visit to my study."

She licked her lips. "How romantic."

He kissed her gently, his hand sliding up to caress her breast. "Thank God you didn't change into something sturdy. I believe I'm going to take you right here after all."

She would have allowed it without hesitation, but Jack stopped himself and sat back on his heels. "Listen. Someone's coming."

"Oh, dear." She adjusted her dress just as Walter and Frank Crowne rode up to the fence.

The older man was grinning from ear to ear. "I see you haven't lost any time enjoying married life, son."

"Didn't I tell you she was a tramp, Pa?"

Walter pulled a pistol and leveled it at Jack, who had started to rise to his feet, his fists poised to avenge the insult. "Settle down, Ryerson. Frank, keep your goddammed mouth shut. And Miss Trinity? I apologize for that remark."

"It's Mrs. Ryerson," she reminded him haughtily.

"That remains to be seen, doesn't it?" Walt returned his pistol to its holster. "Speaking of romances that won't last, keep that girl of yours away from my Randy. He's not worth a darn these days because of her."

"I've taken care of that," Jack assured him.

"Well then, I guess you two can get on back to doing what you were doing."

"Shut up," Jack said, his eyes narrowed with disgust.

"We'll see you in court." Walt laughed heartily, then the two men rode away.

Trinity touched her husband's shoulder. "I know it's maddening, but in a way, it's good he saw us together this way. Now he knows that the marriage isn't a sham."

"He knows you've been letting me make love to you. I think they always assumed I'd insist on *that*. From the sound of it, he's still going to force the orphanage to challenge us."

"They'll lose."

"Will they? I've learned not to take anything for granted where that bastard's concerned. He used his influence with the bank. He's not above doing the same with some dishonest judge." Jumping to his feet, he reached down for her hand. "Let's go. I've got a lot of work to do."

She wrapped her arms as tightly as she could around his chest on the ride home, but still he felt hundreds of miles away, and she cursed Walter Crowne for the endless wedges he was driving between them. She also found herself worrying anew about Louisa. Was she still seeing Randy? What would Jack do if he ever discovered such a thing?

And worse, what if Randy was no better than his brother? Just the sight of Frank had made her sick, and if Jack hadn't been there to protect her, she knew she would have been terrified. Was Randy really as gentle as everyone claimed, or was there a disrespectful brute lurking under that sunny smile?

Despite all her musing, she was fundamentally unprepared to find Randy Crowne himself standing outside the corral gate with Louisa on their return to the ranch. Without seeing Jack's face, she knew it was contorted with anger, and she squeezed him gently, admonishing him. "Be very careful, Jack. The last thing this feud needs is more violence."

He lowered her to the ground without answering, then dismounted and strode over to the couple. "Louisa, go inside with Trinity."

"No, Jack," his cousin responded, her tone soft but firm. "Randy isn't here to fight. Please just listen to what he has to say."

"Trinity? Please take Louisa inside."

"Come on, honey," she murmured. "They're just going to talk. I promise."

Louisa wrapped her arm around Randy's waist and jutted her chin forward in a show of complete defiance. "I knew you wouldn't treat us with respect. I told Randy we should just run away together, but *he* wanted to talk to you."

The blood drained from Jack's face. "Run away?"

"If need be. We're in love and we want to get married—"

"We want to get married *someday*, sir," Randy interjected hastily. "I'm willing to wait as long as you want me to."

"Then you'll wait forever." Jack ignored Louisa's loud gasp as well as Trinity's muted one. "Haven't you been paying attention, boy? Your family has done everything in its power to ruin my wife's life."

"I'm not my father, and I'm not my brother. And begging your pardon, sir, but you're not Abe Standish. I don't have anything against you or Mrs. Ryerson. I just want to spend time with Louisa. I'll follow your rules, sir. Just tell me what they are."

"I saw your father today," Jack told him. "He asked me to keep Louisa away from you. It's the first thing he and I have ever agreed on."

"He's against the match," Randy admitted.

"There is no 'match.' Just a perverse infatuation that ends *now*."

Randy's cheeks reddened. "If you'd listen—"

"There's nothing you can say," Jack assured him. "I'm Louisa's legal guardian. If I even suspect you've come near her again, I'll pack her up and send her back to Boston on the first available ship."

Trinity bit her lip, almost hoping Randy would say something wildly romantic, like he'd be on that ship, too. He was such a handsome boy, with a smile that could make any young girl melt. But he was clearly not ready for this sort of confrontation, let alone love or marriage.

If only Jack could see that, she thought wearily. *If he lets them visit here, under his watchful eye, Louisa will almost certainly grow tired of him.*

"Jack?" she murmured. "Can I have a word with you in private?"

"Absolutely." Jack stepped up close to Randy. "My wife wants to speak with me. Since our conversation is over, why don't you just be on your way?"

The boy gave Louisa an apologetic wince. "I don't want any trouble, honey, so I guess I'll be going."

She nodded stiffly. Then, with a haughty glance in

Jack's direction, she sprang forward, planted a kiss on Randy's cheek, then darted off toward the ranch house.

"Louisa!" Jack roared, but Trinity caught him by the arm before he could stride after the girl.

"Wait, Jack," she said, soothing him. "He's leaving. See?"

They watched as Randy swung into his saddle and galloped away; then she slipped her arms around Jack's waist. "It won't last. That was clear to me, and would have been to you, too, if you hadn't gotten so angry. You're such a grand feuder," she added, kissing him lightly.

"He didn't put up much of a fight," Jack mused. "Perhaps you're right."

"If he had fought for her, she would have been dazzled. But that was a rather lackluster performance. By him," she added hastily. "You, of course, were heroic, as usual."

He grinned. "I'd like to stay and be insulted, but I have a ranch to save."

"Try not to think about Louisa," Trinity advised. "I'll find a moment after dinner to talk to her. You should concentrate on reading Grandpa's journal."

"Thank you." He seemed about to say more, then just kissed her on the cheek and strode off toward the house.

She touched the spot his lips had brushed, wondering what thoughts, beyond vengeance against the Crownes, were on his mind. *Isn't that enough?* she scolded herself. *A ranch to save; his entire fortune at risk; and a powerful family determined to ruin him—and to ruin his cousin, too, if he's not vigilant. There's no room in his life for romance.*

"At least," she added philosophically, "he's probably not spending much time thinking about Erica, either. That at least is a blessing."

Wandering around to the front of the house, she joined Clancy on the porch, where the foreman was enjoying a well-deserved rest in one of the whitewashed rocking chairs. He greeted her warmly, then turned his attention back to the little boy sitting at the end of the lane leading to the ranch.

"He's out there again?" She sighed as she settled onto the top step. "Doesn't it break your heart?"

"It surely does."

"Jack wants to adopt him, but every time he broaches the subject, Nicky politely reminds him that he already has a father."

The foreman nodded. "A body doesn't want to let go of some notions, no matter how crazy they are."

"But he's missing so much of his precious young life, waiting for something that will never happen. I know it would be painful to admit his father's dead, but the pain would fade and eventually would become bearable."

Funny thing, how you can see that so clearly when it comes to Nicky."

"Pardon?"

"You and the boy, each letting life pass right by, waiting for someone who doesn't exist anymore."

"Who am I waiting for? Oh! For heaven's sake. Did Jack tell you I want a dashing rogue to carry me away? He's convinced of that, even though I never said any such thing."

"That doesn't sound like you," Clancy admitted.

"You're more like the boy, waiting for your father, even though he's dead and gone."

"My father?" she said, shaking her head. "I know full well he's never coming back, Clancy. What a silly thing to say."

"Is it?" The foreman looked directly into her eyes. "Why do you want to go to all those places he went when he was alive?" Before she could answer, he did so for her. "You think you'll find a part of him there so you can feel like you're with him again."

"*Again*?" She rolled her eyes. "When was I ever with him in the first place? He never once took me with him—Oh, dear. Is that what you're saying?"

"I'm not saying a danged thing."

"You're saying I want to go to those places and pretend Father took me there with him," she mused. "So I'll feel as though I was a part of his life. Is that it?"

"*His* life." Clancy nodded. "Not your own. *His* memories, not yours."

She started to protest, then smiled wistfully instead. "You'll be pleased to hear I made a memory of my own today. With Jack. He took me on a treasure hunt."

"Is that so?" The foreman pursed his lips. "Funny thing, how he's got time for treasure hunts and visits to vineyards, him being so busy and all. Kinda flattering, wouldn't you say?"

"Yes. Although I suspect he was evaluating Señor Castillo's winery as a future investment. And part of the treasure was Grandpa's first journal, which Jack wanted to find for his own reasons. So it wasn't just to please *me*."

"I never said he was trying to please you. I figure he

took you with him to please *himself*. That's the flattering part of it."

Trinity licked her lips, enchanted by the concept. Then she touched the old man's shoulder. "Will you do something for me?"

"Anything."

"Go and work your magic on Nicky. Please? If we're to be a real family—and I'm daring to believe perhaps we are—I don't want to leave anyone out."

Without waiting for a reply, she pecked him on the cheek, then dashed into the house and down the hall. Anxious to tell Jack what she'd just discovered about their strangely fortuitous marriage, she had one hand on the study door when it occurred to her she was overdressed; she spun toward the staircase, intent on changing into the silky nightdress of his fantasies.

To her surprise, Mary was standing at the top of the stairs, her face streaked with tears.

"Oh, dear. What's wrong, honey?" Trinity asked, and immediately the child flew down the steps and into her arms.

Stroking the child's hair, she urged her to relax, then murmured, "What is it, Mary? Tell me, so I can make you feel better."

Stifling a sob, Mary handed her a folded piece of paper. "Louisa ran off again. But this time, she's really gone. I found this on her pillow. She probably didn't think we'd find it until suppertime, but—" She covered her face with her hands and burst into tears again.

"Oh, dear." Trinity scanned the first few lines, then began to read aloud.

"Dear Jack,

I knew you would send Randy away without listening to him, but he is so sweet and trusting, he insisted on talking to you. Now you have left us no choice. You are not a fair man. You say awful things about Randy's brother, but you are just like him, filled with hate. But Randy and I are different. We love each other. You always said we should marry for love, but you only married Trinity to save the ranch. You are a hypocrite and I will never forgive you.

Your outcast cousin,
Louisa."

"We'll never, ever see her again!" Mary wailed.

"That's not true." Trinity cuddled the distraught girl. "Jack will find her and bring her back. They can't have been gone for long." She gave her one last squeeze, then pushed her gently away and looked into her bloodshot eyes. "Is there someplace special they usually meet?"

Mary nodded. "She visits with Nicky for a while, then meets him out by the windbreak. I think he even sleeps there sometimes, just to be near her. I knew all about their meetings, but I promised I wouldn't tell."

"This isn't your fault, honey. And it isn't Jack's, either. It's part of the feud—a feud none of us started."

"Louisa always said her love for Randy would heal the wounds between the two families. Like Romeo and Juliet. I think she loves that idea more than she even loves him."

"We need to tell Jack now."

"Tell Jack what?" he asked quietly from the doorway.

She winced at the sight of him, so handsome, so unsuspecting. Crossing to him quickly, she reminded him,

"When Father Corona cautioned you to be patient on our wedding day, I truly believe he somehow knew this moment was coming. Please, *please*, don't get angry or upset."

"I won't. I promise." He held her at arm's length. "Tell me what's happened. What's this?" he added, taking the letter from her hand.

She watched with tearful sympathy as his green eyes scanned Louisa's indictment. "Well . . ." He cleared his throat. "I'll find her. Don't worry." To Mary he added firmly, "I'll find her and bring her back safely."

"She'll just run away again," the girl dared to warn him.

"Not if I listen to what the Crowne boy has to say. And I will."

"Oh, Jack." The two females embraced him with relief, then Trinity insisted, "You must leave right away. They can't have gone far."

He nodded. "Mary, sweetheart, will you run and tell Clancy to saddle Pluto for me?"

The girl nodded, then left the room, still sniffling.

"I was coming to find you," Jack told Trinity with a sheepish smile. "With hopes of luring you into my office for a romantic rendezvous."

"I want more than a romantic rendezvous," she dared to tell him. "But nothing matters until Louisa is back home safely." Kissing his cheek, she reminded him, "Be patient with her. Be loving. I believe she wants you to come after her. To prove to her that you value her and respect her."

"I'll do my best," he promised, then he kissed her on the mouth. "We'll be home in time for dinner."

* * *

What Pluto lacked as a cutting horse, he made up for in speed, and Jack was confident he could catch up with the fleeing couple before they were halfway to Stockton. Catching them wasn't the problem, it was what to do, what to say, once he found them.

If only it were any other boy, he told himself between gritted teeth. The thought of a Crowne touching his cousin, kissing his cousin, daring to seduce her . . .

He shook off his disgust, knowing it would do more harm than good, and decided to adopt Trinity's philosophy: if he allowed Randy to court Louisa, she would tire of him eventually.

And so Jack would do what he should have done earlier that afternoon—he'd lay down strict but inoffensive rules for the courtship.

A high-pitched shriek jolted him back to reality, and he quickly surveyed the surrounding area, praying that the sound hadn't come from Louisa, and praying further that he wasn't too late to save her from Randy's brutish advances. Why hadn't she trusted Jack? Why hadn't she listened? If it was too late, he'd blame himself, and he'd kill every living Crowne with his bare hands!

Then he saw her, blessedly safe despite her proximity to a pair of brawling males. One was Frank Crowne— Jack would have known that huge frame anywhere. And the other appeared to be the younger brother.

It almost brought a smile to Jack's lips as he realized Frank had unwittingly done his work for him. And it made perfect sense. Randy had probably left a note for Walt similar to the one Jack had received, and the

Crownes had reacted with disgust at the thought of a union of the two warring clans. That suited Jack just fine.

Then Frank landed a punch on Randy's jaw that sent the younger man hurtling into the air, slamming against a nearby tree. Jack could imagine the bone-crushing pain, and actually felt sympathy for the boy. But ultimately, Randy was the Crownes' problem. Jack's only purpose now was to collect Louisa and carry her safely home.

But Frank clearly had another, darker purpose, and to Jack's horror, the big man now advanced on the girl, grappling her into a rough, disrespectful embrace, covering her innocent lips with his twisted mouth.

"Crowne!" Jack yelled, pulling his rifle from its sheath. "Goddamn you! Let her go!" Without pausing to think, he fired a warning shot directly over the scoundrel's head.

Frank turned, but rather than releasing Louisa, he faced her toward Jack and used her as a shield while shouting back, "She ran off freely, Ryerson. She's a whore, just like all your women. Time someone introduced her to a real man."

Jack leveled his weapon at the leering face, but didn't dare shoot. Instead, he urged Pluto cautiously forward until he was close enough to communicate in a quieter tone. "Don't be a fool, Crowne. Let her go."

"She feels *real* good," Frank said, fondling Louisa's breast. "Ride on home now. I'll send her along when I'm done with her."

Jack dismounted slowly, giving Louisa a reassuring nod. "Let her go, Crowne. It's time you saw to your brother. He hasn't moved a muscle since you hit him. I think you broke his skull."

"What?" Frank turned his head enough to confirm that it was true, then looked back at Jack, his eyes now filled with confusion.

"Let my cousin go. You need to get Randy into town to see the doctor."

"He doesn't need a doctor. Randy! Goddamn you, boy, wake up!" Frank nudged his brother's leg with his boot.

When Louisa's terrified gaze locked with Jack's, he took advantage of Frank's distracted condition to arch an eyebrow at her foot while moving his own in a subtle but definite kicking motion. To his relief, the valiant girl gulped and nodded.

Then Jack said coolly, "Is his head bleeding, Frank?"

"I can't tell from here." Frank moved closer to the body, dragging Louisa along. Then he prodded the boy again with his boot.

Jack took a deep breath, then gave his cousin a nod. She kicked her foot back sharply, landing a blow on Frank's knee, then wrenched herself free and sprinted to Jack, who continued to keep the rifle trained on his adversary.

"Bitch," Frank said with a growl, but he didn't even try to stop her. Instead, he sank to his knees and began to shake his brother's lifeless body. "Get up, you stupid fool."

Louisa wrapped her arms around Jack's waist, sobbing with all her might.

"Hush now, sweetheart," he crooned. "You're safe now. I'm taking you home."

"But Randy—"

"Randy will be fine with his family," Jack assured

her, but he was beginning to wonder if it was true. The boy still hadn't shown any sign of life. "I have a canteen, Crowne. If you want it, take it. Just move slowly, or I'll have to shoot you."

Frank didn't even seem to hear the offer. He was cradling his brother in his arms, swearing and cursing, but in a voice uncharacteristically soft and loving.

"Get up on Pluto now, sweetheart," Jack whispered. "Here." He boosted her up into the saddle with one arm while still aiming the rifle at Frank. Then he swung himself up behind her.

"Louisa and I are going for the doctor, Frank."

"The doctor?" The big man struggled to his feet, his fists clenched at his sides. "It's too late for a god-dammed doctor! That bitch killed my brother—"

A single shot from Jack's rifle, zinging past Frank's ear, effectively silenced the brute, who again sank to his knees to take his brother's corpse into his arms.

"We'll send the sheriff then. To your ranch. Go on and take your brother home."

Frank clearly tried to muster another hate-filled glare, but failed. Then he buried his head against his brother's chest and burst into tears.

Louisa began to sob again and Jack hugged her quickly, then touched his heels to Pluto's sides. "Let's go, boy. There's nothing more we can do here."

"How is she?"

Trinity gave her husband a weary smile. "She's safe, thanks to you. And she's sound asleep, so won't you please consider getting some rest yourself?"

"I can't believe I put her through this."

"There's enough blame for all of us," Trinity reminded him, joining him on the parlor sofa and cuddling against him. "Don't you remember when you urged me to abandon the feud? If I'd done as you asked, none of this would have happened."

"You're a good wife," he murmured. "But I have a feeling Louisa wouldn't agree with you."

"That's true. She feels all the blame resides in one person." When Jack winced, Trinity explained gently, "Not you, Jack. She blames herself, fully and completely."

"Why?"

"She says Randy didn't want this elopement. She's the one who insisted on it."

He buried his head in his hands. "She shouldn't blame herself. She's so sweet. So innocent."

"I'm not as innocent as you believe," Louisa's voice informed him from the doorway.

Trinity jumped to her feet. "Louisa!"

"You should be in bed, sweetheart." Jack strode across the room to take the girl into his arms.

"I had to talk to you. I c-couldn't talk before. I kept c-crying . . ." She bit her lip, as though fighting another wave of heartfelt sobs.

"You have a right to cry. To be miserable. To feel angry and betrayed. But there will be time enough for that, Louisa. For now, you need to rest."

"I had to talk to you, Jack," she insisted stubbornly. "To apologize for calling you a hypocrite, and comparing you to—to Frank." To Trinity, she added tearfully, "You were right to warn me about him. If Jack hadn't arrived when he did, Frank would have done to me what he tried to do to you."

"But Jack did come for you. That's all that matters for now."

"Do you think the sheriff believed us? About Randy?"

"I'm sure he did." Jack bent down and swept his arm under her legs, lifting her up off the floor. "I'm taking you back to your bed. You need to sleep. I'll sit at your bedside all night if you'd like."

Louisa stared into his eyes, as though humbled by the offer; then she cradled her head against his chest and thanked him in a voice so forlorn, it was all Trinity could do not to burst into tears herself.

"Go on, Jack," she urged her husband softly. "Things won't seem so hopeless in the morning. And Louisa?" She crossed the room to stroke the girl's hair, murmuring, "Tomorrow, we'll have a nice, quiet visit. You go and get some sleep while I look in on Mary and Jane."

Jack gave her a grateful smile, then bundled Louisa closer and headed for the stairs.

Thirteen

Jack spent the night by his cousin's bedside, emerging the next morning looking haggard and drawn, yet stubbornly heading out to the herd while the sun was still low in the eastern sky. Trinity took up the vigil, listening patiently to hour upon hour of tearful self-recrimination until finally, Louisa fell into her first true sleep since her ordeal.

By then, the sheriff was on their doorstep, and Trinity's heart momentarily froze in her chest. But the news was good—or, at least, as good as possible under the circumstances. Randy was in fact dead, but at least his death had been ruled an accident by the coroner. And Trinity had to admit that despite her own fervent hatred for Frank, any other result would have been too cruel for words.

If she harbored any lingering hopes that she would soon be wearing her silk nightie for her husband, or talking to him about the new and wonderful confusion she felt over their prospects for happiness in the future, those hopes were dashed with the news that Walter Crowne had declared war on the Spur, throwing down the gauntlet by offering the ranch's workers tenfold pay if they would leave Jack's employ and come to work on

Crowne Ranch immediately. Jack's expression at dinner was stoic as he recounted the situation. He and Clancy had discussed the matter and decided they couldn't possibly match the offer, except for their three most valuable hands: Little Bob, Sampson, and Clancy himself.

Which meant Jack's own role would be even more taxing, but in a way he seemed to welcome it, and Trinity couldn't really blame him. He needed to keep his mind off his financial situation, which had seemed so promising just one day earlier, and now had been completely jeopardized. If only they could simply sell the entire ranch to Crowne for enough to restore Jack's holdings, she would have insisted upon doing just that. But it was too late. Crowne was out for more than just land now. He was out for blood, and wouldn't rest until he'd broken the Ryersons as well as the Standishes.

With all that was happening, she was sure she'd see little of her husband, and so was surprised when he summoned her formally to his study just twenty-four hours after Louisa's ordeal. Smoothing her hair, Trinity hurried to join him, hoping only that he was going to give her some way, romantic or otherwise, to make his burden more bearable.

He greeted her with a stoic nod. "I won't keep you for long. I know you're exhausted."

"I'm fine." She stepped up to him, smiling shyly. "Is there some way I can help?"

"You can answer a question honestly."

She drew back, alarmed by his hoarse tone. "Of course, Jack. What is it?"

"What did Louisa mean when she said if I hadn't arrived when I did, Frank would have done to her what he tried to do to you?" When Trinity hesitated, he growled. "Don't keep secrets from me, Trinity."

"It isn't a secret, Jack. It's just—it's just something from the past. Years ago, I swear."

"What do you mean?"

She stroked his jaw. "It happened so long ago. It was horrible—I won't pretend it wasn't. But the worst was interrupted by Walt Crowne, of all people, although I'm sure he doesn't know it to this day. I only told Louisa so she'd understand why it was important not to wander too far from the ranch house."

Jack sandwiched her face between his callused hands. "You should have told me. I never would have allowed that animal to step foot on this ranch—"

"That's why I didn't tell you," she admitted. "I didn't want you to think my hatred of them was based on fear. It wasn't—although I'll admit he still scares me. I would gladly have sold them the ranch if Frank's behavior was their only sin. But they ruined Grandpa and then murdered him. That's what this feud is about. Not Frank's assault on me."

"I can't stomach the thought that he laid a hand on you."

"Do you see now why I was so—so utterly seduced when you throttled him?" she asked, her heart beginning to pound anew at the image. "Without knowing it, you avenged me."

"Damn." His mouth crushed down to hers, kissing her with such ferocity it almost frightened her. Then his ardor took another, more heroic turn as he began to nuzzle her neck, praising her beauty while declaring himself to be worthless. Her lover. Her slave.

Within seconds she was drenched with need, and she wrapped herself around him, urging him to take her. Tumbling to the floor, they clawed at one another's clothes while indulging themselves feverishly, until finally Jack was in her, plundering her with long, rhythmic strokes until a world of pleasure exploded around them both.

Dazed, they clung to one another, allowing their pounding hearts to recover. Then Jack brushed a lock of hair from her cheek and murmured, "I need to get back to work."

"I know."

He hesitated, then flashed her a rueful smile. "It's the last thing I want to do. Work, I mean. All I want to do is make love to you."

"Because it pleases *me*?" she teased. "Or because it pleases *you*?"

"Pardon?"

She kissed his cheek. "Just something Clancy taught me about us. One day, when your investment is secure and Louisa has recovered, I intend to teach it to you."

"I look forward to that, Mrs. Ryerson." He stood, then pulled her to her feet and kissed her gently.

"Stay with me for a while, won't you?"

She nodded, then curled up on the sofa and watched with pride as he methodically dedicated himself to saving their future.

Two long weeks after Randy's death, Louisa made her first appearance at the breakfast table only to rush away, sobbing miserably and wrenching in agony. Elena motioned for everyone to stay seated, then bustled after the girl.

"She's making herself sick with all this grieving," Jack whispered, his face as white as his cousin's had been.

"And you're exhausting yourself with your long hours and rough work," Trinity reminded him. "I'm beginning to think the Ryersons are more irrational and stubborn than ever the Standishes were."

The remark brought an apologetic smile to his face. "I honestly believe I'm turning this mess around, slowly but certainly." His gaze shifted back to the doorway. "I'm going to send for the doctor for Louisa. It's been too long, and she looks like she's wasting away."

"Elena says she'll feel better in a few months," Janie told her brother cheerfully. "She's *embarazada*."

"I beg your pardon?"

"It's when you're sick in a wonderful way," Janie explained. "That's what Elena and her *tia* say. They smile whenever they talk about it. So don't worry," she added, reaching for a tortilla and slathering it with a creamy paste of beans and cheese. "She'll be better in a few months."

Jack's voice was hoarse when he whispered, "Trinity?"

"I'll go and ask her immediately. Don't jump to conclusions, Jack."

"They intended to marry, but they never made it to town."

"That's true. So perhaps it's a misunderstanding."

He buried his face in his hands, murmuring under his

breath, and while she couldn't make out the words, she had no doubt as to the sentiment—that this new burden on top of all the others that Fate had heaped onto his shoulders might honestly be the one to crush him.

While undeniably a shock, Louisa's pregnancy piqued Trinity's imagination in any number of unexpected ways. She found herself wondering whom the baby would resemble: Randy, with his darling face but hated Crowne chin? Or Louisa, a stunningly beautiful girl with green eyes that nearly rivaled Jack's in intensity and sparkle?

If you and Jack had a child, she teased herself, *it might have those green eyes, too. Can you imagine anything more adorable?*

She laughed at herself, not only because such thoughts were so unlike her, but also because there had been precious little opportunity for conception since the pregnancy had been revealed. Jack simply never came to bed any more and while she had considered seducing him in the study more than once, she knew she needed to respect his work, however fanatical, at least for a while longer. She knew also that he blamed himself for Louisa's condition and to a lesser extent, for Randy's death. The only way for him to deal with those feelings was to succeed at something—in this case, saving the Spur.

Still, after a full week of celibacy, Trinity began to need her husband in the most unladylike of ways, and she suspected he missed her, too. After all, he might be exhausted and guilt-stricken, but he was still Jack, a supposedly rational man who had proven to be a decidedly irrational, not to mention voracious, lover.

And so she decided to wear her wedding dress and wait for him on her balcony, hoping it would stir erotic memories of their consummation. But when he rode in at twilight, he wasn't alone. Instead he was deep in conversation with Clancy, so she retreated for a moment into her room, poking her head out enough to watch for a seductive opportunity.

She almost betrayed her presence with a burst of laughter when her dusty husband walked over to a horse trough and unceremoniously dunked his head into the water, then stood up and shook himself briskly, as though that were enough of a bath for the moment. Had he always been this earthy? This simple? Practical, yes. But she knew that the ranch had changed him. It had changed them both, had it not?

As if to further thwart Trinity's planned seduction, Janie then skipped into view, shouting, "You're home!" and giggling happily when Jack scooped her up in his arms.

"Did you miss me?" he demanded.

"We have a letter from Erica! See? Mary and I want you to open it right away."

Erica? Trinity grimaced with distaste, then relaxed when Jack's reaction to the letter mirrored her own. "What does she want now?" he muttered.

"Perhaps she misses us," Janie said, scolding. "We miss her, don't we?"

"Not particularly."

Trinity grinned and edged further onto the balcony, enjoying the scowl on his face.

'I'll see to the horses while you read your letter," Clancy suggested.

"Leave Ranger with me. I promised him a special reward for chasing down that darned bull."

"And don't feed my piggie," Mary warned the foreman. "I promised him a treat, too."

Clancy chuckled, then clapped Jack on the shoulder. "You've got a beautiful wife waiting for you upstairs, don't forget."

Trinity bit her lip, surprised and touched by the foreman's Cupid-like reminder. She could only hope Jack would be inspired by it.

"What does Erica's letter say?" Mary was demanding.

"She sends her love."

"Yay! Can we send love to her, too?"

"Yes. We'll do so tomorrow. Go and help Clancy now, before he feeds the pigs without you."

Wandering over to a shady oak tree, Jack leaned against the trunk, then began to devour every word Erica had written.

At first he frowned, which pleased Trinity greatly. Then a knowing smile began to tug at the corners of his mouth, and she groaned in frustration. It was as though Erica were charming him from thousands of miles away! Then he straightened, his eyes sparkling as he returned to an earlier page and scanned it anew.

It had been so long since Trinity had seen that expression—that vibrant, confident, masterful grin—that her knees almost buckled beneath her in awe of it. Except it wasn't for her, or for one of his sisters, or his new life on the ranch. It was for Erica, and Trinity's heart stood still as she struggled to imagine what his former fiancée had written to enrapture him so.

Then his shoulders slumped and his grin dissolved into a look of wistful regret. Shaking his head slowly, he folded the letter and tucked it carefully inside his vest, close to his heart.

And Trinity knew beyond a doubt what had happened. Erica Lane McCullum, a willful, beautiful female with a heart of gold and eyes to match, had come to realize just how insane she had been to allow Jack Ryerson to slip from her grasp. Her passionate fling with her sailor had undoubtedly run its course, and she had realized that her first love was also her truest one.

And so she had written to him, as he had secretly prayed she would do. But his prayers had been answered too late, because he had a bride now. A woman he respected. A partner who trusted and needed him. A family in the throes of crisis over Randy's death and Louisa's pregnancy. An empire still on the brink of ruin.

But for one brief moment, Erica had rescued him from all that, had given him a reason to hope. To dream. And Trinity knew that whatever happened now, she would never, ever forget the look on her husband's face as he'd read that fateful letter.

Jack wandered to the front of the house with Ranger in tow, wrestling with the feelings Erica's letter had reawakened. If ever he had needed proof that she was the world's most frustrating female, she had just provided it. Still, he was flattered. And tempted, despite the fact that the timing was so inappropriate it was literally painful.

If she meant what she'd said in her letter—if her new stepfather actually wanted someone trustworthy to manage his extensive oil holdings and various other investments, it was the opportunity of Jack's lifetime. Unfortunately, he was in no position to take on such a commitment. Not with his full attention needed for the ranch, and his personal finances in a shambles.

The sound of hoofbeats in the distance provided a welcome distraction, and he decided with a frustrated scowl that anything—even a visit by one of the Crownes—would be better than dealing with another hopeless dilemma. Still, when he squinted toward the rider and determined that the man was a total stranger, he felt a wave of suspicion. And when the figure turned off the path unexpectedly and headed for the spot where little Nicky was standing and waving with innocent enthusiasm, Jack's suspicion turned to apprehension.

Jumping onto Ranger's back, he pulled his rifle from its sheath, just in case, then urged the horse forward at a gallop. Oblivious to him, the man rode straight up to Nicky, dismounted, and strode over to him, then pulled the boy into a huge bear hug.

To Jack's amazement, Nicky responded eagerly to the embrace, then whooped with joy as the man hoisted him into the air and grinned into his face.

"It can't be," Jack whispered, slowing Ranger to a walk and staring in disbelief.

"Jack!" Nicky's face was shining in a way Jack had never imagined it might. "Pa's finally here!"

"My God." Jack covered the remaining distance

quickly, then dismounted and approached the pair with wary delight. "Holloway?"

"In the flesh." The newcomer pumped Jack's hand. "I can't thank you enough for watching out for my boy until I could get here."

"*Gregory* Holloway?"

The man winced. "I know what you heard, Mr. Ryerson. All I can say is, it isn't true. My wife . . . my little babies . . ." Tears sprang to the man's eyes, then he hugged Nicky close and murmured, "If I'd lost Nicky, too, I really would put a pistol to my head."

"I'm glad you're not dead, Pa," Nicky told him.

"So am I, son. So am I."

"Is Ma really dead?"

"Yes."

"I thought so. But I knew *you* weren't. Even when they showed me your face."

"I heard all about how you defended my good name, Nick. I've never been so proud. Or so humbled." He hugged the boy again, then gave Jack a rueful smile. "Considering what you thought you knew about me, it was decent of you to watch out for my son."

"He's a fine boy." Jack shook his head in renewed disbelief. "The sheriff was so certain."

"I can't blame him for that," Greg said. "No one in Stockton knew I had a brother, much less one who looked so much like me. Even Nick didn't know. It's a long story, but the short of it is, Mark and I had a falling-out years ago. Over a woman. He loved her, I married her. He kept coming around, bothering her— acting almost crazy with jealousy. So we packed up and moved away. Never looked back, or kept in touch with anyone. It was like I'd never had a brother at all. If I had thought for one minute he'd track us down, I never would have left my family alone."

"You have my deepest sympathies."

"Thank you kindly."

"My family is going to be thrilled," Jack warned him. "Best prepare yourself for a riotous reception."

"Yeah, Pa. Wait till you meet Louisa. She takes the best care of me, next to Jack."

"I'm grateful to her. To all of you," Greg told Jack, his voice choked with emotion.

Jack studied the pair and decided it was nothing short of a miracle. Just what the Ryerson family needed, after too many weeks of feuding and mourning. They'd celebrate for hours, and then Jack would sweep his pretty bride up into his arms and make love to her until morning.

And then it all begins again? Jack refused to accept that thought. If miracles were possible—and Greg Holloway was proof that they were—then Jack wanted his own. A full-fledged reprieve from the downward spiral that had engulfed his family.

And in an instant, he knew exactly what to do.

"Mr. Holloway? Can I ask a favor?"

"Name it."

"Go on up to the house with Nicky and let them make a fuss over you. Tell my wife I have something to take care of, and I might not be home till late. And tell her I intend to return with good news. Perhaps even another miracle." Jack was grinning again as he added mischievously, "Tell her I love her, and to wait for me. *In my study.*"

* * *

Hands in the air so that no one could suspect him of being armed, Jack urged Ranger up the long, dusty lane that led to the doorway of the Crowne ranch house, a sprawling adobe structure surrounded by fruit trees. Several ranch hands, none of whom was familiar to Jack, took one look at Frank's hostile expression and scurried off toward the bunkhouse as though certain something terrible was about to happen. But Jack had become reacquainted with miracles, and so his calm expression and even voice were genuine as he greeted his adversary.

"Good evening, Frank. I'm here to make peace between us, once and for all. I've got a proposition for you and your father."

"You must be insane." Frank pulled his pistol and aimed it at Jack's face. "Get down off there. Slowly."

Jack complied, then arched an eyebrow. "Is your father inside?"

"You've got guts, Ryerson. I'll give you that. You actually think we're gonna let you ride out of here alive?"

"It's to our mutual advantage to put an end to this feud before someone else gets hurt."

"You should've thought of that before you got my brother killed. The feud'll never be over now until every Standish and Ryerson in California's dead."

Jack shrugged. "Once you hear what I have to say, you might decide there's at least one Ryerson you need to keep alive."

"What the hell does that mean? Never mind!" Frank's lips curled into a sneer. "We don't care about your fancy

Boston business deals. With you out of the way, the Spur'll be ours by the end of the year. That's the only proposition I'm interested in."

"So? You're going to kill me in cold blood? I imagine the coroner might not be quite so willing to call *this* an accident."

Frank's eyes blazed. "You're trespassing on my land. I've got witnesses."

"That's enough, Frank," came a tired voice from the porch, and Walt Crowne stepped into view.

Jack's eyes widened at the transformation in the patriarch in just three short weeks. A thousand new lines had appeared on his face, and his proud, straight bearing had disappeared, replaced by slumped shoulders and a lackluster expression.

"I'm sorry for your loss, Walt," Jack told him sincerely.

Frank snorted. "That's doubtful, considering you're the cause of it."

Jack kept his gaze fixed on the father. "In a way, we all caused it, wouldn't you say? It's what comes of feuding. That's why I'm here. To make sure no one else gets hurt."

"There's only one way to end this feud, Ryerson," Walt assured him. "By giving me back my land. If that's why you're here, fine. If not, you'd best get back up on that horse and ride on out of here before Frank does something we'll all regret."

"You're going to let him go?" Frank growled. "Why? Randy's dead because of him. And once he's out of the way, the Spur won't last a month. His widow'll be begging us to buy it back for any price we name."

The elder Crowne shook his head. "You worry me sometimes, boy. You can't just kill a fella in cold blood, no matter how much he deserves it."

"But, Pa—"

"That's enough!" Some of the old fire had returned to Walt's voice. "Come on in, Ryerson. Let's hear what you have to say. Frank? Cool off. When you've got hold of yourself, you can join us."

Jack followed Walt into the house and down one step to a room that seemed to serve the functions of office, parlor, and storeroom. Crates filled with documents and newspapers were stacked haphazardly against the wall, while rough wooden chairs were intermixed with elegant upholstered furniture. At one end sat a huge oak desk flanked by a pair of handsome sea chests, and Jack remembered an entry in Abe Standish's journal recounting how Walt's father, Randolph Crowne, had used those trunks to store his most precious possessions. The chests were trimmed with brass and leather and, according to Abe, each handle concealed the hilt of a tiny, razor-sharp dagger, cleverly masked by the intricate design.

"Sit right there," Walt said, indicating a rustic wooden chair directly across from the desk and away from the trunks. When Jack had complied, Walt settled down behind the desk and leaned forward, staring at his guest with unexpected ferocity. "Make no mistake about this, Ryerson. I hold you and yours responsible for my boy's death. I won't let Frank kill you in cold blood, but that's only because I don't want to see the last of my kin hang by his neck. So state your business, then get off my land."

"Your son's death was an accident, caused by a festering, irrational feud. It's only a matter of time before someone else dies, Walt. You must know that."

"Then end it. Give me back my land. I'll even pay you for it. Not a lot—why should I, when I can have it for next to nothing in a few more months? But it's worth something to me to see you and yours head out tomorrow and never come back. What price do you have in mind?"

"I didn't come here to sell. I came here to warn you you have more at stake in this than you know. Something priceless. Something worth more than any ranch. Your grandchild."

"My—?" The blood seemed to drain from Walt's wrinkled face.

"My cousin is carrying Randy's child," Jack confirmed. "If Frank had had his way the night he killed Randy, he would have killed Louisa, too, once he had raped her. My arrival prevented that from happening." He leveled a stare at the older man. "If Frank had killed her, I would have hunted him down and killed him. You'd be all alone. You never even would have known you lost a grandchild. That's what comes of feuding, Walt. Don't tell yourself you don't have anything to lose, because believe me, you do. We all do."

"A grandchild." Walt licked his lips. "That's something."

"I agree."

"Frank attacked her? I didn't hear anything about that. Is she hurt bad?"

"She's fine. Queasy and tearful—partly from the pregnancy, and partly over Randy's death. But she'll be fine. And she'll be a fine mother."

"In Boston?"

Jack eyed him sympathetically. "I'm not a rancher, Walt. I need to take her home with me. But I doubt we'll be able to leave before the baby's born—she's just too fragile to even consider that. So you could spend a little time with your grandchild after it's born, assuming we can work out the rest of this mess. And who knows? Maybe the idea of visiting a thriving cattle ranch will appeal to the child one day." Leaning forward, he insisted, "The important thing is, the child will be alive. That alone should be enough to make you want to resolve your differences with us."

"Resolve 'em how?"

Jack smiled, encouraged by the simple question. "For the time being, a truce. After that, we might even consider cooperative efforts. There are any number of measures that could help both ranches—"

"It's all one ranch!" Walt pounded the desk in frustration. "You want to cooperate for the sake of my grandchild? Fine. I'll pay you top dollar, right here and now. You can recoup your investment and go on home once the baby's old enough to travel. You say you want to end this thing, so end it. I promise you, I won't let anything happen to your cousin or anyone else you care about. That's the best I can do."

"What are you saying, old man?" Frank's voice was a low, menacing growl. "We have them on their knees. And look what else we've got!" He stepped into view, dragging Trinity along with him, her arm twisted behind her back, a pistol trained against her temple. "We've got 'em both now, Pa. And neither of 'em is leaving this ranch alive."

Fourteen

Jack was on his feet, aghast at the sight of his bride, her hair tousled, her face bruised. Clenching his fists but not daring to charge because of the gun, he growled instead. "Let her go, Crowne. Walt, tell your son to let my wife alone this instant or I swear, you'll never lay eyes on that baby."

"I'm fine, Jack," Trinity told him, but he could see from her swollen cheek that it wasn't true.

"Let the girl go, Frank," Walt told his son softly.

"You're not making the decisions anymore, old man. Losing Randy made you soft. This is your chance for revenge. Can't you see that?" He began to speak with the eagerness of a child intent upon impressing a parent. "We can make them deed the Spur back to us right here and now. Ryerson'll do it to save his wife. You can own it again, just like you were always supposed to do. It's your birthright. And mine."

"And my grandson's."

"Grandson?" Frank murmured, then he began to shake his head frantically. "Is that what Ryerson's been telling you? That his cousin's got herself pregnant? Even if it's true, it could've been any man for a hundred miles—you know that. If that girl gave herself to Randy without making him marry her first, how many other fellas have had her?"

"Shut up," Jack warned. Then, without taking his eyes off Frank, he murmured, "Walt, tell him to let Trinity go. Now."

When the patriarch didn't answer, Jack glanced in his direction and was alarmed at what he saw. Greed had returned to the ranch owner's face, overshadowing his grief over the loss of a son and his elation over learning of a grandchild. The feud—that monstrous evil that had enslaved this man for so long—had reasserted control over him, body and soul.

"What do you say, Ryerson?" the old man asked. "Will you sign the deed—right here, right now—like Frank says?"

"Yes. Let my wife ride safely away, and then I'll sign it over to you."

"Stop your wriggling, stupid bitch." Frank yanked Trinity's arm more tightly behind himself with one hand while sucking at the bite mark she had apparently inflicted on his gun hand.

"Trinity, don't," Jack said, pleading, but to his distress, she kept struggling.

Frank grappled her roughly. "She thinks I won't shoot her, but I will. And then I'll shoot *you*."

"Trinity?" Jack shook his head.

She stopped for a second, then wrenched almost free with one Herculean effort, but Frank grabbed her as she dashed for the desk. Then he forced her down into the nearest chair, pressing the barrel of the pistol tightly to her head once again.

"Damn." Jack stepped closer, keeping his eye on the

weapon. "Trinity, I'm begging you, don't fight him anymore."

"I won't," she said, locking gazes with Jack. To his confusion, her eyes were twinkling. Why? She was behaving as though *she* were the one in control.

"Do what you have to do, Jack," she said, her tone submissive. "Sign the deed if you have to. I spent all last night reading Grandpa's journal, and I know just what he'd tell me to do if he were here right now."

"The journal?" Jack struggled not to look at the sea chest that was mere inches from Trinity's hand. "I believe I understand what you're trying to say."

"Draw it up, Pa." Frank's voice was laced with excitement. "After all these years, it's ours again, and it isn't gonna cost you a dime. Why should it? Standish stole it, and now it's like she says: Standish himself is advising them to give it back to its rightful owner."

Walt nodded, then reached for paper and pen. "Our men saw you ride up here of your own free will, Ryerson. Trespassing on our land, taking your lives in your hands just to come here and end the feud the only way it can be ended. We've got witnesses to that. It'll be our word against yours and they'll believe us, 'cause no one will believe you were fool enough to come here unarmed unless you intended to give me back my land."

"I'll sign whatever you want." To Frank, Jack added, "You'll be the witness."

Frank nodded. Then, clearly lulled by the change in Trinity's behavior, he edged closer to the desk, keeping the pistol trained on her but concentrating his attention on the words his father was writing.

Jack remembered how Louisa had acted bravely,

kicking Frank on Jack's signal, enabling him to rescue her. Bold, adventurous women—thank God those were the sort that surrounded him! And the boldest of all was his bride. Had he honestly dared wish, even once, that she were otherwise?

Taking a deep breath, he gave Trinity a nod; then her hand flew toward the chest, pulling out a shiny dagger and burying it in Frank's thigh. The big man yelped just as Jack grabbed his gun hand and wrestled it above his head. Then they struggled to the floor, each desperate to gain control of the pistol, each relishing the chance to inflict pain on the other as payment for the misery they'd endured these last torturous weeks.

Then the weapon fired.

"Jack!" Trinity shrieked. "Oh, please, no!"

"I'm fine," he said, gasping for a breath. His hand was still locked on the pistol, as was Frank's, but both men had momentarily stopped their struggling in order to take stock of their condition. Jack's shirt was drenched in blood, but he quickly discovered the source—a gaping wound in Frank's chest.

"Damn. You're hit, Frank."

"Yeah." The big man began to wheeze as he struggled to sit up, then fell back down, instantly exhausted.

"Stay still." Jack wrenched the pistol away with one quick movement, then laid it on the ground and tore the fabric away from the wound. "It doesn't look too bad. Trinity? Take a look."

"No! Stay where you are," Walt Crowne warned. "Ryerson, move away from my boy. And keep your hands where I can see them."

Looking up, Jack saw that the older man had found a

pistol of his own and was pointing it at him. "Fine," he murmured, grateful that the rancher wasn't targeting Trinity. Raising his hands above his head, he stood slowly, moving between his bride and Walt. "Tell us what you want us to do."

"Just go. I'll take care of this. Get out before I change my mind." His voice began to quaver. "You were right, Ryerson. If we don't stop this here and now, we'll all end up dead. Frank?" He edged around the desk, keeping his eye on Jack and Trinity as he approached his son. "Can you talk, boy?"

"Make him sign it, Pa," came the gasped reply.

Walt shook his head. "It's finished, son. Just lay back now. I'll take care of you in a minute." To Jack he insisted, "I want to see that baby when it comes."

"I'll arrange it."

"Go on then. Get out."

Jack nodded, and had just begun to usher Trinity from the room when Frank's snarling voice stopped him with a bloodthirsty "Ryerson!" Whirling, Jack groaned at the sight of the pistol once again in his enemy's hand.

Shoving Trinity through the doorway and into the safety of the hall a split second before a single shot rang out, Jack recoiled in horror, first because he was sure he had been in the bullet's path, and then because he realized that the shot had come from Walt's gun, not Frank's, and had virtually blown Frank's hand from its wrist, causing torrents of blood to gush freely.

Allowing his weapon to crash to the floor, Walt Crowne fell on his knees beside his son, cradling him in his arms while trying to bind the gaping wound, lamenting all the while. "You can't just kill a fella in cold blood, boy, no matter how much you hate him."

It was a heart-wrenching sight, but Jack had learned a valuable lesson, so he retrieved both pistols and handed them to his bride before joining the mournful father. "Let's get him into town. I'm sure the doctor—"

"It's too late for that," Walt said, sitting back on his heels, his eyes swimming with tears.

Jack pressed two fingertips to Frank's throat, confirming that indeed no pulse was present.

"Listen to me, Walt—"

"Just go."

"Come on, Jack," Trinity murmured, taking him by the elbow and urging him to his feet. "They need to be alone."

As the couple reached the doorway, a plaintive voice asked, "Are you going to let me see that grandbaby?"

Before Jack could answer, Trinity spoke clearly. "I'll see to it personally, Mr. Crowne. No one knows better than I how much a child needs its grandpa."

The old man gave her a grateful sigh. "I didn't kill Abe. I know you think I did, but I didn't."

"I believe you."

"Frank might've done it. I reckon we'll never know."

"It doesn't matter anymore," Trinity told him quietly.

Walt nodded, then gathered his boy back into his arms and began to sob.

Jack's arm was wrapped tightly around Trinity's waist as he led her into the cool night air, and she reveled in the feel of him—his strength, his courage, his protectiveness. He had saved her life; saved the ranch; saved her from spending a lifetime chasing, and being chased by, ghosts. In place of feuds and loneliness he had introduced her to love—the kind of love that made hearts soar and families thrive.

She remembered the stab of foreboding she had felt when Greg Holloway told her what Jack had said: that he was off in search of another miracle. Instinctively, she had known exactly where he had gone—to end the feud that had imperiled his family since the fateful day when he first rode onto Standish land. The return of Nicky's father had inspired him to want his own life back, or at least as much of it as he dared take.

"Look at me, darling." He tilted her face up to his, then stroked her bruised cheek. "What did that animal do to you?"

"He hit me, but just once. And I suppose I invited it, by coming here all alone. I panicked when I realized where you'd gone."

"I should have known you'd follow me."

"Because I love danger?" she asked with a rueful smile. "You have me woefully confused with Erica, darling. I detest danger with all my heart."

"So do I."

She had noticed his wince at the mention of Erica's name, and reminded herself of the decision she'd made while galloping to Crowne Ranch. He wanted a miracle, and the greatest miracle of all would be for her to let him go. With the feud behind them, they had no more need to be married. What he did need was the sparkle and excitement Erica's letter had inspired in him. And while it broke Trinity's heart, she couldn't bear to deprive him of that. Not after all he'd done for her.

Slipping her arms around his neck, she forced herself to smile up at him. "Everyone's safe now, darling, thanks to you. Nicky has his father—you were right to call that a miracle. And you were right to come here in search of a miracle of your own. You deserve that more than anyone, and I'd never stand in your way. So?" She brushed hastily at a tear that had escaped down her cheek. "Don't you think we should talk about Erica's letter?"

"You know about that?"

She gulped and nodded. "Now that the feud is over, there's nothing stopping you from—well, from following your heart."

"It's tempting," he agreed. "But there's still so much to do here."

"Clancy can do it now, with Mr. Holloway's help." A tiny sob escaped from her throat. "You're free to go."

Jack pulled her against his chest, burying his face in her hair. "Is that what you think? That I want to go off to Pennsylvania and investigate some dirty old oil fields? When my cousin is expecting a baby and my wife still hasn't had a honeymoon?"

"Oil fields?"

"That's where Erica's stepfather has most of his investments, and I'd be lying if I said I wasn't tempted to take him up on his offer. There's a fortune to be made in oil, and I'd love to be a part of it, but it can wait. After all—"

"Her stepfather?" Trinity pulled free and stared up into his eyes. "What are you *talking* about?"

Jack chuckled. "I thought you said you knew about the letter. Erica's mother remarried recently, and her new husband has extensive investments he'd like me to manage."

She could barely hear his words over the roar of relief pounding against her temples. "That's what you found so tempting about her letter? An investment opportunity?"

"Of course. What did you think?"

"Oh, Jack!" Throwing her arms around his neck, she hugged him wildly, then dragged his head down for a long, luxurious kiss. "You frightened me to death, Jack Ryerson. Do you have any idea how much I love you?"

"And I love you." He stroked her bruised cheek with his thumb. "It's the most amazing thing, too. I never really knew how staggering true love could feel."

"Tell me," she suggested in a whisper.

He licked his lips, then admitted, "It feels like chaos, yet I can't imagine my life without it, or my world without you in it. You make me feel vulnerable and irrational and worthless. Yet at the same time," he flashed a rueful grin, "I feel invincible."

"Because you're my hero."

"Yes," he murmured. "Yes, I believe that's it."

She rested her head against his chest and exhaled with relief. "I can't live without you either, Jack. It really is a miracle, isn't it?"

"Yes, and I'm determined to be worthy of it." Stroking her hair, he promised, "As soon as the baby is born and everyone is safely back in Boston, I'm taking you on a honeymoon."

"We may not have to wait that long. Mr. Holloway is

determined to stay on indefinitely and repay you by helping with the ranch. And—" she pulled free enough to smile up at him—"he may discover a second reason to stay at the Spur, if Louisa has anything to say about it."

"Pardon?"

"She seemed quite taken with him, and he with her," Trinity explained, remembering the magical moment when Nicky had pulled Louisa by the hand to meet Greg Holloway, telling his father how the pretty girl had been the only one to believe him, and how she had sat on the porch with him, waiting for Greg's arrival. Louisa had blushed and stammered, while Greg had murmured his thanks, his eyes wide with appreciative interest.

Trinity bit back a grin. "What will you say if he asks your permission to court her?"

"*Court* her? When *he's* in mourning and *she's* pregnant?" Jack objected, then he caught himself and grimaced ruefully. "I'm not going to make that mistake again."

"That is your motto, after all, is it not?" she said, teasing. "Never to make the same mistake twice? Isn't that why you insisted on comparing me to Erica at every turn?"

"You are an entirely different mistake than Erica ever was," he retorted playfully.

"Entirely different? Do you truly mean that? At last?"

He nodded, then cupped her chin in his hands. "I meant what I said about that honeymoon, too. Before the year ends, I'm going to take you to Greece, by way of Morocco and Egypt."

"Morocco?" She tossed her head impatiently. "Don't you mean Pennsylvania? And after that, there's the challenge of turning the Castillo ranch into a full-fledged winery!" Enjoying his shocked expression, she insisted, "I can't imagine anything more exciting than travelling with my husband, finding new investments by day and making mad, passionate love all night."

"Nor can I," he murmured.

"Of course, once we have children, it will change. But I'll have the girls to keep me company while you're away. And from time to time, you'll take us all with you."

"Children?" He coughed as though clearing a lump from his throat. "Even then, you won't need to stay behind, darling. I promise you that. There will be nannies and governesses—"

"And I'll welcome their assistance," she agreed. "But the adventure of being a mamma is one I intend to experience fully."

The look of jubilant amazement on his face touched her heart. "It seems I may have some small trace of maternal instinct after all."

"I never doubted it," he told her gently. "I only feared you'd never believe it about yourself."

"Any more than you'd believe you were a hero?" She twined her arms around his neck. "It seems we really are perfect for one another, fantasies and all. Which means we owe Russell Braddock an apology, wouldn't you say?"

"I owe him more than that," Jack told her, his voice hoarse with amazement.

"And Grandpa, too," she urged playfully. "He's the one who forced you to marry me against your will."

Jack grinned. "And don't forget Erica. If it hadn't been for her—"

"Jack Ryerson!"

He silenced her with a kiss, then scooped her up into his arms and carried her away with him forever.

You can E-mail Kate at: <u>katedonovan@hotmail.com</u>

From Best-selling Author
Fern Michaels

DO YOU HAVE THE
HOHL COLLECTION?